I0822556

Devil's Elbow

Books by the same author

LIGHTWOOD
RIVER ROGUE
THIS IS ADAM
DEVIL'S ELBOW

Devil's Elbow

a novel by

Brainard Cheney

MM John Welda BookHouse

2012

Published by permission 2012 by MM John Welda BookHouse
P. O. Box 111, Eastman, Georgia 31023

ISBN: 978-0-9839365-6-5 (Hardcover)
LCCN: 2012919408
The Lightwood History Collection: Book 5
First Edition

CONTENTS

to the memory of

STANLEY JOHNSON

(who contributed to this effort)

FIRST RETURN

*

Judy

Chapter 1

THE RESTIVE redheaded young man, at the moment slumped down in the grimy plush train seat, began to hear a voice in the low wash of time's roar. Though not his own, it was disconcertingly familiar. He was, exacted by a new life, riding the day coach all night from Nashville, in Tennessee, to his old home, Riverton, in southern Georgia, that signal Christmas of 1926. The underbeat of car wheels seemed to contribute a stammer to the fell refrain that made it strike even deeper in him: "T-Taking you to the turkey roost . . .t-taking you to the turkey roost." This did not answer any question in his mind at the moment, but somehow gave his motion what he would have called, had it come to it, an eschatological rhythm.

The adjective was a recent acquisition that he sought occasions to use, though he could not, to be sure, include it in his newspaper reporter's vocabulary. Nor would he, for that matter, allow any real ground for eschatology, except for the sake of argument. But whatever called, his progress was in dramatic contrast to that of his last journey on this train that had taken him to his mother's deathbed six months before. In a way, his return was an aftermath of the event, and he hoped it would prove to be nothing more. Supporting this hope was a glimmering sign in the night-black windowpane to his right that never came farther than the corner of his eye: a girl's dimpled face, grained against the irony of her smile.

The question uppermost in Marcellus Hightower's mind was: Could he float a new loan on the homeplace to get it, as a riverman would say, around Devil's Elbow? Not actually a new loan, but a renewal of the mortgages already on it. What would this enterprise demand of him? The thought gave rise to inner tremors that took the edge off the pleasure of anticipation. He was to celebrate Christmas with old friends in Riverton, and visit his elder sister in the neighboring town of Lancaster. He would also see Adam, Adam who still rented a farm from the Hightowers and looked after the place and who still meant a lot to Marcellus. But Adam was so much a part of the exactions of his undertaking that he thought of their reunion with mixed pleasure.

The train had been interminably slow on his belated and conscience-stricken way to his mother's bedside, in June. He had got there almost too late, too late for his penitence and barely in time for a moment of recognition, before she fell into the irrevocable coma. An uneasy suspicion came over Marcellus now that—slow or fast—the rhythm of the train remained the same: "T-Taking you to the turkey roost." But the phrase was idiotic! It was only that he dumbly resisted this reentry into his past. Why? he asked himself captiously. He didn't intend to stay. And Dan Walker might be taking him on a turkey hunt at that. He shuddered involuntarily. The hollow windy voice spoke not of feathered game. At any rate, it was only a rabbit that jumped over his grave.

He got to his feet. He stood only head and shoulders higher than the back of his railroad chair: a bit over five feet seven—not that he didn't know the fraction exactly, two-thirds of an inch. The width and thickness of his shoulders and size of his head gave him a heavyset appearance, though he was actually on the lean side. As he turned obliquely, stretching and eyeing a silver watch on his uplifted wrist, chin and cheekbones lent his squarish face a flinty look, and his small deep-set eyes were hooded like a hawk's. His sharpened profile was forbidding. The bandbox air that smooth hair parted in the middle, well-fitting coat, and neat bow tie gave him was spoiled now by his yanking the paisley knot untied and coming out of collar, vest, and jacket.

On the earlier return (before he took the newspaper job at seventeen fifty a week) he had been getting into his Pullman upper berth by this time. He had always chosen uppers because they were quieter and he liked jumping for the curtain rod and swinging himself up. He glanced about him now with an aseptic smile. Just ahead of him, a wooly, ill-assorted pair of socked feet extended over the arm of the bench into the passageway. Across the aisle, farther on, a woman's disheveled hair floated above the bulge of a white pillow. The scene had a greasy look, a body and lunch-box smell. He wrinkled up his odd nose—which would have been well designed had it not been bradded on his face—and sniffed. But he told himself that he had better invest a quarter in the available sleeping accommodation, and follow suit.

Yet somehow he couldn't bring himself to it. He slid down into his seat again and consulted the night window. Its perspective gave him passage out of the room. His sensitive face softened, eyes agleam. He was back in Nashville. The gruff, gray-moustached judge by whom he sat was murmuring to him, "What would *you* do with her, son?" And he recovered his feeling of self-importance and its consequent restraint of novel responsibility. Actually, he held no official capacity at all. He was gleaning the court for his column, which had been running only six weeks. One of them, back again for the third time: the innocent country girl who got her traveling salesmen drunk and rolled them. His police Honor's confidence in him had astonished Marcellus.

The glow on his countenance represented other recognitions, too. Some time back he had won his police reporter's "badge," having stolen a gallon of drinkable confiscated liquor out of the lieutenant's office. He now got free drinks at three speakeasys that lay between the station house and his newspaper, was admitted to all the town's gambling halls, and the croupiers and whores called him Shorty. However, in the late summer, his life had taken on the aura of a more select and intellectual underworld through his sharing a flat with the paper's sports editor, Bill Trice. He too had been a police reporter in his day, and a great one. Trice was an education all by himself, if you could take it.

It was Trice who had introduced him to Nashville's Bohemia. Though it had been Bayless Lull who initiated him, out at Spencer's Bluff, the elevated edge of a symbolical river. Elated, too. It was a Baudelairean conspiracy to be drunken, and snotty in its way, on the Cumberland, there where Big-Foot had left his outsize print on a sandbar, going west. He had been impressed by the roster, though he got it only sotto voce from Trice: Bob Blue, humorous columnist for King Features; Rutherford Jones, modern composer; Bill Carson, navy recruiting doctor and world traveler; Hack Putnam, guitarist who knew all about white spirituals, taken in despite his teaching Latin at Vanderbilt; Honus Murphy, six-foot-four, who could shoulder-tote a canoe down or up the Bluff's eighty steps, but admitted mostly because of his wife, Delia called Delilah; and there were some others. But central, though no one would admit it (least of all would they admit it), were Clarendon Lull, who got kicked out of Vanderbilt for the satire he wrote on old Hound's Tooth, the humanities dean; and Bayless, his indispensable wife—Bayless, whose casualness covered astonishing knowledge, wit, tact, sympathy, and generosity—not to mention her beauty.

Marcellus was on his feet again. He retrieved his coat, hanging below the luggage rack, swung it under his arm, and made his way down the aisle to the smoker. It was empty, or almost: the Negro flagman lay sleeping on one of the leather benches. He made his way by him, sat down next to the window, and began filling a straight-stem briar pipe with two Greek symbols carved on the bowl.

By the time he had it lit, the lanky flagman had roused himself to a sitting position. Somnolently, he pushed an ashstand with his foot over to receive the burnt end of the kitchen match Marcellus held between his fingers. "Thanks!" he said, between pulls at his pipe. "Don't I know you?"

The disjointed black man gathered himself together, buttoning his blue coat. "Might." he admitted, as if silence were protective.

"If you had on a white coat, I would take you for the porter on the Nashville sleeper."

The man picked up his cap coldly. "Never there."

Removing his pipe, Marcellus blinked at him. "You know Judge Mathews, in Nashville?"

"Never there, neither," the flagman said with a detached understanding. His dim face relenting toward a smile, he added "I know about him, all right."

Marcellus bored in on the grin. "I'll bet you do!" he said with insinuation, thinking the Negro was so black his looks were hard to take hold of.

"That looks like a college pipe you got there," the flagman said, willing to be genial on a more proper subject. "Did you cut them letters in it?"

"Thank you, thank you! But it called for a better carver than I am." Marcellus gazed at the lettering on the dark brown bowl, and his eyes took fire. With an abrupt upthrust of chin, he came to his feet and strode across the compartment. Turning, his focus on the distance, he waved his arms and began to declaim under his breath—or more exactly, through his pipestem:

" 'Oh, how wonderful it is to be young,
How wonderful it is and how odd—
To astound all the neighbors with theories
And not to believe in God.' "

He paused, beating fist on palm measuredly to pick up the next stanza. "Something, something—

" 'To lie brown and naked beside fierce waters
And make all the farmers look to their daughters.' "

The flagman put on his black kepi and leaned an ear toward the window, as the fist-palm pause resumed. "Like a torpedo on the track?" he asked cryptically.

Marcellus shook this off and swung back across the room in triumph.

"To come scaley and old, with a pair of weak kidneys and a stick that trembles and have to believe in God—

"Isn't it odd!"

The flagman was peering through the windowpane. "Passed the fusee!" he announced. Then turning back to Marcellus, his face losing some if its dark severity, he went on in a tone of admiration, "You a shonuff poet! That fine!"

Marcellus snapped the pipe out of his mouth. "Oh, it's not mine! A real poet wrote that! Red Lull, in Nashville. Though it's not known off the Bluff—that's our little group there. But Clarendon has published a number of poems. He's a 'Fugitive.' " Marcellus said this as if he were saying he's a thirty-second-degree Scottish Rite Mason. "He's a novelist, too. Working on one now called *The Great Sickness.*"

The flagman nodded politely and began to get to his feet. Marcellus waved him back onto the bench. "But my special poem is *Ming*, 'master of a perverse fate, these two burdens yet must carry'—" He paused abruptly and took his pipe. The words piling up on him were: "There's one woman he cannot rape, another he cannot marry." It came to him confusingly that they wouldn't do between him and a colored man—especially one so strangely black. He shrugged and wagged his head sheepishly. "Well, you know, I've never tried to say that one sober. I have to have a few drinks before I can remember it."

"Kerreck!" the flagman said, on his feet again. He took a stride to the compartment door and peered up and down the passageway beyond. "And you got something in your luggage, I could go get it?"

Marcellus laughed stridently, saying, "They make better liquor where I'm going than where I came from." He didn't quite like this turn of things, but he saw that the flagman was smiling with more genuine feeling than before.

Still in the doorway, nodding and grinning, and without any perceptible movement of his loose pale gray lips, the flagman ventriloquized in a disapproving voice: “Come old or come early, *He* already there—the police judge of ‘em all!”

Marcellus snorted as he realized that this comment was aimed at Lull’s verse. He frowned, scrutinizing again the dull, dead blackness of the noncommittal face. The long eyelids lifted to give him the gray whites, with holes in them that led nowhere. Marcellus’ frown deepened into a shiver. He began knocking out his pipe, conscious again of the train’s rock and roar. “Guess I’ll get back to my seat,” he said.

The flagman limbered and grinned as if Marcellus had made a joke; this time, one so amusing that he exposed a gold jaw tooth. “Got to get up front myself,” he said genially, “to flag us by that red light.” He disappeared from the doorway.

But the gleam of the gold tooth, like a surprise ending, seemed to remain with Marcellus after the flagman had gone, and presently he refilled and relighted his pipe. The night window caught the corner of his eye again, and he smiled back at it and rocked across the smoker, coming stoutly with the last lines of *Ming:*

“ ‘But if you think he doesn’t know what to do, you’re wrong, by Harry!

“ ‘He marries the woman he cannot rape, and rapes the woman he cannot marry.’ ”

Melanie’s dimple had gone into a twist at this, a quizzical interrogation point.

She had been Bayless’ idea. He would have liked to fall in love with Bayless, but he supposed she had more lovers and would-be lovers than she could say grace over already. And her hands full, what with keeping Red’s love affairs on an even keel, too, and harmony in the community. So Bayless had found a girl for him: "She's cute and clever, not one you want to marry, but fun to be with."

"Sounds good," he had said, "if she don't want to get married, either!" But his double take on her had been a curious thing!

He had met Melanie in the semidarkness—just before they got into the rumble seat of the Lull's car. And on the ride out to the Bluff, agreeably he had found her as hep to the ways as the words of Bohemia, and her lips fresh. When they had got into the light in the main room of the Lulls' camp, he had seen that she was real young. A slip of a thing. She had looked almost virginal, with those bright dark eyes, under quick mauve, satiny lids—both shy and sly. Her sharp asides had surprised him. And he had been shocked to find that she was only a junior. Still, she was one of Red's students in poetry, and he had taken a fancy to her.

Marcellus might have seen in that light, too, something a little familiar about her looks. When Melanie had let out her former life on their second date she had said she had known at once who he was, but thought he wouldn't remember her. She had been only a child called "Plump" at that distant brief meeting, and he had scarcely been aware of her existence. Anyhow, in seven years she had lost all of "Plump" Crosby's chubbiness, and he had not recognized her.

Now, when he tried to recover the details of that encounter, he found that for some reason he didn't want to remember "Plump." This double image disturbed him. Marcellus slumped onto the leather bench by the window and pulled on his pipe. The plump little Melanie of that time had come from Macon, he remembered. Melanie and the Riverton girl she was visiting were at the Ransom's ostensibly to play with Mona Ransom, but Melanie had taken more interest in big brother David; had run after him, picked at him.

Already the swellings under Melanie's middy blouse were conspicuous—disturbing to him and, he had assumed, to David, too. She could scarcely have been more than thirteen, but her breasts were sixteen, maybe eighteen. It was plain she was proud of them. And she was a city girl. When he saw her and David coming out of the "company" bedroom together, into the back hall, he wondered what had gone on between them. Oh, he didn't seriously believe very much. But he was gourd green then, and wildly fanciful! And somehow it made him diffident still, when he and Melanie had spoken of the occasion, there in the parlor of her sorority house. Didn't they meet at a cane grinding at Ransoms'? She had seen him there, she said, but she didn't think they were ever introduced.

That wasn't, however, the first time that she saw him. She and "Goldilocks," her hostess, were having ice cream in Courtney's drugstore, at the long back table against the wall mirror that was part of the partition between the drug mixing and the public rooms. It was the table where the grown-ups usually gathered, but they had appropriated it and were sitting opposite each other to look in the glass and see who was coming in the door, before they issued their greetings. So she had seen Marcellus first in the drugstore fixture.

She could describe his clothes: moleskins and woods boots and plaid wool shirt. And he had red sunburn on his face. He had come in with a colored man, a remarkable-looking mulatto who stuttered. They were talking. Marcellus had paused to greet David Ransom, behind the soft-drink counter; but had looked right through her, without seeing her. He and the colored man had gone behind the counter where David stood, and the three of them had filed on into the back room.

In the smoker Marcellus took out his pipe to mutter aloud and wag his head. There they all were. On the brink of things. David,

Adam, himself. And precocious little Melanie taking them into her looking glass, into her future—but not seeing—nobody seeing the specter of violence glaring over their shoulders. The roar came closer.

Chapter 2

TEN-YEAR-OLD Mona, dark eyes shimmering, lips wavering in a defensive smile, ducked toward her plate of macaroni pie. But after a moment she came up to shake her head of bobbed tow hair, and retort, "I don't care: if my big brother likes her, I like her, too."

And he, Marcellus, had replied: "But your big brother likes a lot of 'em. And they like him. Don't they? Squirmie Irmie, heh, heh, heh!" That conversation had taken place in the late afternoon of the second Sunday in January of 1921, before the long seeming of irrelevance ended.

Irrelevance? He and Mona hadn't been talking about Squirmie Irmie, but about the Methodist preacher's daughter. And the term of ridicule he threw in was a substitute for the name he couldn't recall, the name of the little girl he had seen there six weeks before and hadn't quite liked. How remote can a person be from the scene of action and still be important to it? Marcellus wondered, unconscious now of the train that bore him onward to the country of this past, yet sensing a portentousness in the mention of Melanie—Melanie, who had been only a byword in bantering over the preacher's daughter, David's "girl" in that scene of ironic irrelevance from which David's absence went unnoted.

Marcellus and Mona were still at the table in the Ransom dining room, in which the high ceiling and walls of white plaster, above dark wainscoting, were then shadowed in lavender from the shaded swinging lamp. They were eating an early cold supper so that the children could get to an Epworth League meeting at the church on time. Mona's two next older brothers, aged twelve and fourteen, had already gobbled down their meal, and gone.

Earlier in the afternoon Carruthers Ransom had asked him about the absent David. Carruthers was uncle to the orphaned Ransom children, and they lived with him and his wife. Marcellus had encountered Carruthers at the Methodist Sunday school, where he was superintendent. Marcellus came because there wasn't anywhere else to go in Riverton on Sunday afternoon. Carruthers had said, "I see David didn't get back."

Marcellus thought he detected a tone of criticism, and he said defensively, "Well, he may have gone to church out there!"

This only brought a cackle from Carruthers, who added, "Yep, David probably said his prayers under a turkey roost."

Marcellus had at times thought of that two-day interlude as a nightmare of delayed reaction, a sleepwalk, in which they all danced along the tall ridge roof of the Ransom house, right on over the edge. But hadn't their lives been—certainly his own life had been—a sleepwalk up to that very hour? Irony is always retrospective.

His words of farewell to David at breakfast on Friday were the bitterest to bear. He and David were eating a quarter of an hour before the rest of the family for him to catch "Joe Brown," the local train, northbound. Marcellus had been going with his tie cutting only about six weeks, but was doing well enough, he thought, to expand his operation. He needed to make real money. After all, that was why he had quit Vanderbilt and come home: to save the place and provide for his mother, in Philadelphia. So he had asked David to go, on the following day, out to the Hightower place to take up the week's accumulation of crossties and pay off his hands. This would allow him to travel to two or three other towns in the vicinity to subcontract for additional ties. Saturday would be the best day for it. David, it happened, was at loose ends, having given up his job as soda skeet to his brother, Paul.

The high-ceilinged dining room was dim, the cover having been drawn back from one end of the table only. They sat, poised amid the chill shadows, sipping coffee automatically. Marcellus was saying: "You'll have to watch Guyton, that yellow Guinea nigger. He'll plug knotholes on you. And smear doty spots with mud."

David's mouth puckered and his eyes shimmered in response, but he hadn't spoken, when the kitchen door beyond the far end of the table swung open and Aunt Mary, the mountainous, gray-haired, mulatto cook, swept in, bearing a plate of hot biscuits.

Both stared at her with misgivings, and David, imitating her preacher intoned, "Lord God, Aunt Mary, you going to git Shorty left!"

But Marcellus said: "Hand me the syrup pitcher, Dave! I'll have time for a couple."

They finished the pile before they finally quit the table and had to run for it to get him to the train. So it was that he almost forgot to tell David about the flock of wild turkey, roosting in the upper swamp. And about the old swamp rat, who knew where the tree was. *Almost.* But he didn't.

Later that day, at the railroad junction where he had to wait an hour to take a train in another direction, he confronted his conscience about David. This uneasiness, however, had nothing to do with David's going to the swamp, turkey hunting. He had asked

David to take up his ties and pay off his hands as a personal favor. He should be taking him into partnership. Marcellus was nursing the potbellied stove in the depot's empty waiting room. He opened the door on the red-hot embers, preparatory to swinging the coal scuttle at them. The incandescence in the depths of the stove sharpened his sense of his own callousness. David had passed his job on to Paul, his older brother who always behaved as if he were the younger, because Paul had quit his job in Jesup before Christmas and come home and had got to running around with the wrong crowd. Paul needed to be working. It was the sort of thing David did that made you feel so self-centered.

But hell! Marcellus slammed the door shut. Who else would make as good a working partner? He had been thinking about talking his situation over with David, even before he stepped aside for Paul. Marcellus had three thousand ties hewn and most of them hauled to the railroad. But the thing was that they hadn't yet been accepted by the company contracting for them. He hadn't seen a dollar of their money. Moreover, he needed to keep his costs battened down, for he would soon have to pay something on the mortgage on the place and send money to his mother.

"He r-reckless 'bout his drinking." Squatting on his haunches beside the pump, under the big water oak in his yard, Adam had halted Marcellus' question on David before he could ask it.

"It might be reckless in somebody else!" Marcellus had thrown out, from his seat in the old winehouse doorway.

Adam's lips had worked convulsively behind his scraggly gray moustache for an instant. "I-I know. He's stout as they come. And mighty apt, mighty apt. And got a way with everybody. Nobody's a stranger to him. A finer young feller ain't never lived." He shook his head. "But it ain't wary to drink with Tom, Dick, and Harry."

Marcellus had laughed incredulously and come to his feet. But he had held his tongue. He got up now in the empty waiting room and stumbled about the benches, bumping shoulders with the vision of his friend—the muscular, broad-shouldered David, just under six feet, with a wrestler's build.

The composed, good-natured face, with its longish jaw, strong nose and mouth, and crisp blond-mahogany hair combed back from a broad forehead in a pompadour, smiled familiarly on Marcellus. David was, above all, the smile that lay in his luminous brown eyes, bearing always in their depths the elusive light that played between the merriment and melancholy. Marcellus considered his eyes for a moment now, as he had many times before. Although he and David had been intimates since they were small boys, had played, fought, studied, courted, had even swapped dreams and ambitions together, those dark magnetic eyes remained mysterious for him.

It wasn't that he had no knowledge of the mystery, the thing that had set him and David apart in the world and drew them together: their fatherlessness. His father had died just a year before David's died. And he had led David into the strange headless state of being a boy without a father, had comforted him before a derisive curiosity on the school grounds: "Did you cry when your pappy died?"—the callous jest, the taunt that somehow seemed to slash at your privates. It had bound them together against all boys who had fathers. Yes, side by side, they had stood before the long dark that had no shape. Yet, hadn't there been more? Even in death David had gone beyond him; Fate had taken him on beyond. For, a year later, David's mother had died, too.

Why hadn't he taken David into his confidence? Marcellus heard the moaning sound of a train whistle, and got to his feet, without trying to answer his question.

That Monday came early and gray, and Marcellus swallowed his fried eggs and coffee, without even waiting for a hot biscuit, cranked his pickup truck with an anguished grind, and clattered off for town on three cylinders. Rounding up his hands to go to the woods on Monday was always, as he said, belated, bitched up, and bitter. When he turned the corner onto Main Street and parked in front of Carruthers Ransom's grocery store, only five of the twenty-two tie cutters that he hauled from town regularly were there, under the sidewalk shed.

He took Tom, his bellwether, and went to the Quarter to run them up. One was sick in bed; another had gone off with a man's wife; two were in jail; and three he could not find hide or hair of, at all. It was noon when he finally set off for his woods with three-fourths of a load.

After he had them distributed over the location, and the flat, double counterpoint of their saws and axes was on the air and he was about to go on to Adam's place, he saw that it was already one thirty. And, frowning at his watch face with the realization of how late in the day it was, a sudden feeling of mystification and annoyance took him. And he thought that it wasn't like Dave to go on off, without leaving him some sort of word, somewhere!

He found Adam at his woodpile, throwing off a load of lightwood logs. He hadn't seen David since Saturday, he said. When Marcellus told him that neither had David's uncle at Adair and that David had not shown up at Riverton, Adam came down off the wagon, telling his boy, Telfair, to finish the job. He stared at Marcellus, shot holes coming into his eyes. Then he said, glancing away thoughtfully, "H-He come by here, come by 'bout an hour 'fore sundown. Borrowed four shells. Said he'd found he didn't have nothin' but bird shot in his huntin' coat." Adam's jaw worked convulsively for a moment before he went on. "He was going t-to t-take a crack at those turkeys you had told him 'bout. Asked me if I knew where they were roosting—but I didn't."

Adam, advancing on Marcellus, met his gaze in a long look, both of their faces growing expressionless before they broke apart, to move toward the gate. Adam resumed: "He asked me, then, if I knew where he might run up on that old swamp rat Buck Fykes. And I told 'im 'bout Buck having a shack down by the old ferry landing."

When they were at the pickup truck, Marcellus got back under the wheel and opened the door for Adam. Adam paused, with his foot on the runningboard. "I wasn't sho' David knowed the way through there, and I walked with him to the ferry road and a little piece down hit. I stopped off 'bout where that old steamboat boiler lies buried. And I watched 'im out of sight. He was walkin' on, brisk, his gun cradled in his arm. He had on army britches and a army shirt under his hunting coat. And a green felt hat."

Marcellus raced the motor impulsively.

When they got to the commissary, they did not halt on the front porch to swap talk with the half-dozen tenant farmers loafing there, but strode on through the long, high, old-fashioned wooden building to the office at the back. Here Marcellus had Adam repeat his story to Andrew Ransom, Carruthers' younger brother, fair and fleshy, whose usually amiable face, now sober, stiffened visibly as he listened. He pushed against his desk to swing his swivel chair about. "Since you stopped by here a while ago, Shorty, I've seen Pete Ambrose and old man Stoney," he said. "They haven't seen anything of him."

Andrew Ransom and Marcellus exchanged a staring gaze, then hastily broke it off—Ransom glancing through the glass window of his office. "I think I see somebody else out there," he said, getting up abruptly. "Wait a minute." Marcellus had looked, too, and nodded quickly.

Then they both became more deliberate, Ransom slowing his stride as he got into the outer room, and Marcellus modulating his voice as he called out, "I'll phone Bright's. He could have gone up there, shad fishing."

But these inquiries brought no news of David. Marcellus reasoned now that it was time to call Carruthers Ransom at Riverton, though a dumb reluctance took him as he cranked the phone. He reported David's not turning up prudently, but when Carruthers asked, "Do you think something could have *happened* to him?" Marcellus broke out with, "*Anybody* can get shot accidentally, hunting." He startled himself by this, and the catch that came in his throat astonished him even more: he couldn't conceive of David's shooting himself.

Riverton was only a little over five miles away, and there was a good hard dirt road to Adair. In thirty minutes, Carruthers arrived with Robert Bruce, the mayor, and the town marshal. There were three carloads of men with them. A dozen more from around the commissary joined the party.

Since Adam, the last man known to have seen him, put him on the swamp road to Hightower's old ferry landing, the crowd went there. They had no trouble locating the rough plank one-room shack on the low bluff above the landing where the old swamp rat Buck Fykes was said to hang out. But it was quite empty. And the marshal, Rup Willis, after going through it, reported that the occupant had recently broke camp, and in a hurry.

Marcellus was wondering how he could deduce all that from a cold potbellied stove and a ragged piece of mildewed comforter. But old Hinshaw Slappy, his neighbor, turned up at Marcellus' elbow at this point to report, "Buck's boat's gone, lock and chain!"

This jarred him more, for if anybody knew this swamp and what went on in it, Hinshaw did. Fykes had run off. What did it mean? Marcellus suddenly felt himself weak in the knees. But before he could assess this news, Slappy gave Marcellus' impulse more coherent direction. Buck had a helper, he whispered lachrymosely—a 'bout-grown boy named Slitcher. He lived with his uncle, on the Amos place.

A half hour later, Marcellus, Carruthers, and Rup Willis located the Slitcher boy in his uncle's backyard, digging sweet potatoes out of a winter bed. He was down on his knees and didn't get up when they came over to the fence to talk to him.

Carruthers, his spare frame pitched over the top of the fence in his downright way of doing things, reported their mission and information and asked whether he had seen David Ransom or heard anything about him.

Slitcher's dirty, thin, hard-eyed face, as he looked them over, had little that was youthful about it, and it was surely not boyish. He lowered his gaze again and began tossing potatoes into the mouth of a croker sack, as if he were reflecting on the matter. Yes, he said finally, He had seen a man that fitted that description. The fellow had come to get Fykes to tell him about a turkey roost. Slitcher tossed a few more potatoes into the sack, then rose up on his knees and lifted his face to them, as if he were going to make a clean breast of it, Marcellus thought, but of course he wasn't. His tone was faintly argumentative. "I knew where the roost was, too, and I was getting ready to leave. I was coming out here to my uncle's, then. And I told 'im I'd go by with 'im and show 'im the place. It was just about on my way." He sat back down and returned to his task.

Rup Willis spoke up. "Did you do that?"

“Yes,” he said, “And I left ‘im there, near the roost.” He pitched in another potato, then rose again to face them. “That’s the last time I seen ‘im.”

Despite this hard-faced fellow’s dimly hostile manner, his story could be true and probably was, Marcellus thought, but where did it get them? He was conscious of Slitcher’s shifting gaze before he spoke again, spoke to the point that was in everybody’s mind then.

“Didn’t y’all run into Fykes?”

“Didn’t you know he’d run off down the river?” Rup shot back at him, in a show of his professional talent.

Still holding their gaze, Slitcher’s hands moved to toss another potato in the sack. “No,” he said, “No, I didn’t.”

Rup said, “Well, it looks like he has. The camp’s cleaned out and his boat’s gone, lock and chain.”

Slitcher opened his mouth in what could have passed either for a gasp or a mirthless laugh, for it was soundless. Then he said loudly, as if to himself, “So that’s why he wanted my boat paddle!”

This ended the inquiry. They looked at one another, and turned back toward the car they had come in.

Slitcher called after them: “But I ain’t surprised. He takes off whenever the notion strikes ‘im. On the river.”

Later, Marcellus was to laugh wryly at the craftiness of Slitcher’s postscript, to laugh in harassment at this first and the many other versions Slitcher gave of the encounter and at the uncertainties that were to echo from them. But then, at that moment, he took a little comfort in it, half thinking—it was really only a hopeful upsurge—that Fykes’ flight might be a coincidence—thinking that maybe there hadn’t been any reason for Fykes to run off.

But fifteen minutes later, at Adam’s place—there beyond his back field, near the mouth of the swamp road where a giant bonfire burned and men were coming and going, as if it were a military camp—fifteen minutes later, as they were driving down the lane, a great, diffused shout went up. Marcellus could not make out the broken cries, but he sensed distress in them. It cut off their own talk. No one in the car spoke a word, as Carruthers speeded it up to get out of the lane to the blaze.

When they had got through the back gate and pulled off to the side of the road, they saw three men hurrying toward them, bearing things in their hands. Others followed on behind. Marcellus was first out of the car, and advanced to meet them.

Then he saw in the wavering firelight that it was an unbreached shotgun that the potbellied sign painter Munson was handing him. "We found these things under a log," he was saying, "in the swamp, covered up with leaves." The man beside him was holding up a canvas hunting coat.

Marcellus' face stiffened, and he stared at the coat without touching it. He did not need to. It was plainly David's. He turned numbly away, without speaking. But only to face the third man, who was holding up a soft green felt hat, with a grosgrain ribbon around the crown—the crown that had been so close a part of the once invulnerable David!

Chapter 3

HE TURNED his back on the crowd at the bonfire and stumbled off into the gloom, still holding the shotgun in his hands as Munson had given it to him, unbreached. When he had got in among the thickening pine saplings he came to a halt, staring at its loaded chambers, the two bright brass disks that glinted in the firelight, their percussion caps dimly visible. But he did not see the cartridges. He did not know the gun was in his hands. David looked up at him from the breach.

He had sent him to the woods. He had told him about the turkeys, the swamp rats. What had he done to David? The question tore at his ribs like a dog.

As he stood there, gripped by the vision, the eyes smiled in their melancholy way to give his question the hidden danger of a switchblade knife. The depths opened up, glittered, and Marcellus cried out hoarsely, "No!" This was morbid. It had never been more than a suspicion, a discountenanced suspicion. He had put the sharp feelings toward David from him. He couldn't even remember the squirmy girl's name! The thing hadn't even been in the back of his head when he asked him to go to the woods. David couldn't have *known* of his suspicion anyhow. The smile did not commit David, he told himself with relief. It had always been David's smile. Yes its leniency drained Marcellus of all assurance. He was alone. For David was gone beyond him again—to leave him a new shame, both betrayer and betrayed. How had he not known? Any man can get killed. Any man. But it was there all the time in his gaze. How had he not suspected the secret of that smile? How had he not seen it? What had blinded him to its meaning? What had blinded him concerning David?

An odor of oat straw and rotten eggs rose in his nostrils, and the back of his throat went tight and dry and numb. He moved off, still holding the unbreached gun in both hands—and the face, that now wore the look of another day.

How he and David, at twelve years of age and strictly brought up, happened to be left for the better part of an afternoon with the wild, loose, grown-up Rawlings boys on their remote, broken-down swamp farm was hard to reconstruct now, but it had to do with David's absentminded old Cousin Tommy. Marcellus had never seen the Rawlings boys before, and was uncomfortable with them from the start. All three of them had long lean faces and split-level eyes, and looked like sallow Siamese cats. They spoke in an indolent heckling manner, using only their own inside expressions, as if they were talking dog Latin. They called Marcellus by his last name, mispronouncing it in a way that was close to making fun of it. And Carver, the oldest, went around with a switchblade knife in his hands, whittling on something. Their tormenting of the Negro boy they kept around to make the butt of their jokes gave Marcellus the dry grins. He didn't like it, even though Jughead, as they called him, was lanky and big-footed and boggled at the knees when he walked, as if his head were too heavy for him, and talked in a voice that went up and down comically—even though he seemed to endure their hazing. Marcellus knew his mother wouldn't countenance his poking fun at a Negro. He sensed too, if less consciously, that the Rawlings boys had to be making fun of somebody, *somebody,* all the time. And this made him more uncomfortable still.

Yet none of this prepared him for what he and David looked on through the crack in the unchinked pole shed near the barn, where they had all been called by Carver. At first, seeing only Jughead in the middle of the dirt floor, Marcellus was mystified, though he still wore his polite, uncomfortable grin. Then he discovered the duck-legged Negro girl, bending over, looking into one of the hen nests against the wall. Before he had time even to suspect what it was about, Carver spoke: "Look a-here, Jughead's done slipped off in this-here dark place to git to his woman. Tell'er she needn't to be leaning over, making like she's looking in that hen nest, Jughead. We know what you-all come in here for!"

The Negro's head boggled out of balance, and he said in his uneven voice, "Now, Mister Carver, please don't talk like that!"

The Rawlings boys all laughed. Marcellus, his face stiff and warm, glimpsed David, beside him, getting red too. The Rawlingses kept it up, laughing as if they were picking at an itching sore with morbid pleasure. Jughead—his eyes walling, his face working, turning round and round—began to cry. The duck-legged girl came to him and took his hand, yelling out at the eyes at the cracks in sullen desperation: "Y'all oughter be shamed of yourself! I'm going to tell your mommer, Mister Carver!"

The Rawlingses let out turkey-gobbler hoots that dribbled off, then quit. Marcellus could see between the cracks, at the opposite corner, Carver notching a log as the pause lengthened; then he said, "If you don't want to git that black throat of yourn slit, you better keep your damn trap shut!"

Marcellus had heard of boys who played at putting a dog to a bitch in heat. But human beings! His legs began to tremble, and his stomach did a flip. Surely he must be wrong? He turned to David to encounter his own appalled suspicion in David's eyes.

Carver removed their doubts. It wasn't only his beastly words, though Marcellus took them in—"make her git on her hands and knees"—but his laugh and the glinting blade of the knife and the bloodless pitchfork finger that swam in Marcellus' vision and twisted in his stomach with the realization that they would slash open and tear away the last shred of clothes, the least bit of privacy and, really, humanity left to Jughead and the girl. And Jughead's yellow-green face, quaking, going to pieces before him, sucked him in through the crack, into the slit-eyed ring, into Jughead's skin—the quiet hopeless crying making Marcellus' bones ache. Even now Marcellus could feel the nightmare quality of it. He hadn't been able to look away.

He wouldn't have been able to move, either, if David hadn't taken him by the hand—they slipped around the corner of the shed. But it was in front, when David swung open the door and called to Jughead to come on out, that Marcellus had turned to stare at David in astonishment and gratitude and had seen that, in spite of the pulse at his throat, he took his time to meet Carver's gaze, and smiled. Then David had turned the joke on the Rawlings boys by looking around the tree between them and their house and calling out. "Yes'um, Mrs. Rawlings. You better come see. I don't know what these boys trying to do to Jughead!" Carver had jumped ten feet, and everybody laughed.

His own reaction had been tardy and stiff. And the shame of his cowardice was with him still. Though it hadn't been so much his fear of bodily harm as his fear of the Rawlings boys' ridicule that had paralyzed him at the crack that afternoon. A long time ago. But David smiling, David had dived into the river Styx, *that* afternoon. Becoming aware of the shotgun in his hands, Marcellus snapped it together. He had pulled the trigger on David, and the unshakable gaze there before the Rawlings boys had vanished in the haunted look. The assurance of that boyhood day had nothing to do with the squirmy girl or with Marcellus' pulling the trigger. Nothing. Adam's words sneaked hatefully back into his mind: *It ain't wary to drink with Tom, Dick, and Harry.*

A hand clasped him by the arm. He heard Carruthers Ransom's corn-pone-plain voice: "Shorty, we better get going. Do you want to ride over with me and the constable to pick up that Slitcher boy now?" As Marcellus moved off with them, Carruthers added, "You might as well hold on to that gun."

Chapter 4

THE MOCKERY of it was in the echo that came back into Marcellus' head for the first time that night in the swamp. "Thank ye, Mr. Hightower."

The thing that he had done, when he returned from Vanderbilt that winter to save the homeplace, was to set up living quarters in Adam's yard. He never gave this a second thought at the time. Before he went off to school he had always spent about as much of his leisure around Adam's place as anywhere else. Mostly in the woods and on the river, but under Adam's hand, hunting, fishing, rounding up hogs and cattle, rafting timber. Since he was big enough to get from Riverton over the seven miles to the Hightower holding, he had been coming there—almost since his father died and, as he believed, put him in Adam's care to bring up right. Often enough he had bunked in the yard and, on occasion, he had slept at Adam's house. The question never came into his head.

Strictly speaking, the old winehouse was not a part of Adam's domicile, however, and Adam could look at it that way. Besides, he, Marcellus, was only camping there. But Adam had been positive about sending food out to Marcellus in the winehouse and not asking him to his table. He chose not to understand Marcellus' hints about how inconvenient and unnecessary it was for him to do so.

Of course, Marcellus had known better than to try to talk to Adam about the part-time job he had taken at Fisk University that fall, in the practice of race liberalism. Still, in his callownesss, he hadn't guessed that his staying at Adam's yard was a matter of concern to him (and not only to Adam, but to his own white friends in Riverton) and a source of the active hostility of the poor whites of the neighborhood—had not guessed it until that bonfired unbelievable night.

Marcellus had at the time failed to sense mockery in the unctuous words of the old swamp rat Buck Fykes that unfortunate day in Adam's lane. "I thought I'd tell ye. Thought you mought like to take a shot at 'em."

And he, retorting quickly, "We don't own the swamp anymore."

Buck, after a time sidling closer: "I kin show you where they're roostin'. Hit's not in the low swamp. Hit's not on company land." He had broken away here, and the old man had called out sharply, "And I get two, I'll bring yuh one of 'em?" He had shrugged again and snorted, moving on. But Buck had yelled after him, in what he later decided was a hostile tone, "How about hit?"

The insistence of it had moved him to nod over his shoulder, saying, "I can't keep you from it."

Buck had yelled then, "Thank ye—Mr. Hightower!" (It had sounded like "Hiretire.")

It was actually the boy, Dunk Slitcher, that he and Carruthers and the mayor and the district constable were talking to, there by the bonfire. And, of course, the boy didn't say anything of the sort. But the echo had sounded in Marcellus' ears then, and many times afterward during the days they were hunting for old Buck.

The district constable, Mal Brewer, had gone back with Carruthers and Marcellus to get Slitcher. Dunk had come readily enough, still feigning concern and the wish to help, though he professed to know no more about the hiding of David's things than they did.

With men still coming out from Riverton and from all over the south end of adjoining Clarke, the county they were in, there were by this time a couple of hundred of them scattered over the woods and the swamp. The nerve center had moved with Slitcher from the bonfire in the pines behind Adam's place to the bonfire now burning in the upper swamp under the edge of the tall magnolia tree, alleged to be the turkey roost that David had sought. There were droppings about, on the bushes and ground. It could have been turkeys that roosted above. But those wary birds, if they had ever been there, were long gone, had probably quit the swamp altogether, for already searchers who had covered the crosstie woods earlier were now abroad in the swamp at all points of the compass. They took their direction from Mayor Bruce, pivoting on the turkey roost—or trying to. Several of the posses got lost. And there were many bonfires built in the swamp that night, to light the way, though actually they served more to increase the confusion.

The circle about Dunk included by this time the Clarke County sheriff and, too, another Slitcher uncle, from a distance, a mill hand, a mouthy fellow called Simon. Dunk, his face still dirty, but now shadow-marked and wavering in the firelight, stood in the circle with the sheriff beside him, nearer the blaze, while questioners were about in knots, farther from it. The fire's long, leaping tongues made the mauve-bottomed magnolia leaves about it crackle and pop and sent aloft waves of heat and smoke that turned the green-gray density of brush, vine, and tree into phantasmagoria of shifting monster shadows.

By this time, too, the fiction of Dunk's neighborly solicitude had worn threadbare, and the presence of the big stolid sheriff, blunt-faced and ambiguous, under a powder-gray broad-brimmed hat, suggested custody as well as protection. Carruthers' keen voice still led the way, though Mayor Bruce, the district constable, and Marcellus were taking part. The thing was that Dunk's story got them nowhere. They had already walked him around the tree to point out where David had stood, and he stood at each moment of their putative conversation, going over parts of it again and again. Dunk had wavered some and reconsidered on closer questioning, but they were turning up no real loopholes in it.

Marcellus saw Mayor Bruce and Carruthers Ransom look at each other; then the mayor moved on Slitcher. A spare, towering man of a natural elegance, Robert Bruce was Riverton's chosen leader and, Marcellus thought, idea of nobility, too. He nodded to the young tough gravely. "Dunk," he began, in his polished bass, "you say you haven't seen Buck Fykes since you left him at his shack on the river, Saturday afternoon?"

Slitcher's shallow hard face shifted, his eyes catching the firelight like a coon's. "That's right," he said.

"You didn't see him at any time on Sunday"—Bruce's poised inflection seemed to affirm; he lifted his prominent nose—"at your Uncle Herman's place?"

Slitcher blinked at him suspiciously. Bruce's grace of bearing was such that the person he spoke to was usually not only inspired by his example but elevated by his regard. But Dunk only barked hostilely, "I said I didn't see 'im!"

"You were at your uncle's on Sunday?" the mayor asked softly, his heavy lower lip bland.

"All day," said the boy.

Bruce repeated, as if he assumed they were playing by Marquis of Queensbury rules, "You were there all day and you didn't see Fykes?"

"No, I didn't see 'im," said Slitcher, adding defiantly, "'cause he wasn't there!"

"Do you know any Hadleys?"

"Hadleys?" There was a flicker of uncertainty, then, emphatically, "No."

"They live over in your uncle's neighborhood."

"Never heard of 'em."

"You don't know Tom Hadley?"

"No. No, I don't!"

Bruce tonelessly: "Tom Hadley, who knows you, nevertheless—all of you Slitchers—says he saw Buck Fykes in Herman Slitcher's backyard about ten o'clock Sunday morning."

There was a pause, then the boy's head wagged from side to side as he retorted in vehement jerks: "Not—on—no—Sunday morning. He might of seen 'im there the day before."

"He says Sunday."

A tall, sloping-shouldered man moved from the outer edge in toward the fire. He was more leathery and wrinkled, but had the same shallow features as the boy. He shrugged and laughed. "That must be the one they call Lying Tom!"

Mayor Bruce lifted his long fine face impassively to take him in.

"I'm Simon Slitcher, Herman's brother and this boy's uncle," the man announced on a vindictive note.

Bruce nodded, then, speaking to his earlier remark, said "We'll see who's called what, perhaps," and turned from him, beckoning Andrew Ransom, some distance away.

At this moment Dunk hung his head, then did a sort of club-footed double shuffle that suggested a change, either of mind or heart, and that brought him again before Mayor Bruce. "I'll tell you, Mr. Bruce, I've been holding something back," he said hurriedly, giving his uncle a passing glance as he lifted his gaze. "I didn't mention it 'cause I don't know that it means a thing. I don't know it." He turned a little away and glanced at the faces about him, his eyes dark with anxiety. "Mr. Bruce, there wasn't nobody else with us in the *swamp,* when I left this Ransom fellow. But I passed somebody just after I come out of it, in among those field pine below the old nigger's place." His voice took on dramatic pitch. "And he was headed for the swamp, headed right toward the spot where I left Ransom. A-totin' a gun."

Carruthers and Marcellus drew closer, but there was a guardedness in their sharpened faces. The mayor said firmly, "I take it that it was somebody you know?"

"Yessir." Slitcher's head jerked in a quick double nod. "Yessir. It wasn't nobody else but that old Atwell nigger, his self." He barked the last words stiff-armed, hands laced together before him, as if he were leaning on a parapet.

The mayor, the popeyed district constable, Carruthers, and Marcellus all examined the set face impassively for a long moment, then exchanged glances in silence. Bruce spoke with an ironic modulation that was, perhaps, lost on Slitcher, though it was not without effect. "Dunk, you did hold back on a remarkable detail." Marcellus snorted and turned away, Andrew Ransom's murmur as they passed each other was inaudible, but his tone was incredulous.

Slitcher repeated defiantly, "It wasn't nobody but the old nigger with a shotgun in his hand."

So Dunk was *lying*, and lamely, Marcellus thought, still somehow feeling surprised. But the reality of it grew suddenly grim when, glancing about the circle, he discovered that Simon Slitcher had dropped out and disappeared into the brush. Marcellus went to locate Adam.

This he was able to do after a few minutes, scarcely a hundred paces away, near the old ferry road, where the posse Adam was guiding had built a bonfire to warm themselves by and blow a bit. Marcellus found that he hadn't moved any too fast. As he got there he saw another batch swarming in from the road and mingling with those at the fire and talking loudly. "Did you hear about the nigger?" he caught, in a high cracker drawl, above the noise.

The swamp was more open here on the roadside, and Marcellus stood a little away, looking the crowd over. He didn't seem to be able to recognize the newcomers, but they had, in country idiom, a hammerheaded, ragtail look about them. He did identify Big Sam Crews, a slow-witted teamster, who looked like a caricature of General von Hindenburg, with his red moustaches and secondhand army officer's overcoat. He picked out Simon Slitcher, too, on the outskirts. And recognized, threaded through the lot, other Slitchers. He did not know them, but they had the same sort of heads as Simon and Dunk. Marcellus decided the peculiarity was the slanting of the forehead and jaw—the whole face, with its sharp shallow eye sockets, all at the same angle. And each had a forelock that grew out of the brow, like a tuft of wire grass. He picked out five Slitchers among the noisy scatter moving into the clump at the fire, Marcellus thought, like babbling rabbit dogs.

He picked up chilling talk: *They done made Dunk tell who hit was. . . .He seen this Atwell nigger aheaded into the swamp right where he left Ransom. . . .Yeah, that stutterin' nigger. . . . Had a shotgun. . . . Naw, Dunk didn't hear no shootin'. . . .But the nigger knows more'n he's tellin'. . . . The sheriff? Hell, he thinks they elected 'im over in Ochehatchie County! But the nigger ought to be made to talk!*

They were really going to try to pull something. Marcellus had never faced such a thing before, and stagefright made his legs tremble, prompted the drizzles he already had. He saw no weapons, though some of them must have pistols on them. The feel of the barrel of David's shotgun in his hand was suddenly comfortable. It was well that he had taken charge of it. And just as well, too, that he hadn't unloaded it. It could still speak for David, if it had to! He saw now, his pulse sharp, Adam approaching the fire with an armful of wood. Shouldering the gun, he moved toward him. When Adam had replenished the blaze and turned away, he was standing beside him. In the glance they exchanged Marcellus realized that Adam was fully aware of his own jeopardy.

At that moment he sensed that someone was bearing down upon them, and heard at his back Big Sam Crews' booming voice. "If the sheriff won't, fellows, maybe *we* can git something out of this here nigger!"

Marcellus wheeled about to confront him, and Crews, in surprise, deflected his course and sidled away toward the fire beyond them. As they were threading their way through the crowd, he heard the approval for Crews' threat. The rowdies were egging one another on. And behind him, before they got out of the thick of it, "Maybe a little barrel treatment would help 'im to talk." Making their way out, they turned in time for Marcellus to see as well as hear. From under the shadow of his black hat, a hard-cheeked fellow barked, “Barrel, hell! Let’s git a rope.” There, all about him, their faces tightening, eyes flaring, men began to stride jerkily back and forth around the fire.

Marcellus followed Adam away from the crowd to a big ash tree, and they took their stand against its trunk. A half-grown Riverton boy, who had somehow escaped being sent home at sundown, came by, picking his way through the brush near them, and Marcellus yelled at him. “Hubert, go get Mr. Robert as quick as you can!” referring to the mayor.

In the rutted mud flat, under the high trees, where the fire blazed, the men in motion, in their woods boots and overalls and crazy quilt of coats, might have been awkward Indians, dancing to work themselves up to the massacre. Marcellus had a fleeting sense of this, as he gave his attention to the small clump still holding to the fire. He recognized these to be Riverton sawmill hands, and strove for a name that he might appeal to one of them. He didn’t have time.

The man who had talked rope broke away, looking back at the crowd to yell, “Ain’t ye got no guts!” and began to move toward the tree against which he and Adam stood.

Marcellus had been feeling weak-kneed and near panic, but this sent a pain through him that tightened his nerves and brought him a step forward, the gun half raised. David’s gun. The man halted, and his mouth broke open to let out a shrill bark: “Hightower, what you think you going to do with that gun!” Marcellus held to what he had, without moving. After a lengthening pause, the fellow flung his black hat on the ground, shouting: “I’ll be Goddamned! What’s going on here? Are you tryin’ to cover up for a damned nigger?”

Marcellus only gritted his teeth to let his threatening posture speak for him. Watchfully, he eased his gun down an inch.

The talker turned half around to those behind him, now halted in their tracks. His face was a pale black-holed mask, wavering in the firelight. "Damned nigger lover!" he cried out, as if he had caught Marcellus in a heinous crime.

"Nigger lover," echoed a lank youngster, in the crowd. Marcellus saw he was a Slitcher. Stamping on the ground with his big feet, he yelled again, "Yeah, he lives with niggers—sleeps with 'em, they tell me!" This broke the spell, and the crowd got into motion again. At the back a deep-throated lout, lifting his head like a hound, bayed, "A nigger-lovin' son of a bitch!"

Some of them merely marked time, but Marcellus saw that others were inching up on him by half steps. The rope talker had been joined by Simon Slitcher, and the two of them, their heads down, eyes shifting, came nearer and nearer.

The frightful creepiness of this almost hypnotized him; then, between their glinting furtive eyes and his dilated, glittering ones, a spark flared. He felt a stab of panic, and his burning stomach shrank convulsively, jerking the gun in his hands to his shoulder and jerking his words out upon the air.

"First man at the edge of the tree!"

It was as if he had used David's voice as well as his gun—they were strange, hoarse words. But they halted the men.

An instant later, Simon Slitcher wagged his head and fell back, and the man beside him grimaced and nodded. Shifting his gaze, Marcellus saw the sheriff coming out of the brush behind him. He grew conscious of the gun in his hands, and lowered it, his stance limbering. He felt weak and tried to cover it with a grin. "These rowdies wanted to string Adam up," he called out.

“Looks like a Slitcher SOS rally!” The voice was Robert Bruce’s, and he saw that the mayor, just straightening up to his full height, had followed the sheriff out of the brush, into the open.

But the Slitchers were abashed only briefly. Simon was pacing back and forth, to work himself up into another heat. He began in a whine. “All right, Shur’f, why can’t the nigger answer some questions?”

Marcellus retorted sharply, “They tried to mob him, hang ‘im!”

The sheriff moved on the men, raising his hand for quiet. “We’re not going to have any rough stuff here, Slitcher!”

The recent rope talker picked up his hat. “Well, Shur’f, do you want to find out who did the killin’ ”—he jerked the crown down on his head—“or could it be you tryin’ to protect somebody?”

The sheriff turned and fastened his gaze on him, as if he were using binoculars. “I’ll protect any man from a mob, Snavely. If I can.”

From the cardboard crowd a thin voiced called out, “That there nigger lover over there may have some reason to want to protect his nigger.”

This seemed to remind the men of a personal insult, and they got into motion again, bobbling and churning about and popping off: *A damned nigger lover! . . . I hate a nigger lover! . . . Sleeps with ‘em, they tell me!*

They looked as if they were on top of a hot stove, Marcellus thought, staring at them in fresh astonishment. When they had called him “nigger lover” earlier, he had been in too great a fright to react to it. Now he found their epithet shocking, and equally shocking the venom in their voices. They seemed to hate him even worse than they did Adam.

The shifting crowd began to surround the sheriff, growing noisier. Mayor Bruce strode out among them and, raising his arms above their heads, shouted in astonishingly powerful voice, "Quiet!"

This brought a lull, in noise and movement, and the sheriff's crisp words rang out: "Simon Slitcher, you'd better quiet down, or I'll put you under arrest, too!" He settled his gray hat on his head. "We've already kicked up the lard-can still Dunk was running with old Buck, in the lower swamp. Dunk's admitted to it. And we've had word you were selling their pop-skull for 'em up around Dublin.

The Slitcher uncle dropped his face like a man who has hit a slick on a footlog. He sidled away, and the crowd began to go to pieces.

But the sheriff was still apprehensive, as he joined Marcellus and Adam under the tree. "They're going to give us trouble, Hightower," he said, "if we don't get this colored man away from here. And the only safe place tonight is in my jail."

"Jail!" Marcellus glowered, his neck beginning to swell. He looked appealingly at Mayor Bruce. But Marcellus had been shaken by the ragtail assault on him and Adam. And he kept wondering whether he would actually have shot Slitcher and Snavely, if the sheriff hadn't turned up. In the end he agreed to Adam's being locked up for his own protection, if he, Marcellus, were allowed to go along to see that he got good treatment.

Marcellus was only pleasantly surprised when Robert Bruce said, "Shorty, I'm going to see this thing through, too." And turning to the sheriff: "I have my car, Clyde; Shorty Hightower and I will meet you in Clarksville at the door of the jail, *with Adam.*" Marcellus had felt elevated by Mr. Robert's gesture. But when they paused at the nearby fire, where Dunk Slitcher and most of the leaders were gathered, and Carruthers Ransom, also, volunteered to go along, Marcellus decided that there must be something behind their coming with him, besides their not altogether trusting the sheriff.

They showed no disposition to enlighten him, however. They remained quiet during the ten-mile trip to the county seat. At the jail, the sheriff didn't put Adam in a cell, but only in the reception room with the jailer. He gave him a good bed and promised them he would release him just as soon as things quieted down.

It had been a help to have the mayor and Carruthers there to be sure, but Marcellus still wondered at their coming. They didn't drop any hints on the return trip, either. Carruthers kept talking about Marcellus' attitude toward Negroes, saying that he and David had only been amused at Marcellus' letter telling about his job at the Negro college. But when he came back and set up living quarters out at Adam's, they were disturbed. That was one reason why they had urged him to come and live with them.

That might be, but it seemed makeshift talk. Marcellus was still mulling it over when they got back to the big magnolia tree, the turkey roost, in the upper swamp, to find the fire burned low and nobody there. His companions showed no surprise, however, and, without saying what they were about or where they were going, led the way onward, Marcellus soon saw, toward the old ferry landing on the river. He began to wonder if Carruthers hadn't been giving him a going-over to keep them from talking about something else.

And while he was eyeing the lantern in Bruce's hand and thinking this over, he heard the sound of excited voices and looked up to see a glimmer of light through the trees. There followed a gagging, bellowing outburst, like a man having his windpipe played with. Mr. Robert halted and gave Carruthers an excited glance. Then they both broke into a run.

He ran after them, not knowing why at first, but slogging through a muddy slough and up a dim rise to see, in the light from a distant fire, on the riverbank, under a spreading oak, a wide circle of men silhouetted about a dancing figure on the end of a rope—Dunk Slitcher. He wasn't swinging free quite, but his head seemed to be stretched from his body about as far as a man's neck would go without breaking. And on second glance Marcellus saw that his bare feet were balancing him precariously on top of a whiskey jug.

Somebody called out, "There comes Mr. Robert!"

And somebody else: "Let 'im down. He ought to be ready to tell the truth now."

Chapter 5

THE DEEP SWAMP is always dim. Between the trees, spindling saplings, threaded with Spanish moss, create a gray mist. It was this curtain of uncertainty that Marcellus' staring eyes burned through to the flickering silhouettes on the empty backdrop of the river. And his stomach burned, too, as he heaved forward heedlessly, only remotely aware that his companions were moving away from him, were no longer with him. Uncertain footing added urgency to the strides that took him into the circle. But the two men anchoring the rope moved quicker; it slid over the limb and Dunk dropped to the ground like a well bucket.

He lay crumpled in his own shadow until the man holding to the rope still about his neck jerked it and prodded him with a toe. Dunk came to his knees with a heave, grabbing hold of his hemp collar with both hands frantically, tugging at it, sobbing, his thin face swollen and smeared with tears—tears that, at last, had dissolved him into a limber, blubbery boy.

Or, so thought Marcellus, who only with effort controlled the swelling of his own insides—the agonized sound of Dunk's voice grabbing at him to pull him down there with him. And he looked around sharply for Carruthers and Mr. Robert. He could see them nowhere, and confusion was almost upon him, when he heard the admonishing tone of Andrew Ransom's blaring voice and made out the black silhouette of his burly figure against the firelight.

"Tell us the truth, Dunk, and you can stop all of this!" he said, standing, one in a ring of three, bending over to peer at Slitcher.

"Don't let 'em kill me, Mr. Andrew!" Dunk cried out, heaving and rising up on his knees. "For God's sake, Mr. Andrew!"

"Tell the truth, Dunk!" Andrew repeated.

"I'm scared, Mr. Andrew," he pleaded, his body and arms weaving in a supplicating whirl. "I'm scared of y'all. And I'm scared of that old man, too—he swore he'd shoot me to death!"

"Just tell the truth, Dunk!" Andrew said once more, severely, adding somehow with warmth, "We'll take care of old Buck."

Dunk looked about at the circle of men, "I'm just a boy, people! Just a boy, and all alone!" Dunk wrapped his arms about himself to control his trembling body, stiffening his quaking cheeks with a grim mouth. There was terror in his voice and in his eyes. He broke forth again, talking, it seemed, like a crawfish at bay.

"That's right about us having liquor there, that Sa'dy. We did." Dunk's shoulders jerked in a convulsive snivel. "And we 'uz pourin' up a run when that feller come—Ransom. We heard 'im up the road and quit filling the jugs and put the barrel back in the shack. We 'uz done covered up when he got there. He hallooed 'fore he got too close, asked for Buck." The dark eyes swept the circle. "That's just the way it happened, people, shore God!

"Buck called back who was he," Dunk went on. "Ransom told us sumpin' 'bout who he was. Then he asked 'bout the turkey roost. We didn't know how to take 'im. Though hit seemed like that 'uz all he wanted. But Buck was slow to admit anything. We didn't neither one of us want to go off with 'im anywhere, and that liquor lyin' there. We didn't know who else back up in the swamp might of come with him." Dunk interrupted his rhythm to lift his lowered gaze momentarily. "See, I don't deny a thing, Mister Andrew! We 'uz still there, passing it back and forth, when that big Jackson feller—*Grip* they call 'im—come along. He come by often. He live just t'other side and would git one of us to paddle 'im 'cross the river.

He bought liquor from us, too. Grip would drink with us some and pass the time and we got to know 'im. And it seem' like him and the Ransom feller wuz acquainted, too."

Marcellus sustained a sense of shock at Jackson's being in it—shock, too, that he would have let anything happen to David. Grip was a distant cousin of his, a giant of a man, a prodigious drinker and a rough-cut wag, whom he had always considered harmless, and rather liked.

"Then Grip" –Dunk gesticulated by lifting his nose— "sniffin' the air, said he smelled a good smell. And when Buck look over at Ransom, Grip nodded his head that he 'uz all right. You could tell Grip had done had some, but we didn't know how much. There 'uz some talkin' done, and Grip 'uz pretty loud. But all in fun. He kept loadin' up heavy and got more'n he could carry after a while. When he got ready to go on home, he 'uz staggerin' drunk. Ransom was scared Grip couldn't make it—like he might fall out'n the boat. He wanted to go along to hold 'im in." Dunk paused, and Marcellus shook his head ruefully at how like David it sounded. When, after a snivel, Dunk resumed, however, he said, "But then it 'uz Buck held 'im in. And Ransom paddled the boat." He wiped his nose with the back of his hand. "Jackson, he didn't want this Ransom feller to hold ‘im in. And just ‘fore he got in the boat he took back his voucher on Ransom.”

At the mention of the drinking, Adam’s claim about David nudged Marcellus annoyingly. He had never taken any stock in Carruthers’ superstitious view (Carruthers, himself a teetotaler) that no Ransom should ever drink a drop. Liquor had killed David’s father he said. Somehow, in momentary confusion now, Marcellus felt that he and Adam were responsible for liquor coming into it!

Dunk had risen to his knees, his look decisive. “But I didn’t go!” There was defiance in the way he lifted his chin. “I didn’t go along ‘cause they already had a load. This feller Jackson’s a big man. And drunk, too. And the river was up, high. Anyhow, I didn’t want to leave the liquor there like that. So I stayed behind to put it up.” His gaze circled the group again to see whether he was being believed. “Hit’s a fact! I stood there on the bank, watchin’ them ‘til they got ‘cross the steam. I saw the boat make eddy water on the far side and go out of sight behind the willows.”

After a pause, Andrew Ransom spoke. “All right, what happened then, Dunk?”

“I heard a gunshot.” Dunk’s glance made the circle quickly. “But it was some little while, first. I’d done gone on in the shack and was puttin’ up the liquor.”

After another pause Andrew prodded him. Dunk seemed reluctant, wary. “It was a long time *‘fore* Buck come back, a long time—I’d done finished with the liquor and started a fire to cook supper—by his self. It was the boat chain clanking I heard first, down at the landing—and I said to myself, I *wonder what took ‘im so long?”* Dunk lifted drawn features, his eyes glazed as if from some inner pain. “Then Buck come up over the bluff, and I saw he was by his self. . . .And he was totin’ Ransom’s shotgun.”

Andrew, quickly, "Where'd that come from?"

"I don't know!" Dunk came back. "I hadn't missed it until that minute. But I didn't think nothing 'bout that then, 'cause he 'uz holding it on *me.*" Dunk's voice went shrill on the last word, and broke, and heaving a couple of times, he began to snivel. He caught his breath to give the crowd his glance and repeat, "Yeah, people, on me!" Subsiding, then, he went on. "Buck didn't tell me he shot Ransom—nor nobody. Course. He just held that shotgun in my face and said, 'Slitcher, you don't know nothing 'bout this, see? 'Bout no trip over the river, a-tall! And you know how to keep your mouth shut, too, don't you?' Then he jabbed at me with the gun barrel. 'You spill a thing and I'll put you where Ransom is,' he said." Collapsing limberly on the ground, Dunk blubbered, "That's all I know—'fore God, people that's it, that all I know!"

So that was it! Marcellus decided, staring at the hollow-eyed, smeared, desperate face of Dunk Slitcher, still on his knees, there on the empty bank, the secretive river snaking by—still on his knees, like the sniveling end of a man's conscience, talking for his life. *Buck* had killed David! And Marcellus felt murder in his own heart, and hot tears, as he turned shakily away, sweat on his mouth and forehead.

Looking about him then, he saw Carruthers and Mr. Robert in the outer circle and, with a slight sense of disillusionment, he knew what they had done. They had been afraid that Andrew and his crowd might break Dunk's neck. But as soon as they saw him let back down to the ground, they halted on the outskirts to let the boys get a confession out of him. Marcellus thought then that what they had choked out of Dunk warranted the rope, though eventually it would turn out that he had lied again. At all events, Buck *had* run off.

And where was he now? Carruthers and Mr. Robert had reason to put their heads together, there by the fire. It was a hard question. The old river rat had from thirty-six to forty hours' start on them. Though that wasn't the telling point. There were two hundred miles of crooked river to the coast—river bedded in muddy sloughs, wrapped in moss, vine, and tree, swamps a mile to four miles deep on both sides. And why need he go downstream? There was plenty of river above him. Or he might take the other branch at the fork and go up the Ocmulgee. But that wasn't it, either. Buck was in his own lair, among his own kind.

Grip Jackson might be in on the trouble, but he wasn't wholly river rat. He could at least be talked to. Carruthers took Hinshaw Slappy to paddle him and another man across the river to walk out to Jackson's, while a dozen more went back to their cars to drive around by the ferry a few miles below to join him. Marcellus went along with Mr. Robert and Andrew Ransom to the commissary at Adair to get to a telephone. The first call he made was to the sheriff, at the county seat, to come on to Adair and bring Adam with him.

This proved providential, for by the time the sheriff got there with Adam, Carruthers was back from across the river with a lead from Jackson that would take them to Black Ankle, down on the Altamaha River. Carruthers said that Grip claimed to be sick, and couldn't go to Black Ankle with them. He might be sick, but it was for sure he was half scared to death, Carruthers said. He couldn't tell just how deep into it Grip was, but deeper than he let on. Grip claimed that he had been so drunk he didn't take in much that afternoon at the Landing. But he denied that he had disavowed David, or even thought of such a thing; said that one of the last things, he borrowed a dollar from David to pay for his drinks. He claimed, too, that he never heard any gunshot after they crossed the river. And he wasn't even sure but that Dunk was in the boat with them, though he wouldn't insist on it!

But he did tell Carruthers that old Buck was friendly with Hannah Scuffleton, Guv Troupe's woman at Black Ankle, who ran a store and fenced for river rogues. Grip thought Buck would head for Black Ankle to get Hannah to hide him out. And Adam was supposed to be close to Guv Troupe. At the time this had seemed like a hot tip to Carruthers, in fact, to all of them, in their inexperience. The two carloads that ferried across the river to meet Carruthers at Jackson's house had already set out for the Altamaha tough country. And with the exception of Mr. Robert, who stayed on the telephone, all those at the commissary piled in automobiles with the sheriff and with Carruthers and followed after.

Only Adam failed to share in the early optimism. He doubted that Buck had had time to get that far down the rivers. Anyhow, he didn't think *he* could get anything out of Hannah, with that crowd gone ahead of them—with any crowd or sheriff on hand, for that matter. But they insisted on his coming along, and he did.

It was near noon by the time they had covered the sixty miles by highway and four miles by timber trace to the bottom of the Altamaha swamp, to turn into Black Ankle's main and only street—a row of dilapidated board and batten shanties, silvered with age and Spanish moss, the relic of some long-gone peckerwood sawmill. Hannah's store, which differed but little in shape and size, was at the far end of the clearing, now almost reclaimed by the swamp.

Marcellus, who had often heard of Black Ankle and its ill fame, was let down by its piddling appearance. And Hannah Scuffleton (Scuffletonians were mixed: Indian, white, and Negro), a freckle-faced woman with a cast in her left eye, seemed to be too scared by all the gun-toting men and sheriff's badges for any reserve of cunning.

Scared, though a striking feature, stiff-standing purplish-red hair, may have exaggerated her appearance of fright.

Adam was able to talk to her; he was even able to get her away from her counter, with its padlocked, fly-specked show-case, displaying a woman's purple hat of ancient style and a pearl-handed pistol. But even in the privacy of the shed room, she told him no more than she had already admitted to the two sheriffs: she knew Buck, all right, and had for several years; but she insisted that she hadn't seen him, hadn't seen him in six months.

Despite the fact that Mayor Bruce tried to get hold of seasoned rivermen to send out, this first day's experience soon became a pattern. All tips definite enough to be followed up were, but the Riverton volunteer posses sent to the logging camps, boat landings, timber booms, and fishing holes made only water hauls. And the men who rode the rivers in boats to scout the swamps and bluffs did no better.

On information that Buck had been seen at the forks, Marcellus and a former schoolmate, Aztec Smith, went to Doctortown to scour the upper Altamaha, in a motor launch. They almost froze in the January wind, in the open boat, but they did not sight Buck, nor did they talk to anybody who personally had seen him.

Word of Buck did come to Riverton, to be sure, from the Oconee, the Ocmulgee, and from the Altamaha all the way down to the coast. But the man who had seen him never brought the word. And the reports grew wilder, the farther they came. They followed a pattern, too; telling of a little old man by himself in a flat-bottomed boat (usually green) with a covered-over box in the front-end, with something in it that looked like cut-up fish or hog meat. These rumors ran on through the week and into the next.

Before it was over with, however, Marcellus decided it was just as well the volunteers didn't encounter Buck. On the one report that seemed worth following up, he and Aztec had gone downriver to cut off Buck's flight at a railroad bridge. Marcellus lay in wait on an island, with two hundred yards of river on either side of him, for several hours, wondering how in hell he could stop the fugitive without shooting him. That is, unless he wanted to let Buck get in the first shot. Happily, that evening, about dark, Buck was caught in Hall's Swamp some forty miles upriver from them.

It was afternoon of the next day by the time Rup Willis, accompanied by Mayor Bruce, Carruthers, Marcellus, and others got to Hightower's Landing on the Oconee with his prisoner. Riverton's marshal was swollen with pride—as everybody agreed he had a right to be—over his catch, a catch he had made through a tip he got from some of his theretofore entirely worthless kin. For all of Buck's reputation as a river rat, he wasn't pulled out of a hollow log or alligator hole in the swamp, but had been taken under a farmhouse. He had not confessed to the crime yet, but his place of capture, as well as his flight, stood against him. Mayor Bruce had directed that he be brought back to the scene of the killing to locate David's body for them. The story Buck was telling was not at all acceptable, moreover, and it was hoped that this, too, might be worked out while he was there. To this end there was afoot a little plot proposed by the Clarke County sheriff and agreed to by the mayor.

The weather was clear, but cold enough to ice over the sloughs and fringe the river. The Riverton bunch, with Buck Fykes, gathered on the lower end of the bluff, about a bonfire that Adam was tending. A group of farmers and rivermen had a fire going fifty yards above them. And somebody had mended the stove enough to have another blaze in Fykes' abandoned shack, which lay between. It was from the shack that the sheriff emerged and approached the Riverton group, with their scarecrow-like prisoner, who stood with his manacled hands held out to the blaze, wind off the river inflating behind him a muddy secondhand army overcoat several sizes too big for him.

The story Buck was telling put the murder on Dunk. He, too, professed that he hadn't seen David killed. He had gone to paddle Jackson across the river, leaving the two young men at the shack, still drinking. He had heard a gunshot while he was on the other side. When he returned, Dunk met him with a leveled shotgun, and made him help put Ransom's body in the boat. But Dunk, alone, had paddled the weighted corpse back across the stream to a deep hole near the willows, where he dumped it in.

The sheriff tightened his powder-gray hat on his head against the wind as he reached the fire and zipped up his leather windbreaker farther. He nodded briefly at Mayor Bruce and Rup Willis, who stood on either side of Buck, but did not say anything, the casual look on his blunt features telling of a prior understanding. After a pause, lightened by a momentary gleam in the eyes of the men about the prisoner, the sheriff shook his head and cocked it a trifle. "Buck," he began, in bluff tonelessness, "you say *Slitcher* did the killin'?"

The spread fingers shut tensely, and Buck's coupled hands drew in to his chest, in an automatic protective gesture. To Marcellus, who watched from across the blaze, Buck looked as if he might be an evil dwarf, morally subhuman. His gray-whiskered, gaunt, flat, almost noseless face showed only the guarded anxiety of a wild animal. His eyes lifted from their baggy folds, pupil-less yet watery and uneasy. "Mister Shur'f," he said unctuously, in a voice that threatened to crack, " 'Fore God I didn't kill that poor boy."

"I didn't say you did, Buck." The sheriff shrugged. "And I didn't expect you to say you did." He kicked a fallen ember back onto the fire with a booted toe. “But I hear you claim that you put Grip Jackson across the river by yourself.” He glanced at Buck. “Is that right?”

Marcellus had already picked out Jackson’s great bulk among the men about the upper fire. He noticed now that Adam, on his knees beside him, putting wood on their blaze paused to gaze in that direction, and he looked, too. Grip was walking back and forth nervously.

“Why, ain’t it right, Shur’f?” Marcellus heard astonishment in Buck’s voice. He was blinking at the sheriff. “I reckon I’ve put ‘im across by myself a dozen times.”

The sheriff glanced over his shoulder briefly, before he spoke, “I’m not saying it ain’t right. And you may have. But your podner, Dunk Slitcher, says David Ransom was in the boat, too, with you and Jackson—going over. And that he never come back.”

Marcellus saw now that Grip had quit the other fire and was moving toward them. Buck piously wagged his head, like a burred chinquapin, in his worn fur cap. “That young feller couldn’t tell the truth if he had to, Shur’f.”

The sheriff grunted. “Well, both of you’ve got considerable reason for lyin’, I guess.” With another look over his shoulder, he said, “But here’s Grip Jackson now. Let’s see what *he* says.”

Buck’s relaxed forearms again drew back to bring the manacled hands to his chest. When his gaze fell upon Grip, however, he smiled. “I doubt old Grip would know,” he said, with composure.

Striding, hatless, his graying hair tousled above a high fierce brow and looking like giant Grim, Jackson snorted above the wind. But it became apparent that his fierceness was a counterfeit as he called out: “Why wouldn’t Grip know? He knowed he uz so drunk he’d a-fell out’n the boat if’n you hadn’t a-held ‘im in!”

Buck's face spread in a vapid, snaggle-toothed smile.

"You weave and stagger, Grip, but you never fall out'n no boat."

Still frowning, but his voice sober, Jackson said: "Men, I ain't proud of bein' drunk. But I ain't jokin'. This is too serious to joke!"

"Buck knows he ain't jokin' too." The raised voice came from a distance.

Everybody looked about to see who it was, except Fykes, who seemed to freeze in his tracks to the sound of it. Ten steps away, Dunk Slitcher was approaching them—obviously from the shack. The sheriff's surprise. He was handcuffed, also, and a deputy followed behind him at a distance. Dunk strode to within three paces of Buck, and halted, confronting him in silence. Buck seemed silenced, too, by the confrontation—watchful and grim. Yet he held on to his composure.

Dunk, his face darkening, drawing hard on mouth and cheekbone, and his green eyes going black, stared at Buck, till Buck lowered his own gaze. Then Dunk snarled, "Tell the shur'f what you said to Josielee at Uncle Herman's on Sunday morning!" He advanced a step, the accusatory pitch of his voice rising. "How you begged her to cut your throat with a razor!"

The whiskerless sallow patches of Buck's cheeks and his bridgeless nose went gray and he wobbled on his feet as if he might collapse. He turned away, choking, shaking his head. He finally got out, "It's a lie. That don't have nothin' to do with this."

Mayor Bruce shrugged, and the shrug ran around the rim of men. Rup Willis took hold of his prisoner by the arm, and nodded to the sheriff. They began to move off with the two men.

As the circle broke up, the mayor turned and spoke to the crowd. "Well, men, they seem to agree on one point. They both say David's body was sunk under those willows, across from us. We've got grappling hooks here and a couple of boats. Let's get busy!"

It was afterward on the river, by the willow piles, in the razor-sharp wind, as Adam paddled a square-nosed punt, from which Marcellus held behind them a dragline that drew an iron bar bearing hooks along the bottom of the deep hold, that the question came up between them. And Adam said, "Hit's hard to know what did happen, from what they tells us. But if I had to pick a killer between them two, I'd pick the boy."

It was blindman's bluff, Marcellus agreed. But didn't Buck's own guilty conscience convict him? He had been lynching Buck in his heart, and Adam's doubt brought cold sweat and confusion on him even in the freezing weather. "We ought to hang 'em both!" he said.

Reconsidering the mystery now, on the leather lounge of the smoker aboard his homeward-bound train, Marcellus wondered whether it hadn't been a blindfold of fear rather than an inner eye of guilt that convicted Buck. In the six years since, and especially in the six months of his police reporting since, he had come to agree with Adam about it.

Chapter 6

MARCELLUS KNOCKED out his pipe, visited the toilet, drank two paper cups full of water from the cooler in the corridor, and decided that he had better try to get some sleep. But when, at the doorway, he looked upon the undulating flotsam in the dim tunnel of the coach, on the point of floating toward him, he grimaced and turned back. It would be better in the smoker. He lay down on the bench and started to take off his wristwatch, but immediately sat up again. Hell, he wasn't going to sleep: his pulse was still driving like a water pump. In automatic resistance to the onward motion of the train, to his sense of being dragged backward, he stretched out his legs before him and stared up at the ceiling lamp fixedly.

He was able, with effort, to conjure up an image of Melanie, holding out her arms to him. The gesture looked phony. But when she said with a smirk, "He either jumped or fell out of the window" (his newspaper's feather-legged pitch on all suicides), she looked more realistic. He grinned and got out his pipe again. By damn, Melanie was like finding money! Not a cartwheel. She wasn't big enough for that. Hell, a double eagle! Not that he'd ever picked up a double eagle. Before.

He struck his match and let it burn a little, then held it over the pipe bowl. Would he see Judy Courtney in Riverton? he asked himself, with a jerk of the head. His shrug brought a frown. Well, of course he would! She would be home for the holidays—some part of them, at all events. It had been a million years. What would she look like now? His effort to construct the second image brought him to his feet. From the twist on his features, he might have been squeezing a lemon in his mouth. The car swayed, and he tilted off across the compartment to catch himself in the doorway. He hung here for a time, staring at the floor, shaking his head; then he moved back toward his seat reluctantly. His long, hard case with Judy had been like the measles! At five he had been laid up with red measles for a month, delirious; he had had pneumonia, with an antiphlogistin plaster on his chest; everything tasted like rabbit tobacco, and he had to learn to walk all over again when he got up. Marcellus drew in his breath with a quiver and let it out with a sigh. "All right," he said aloud, "that's the thing you hate worst about this trip. But you've got to do it!"

Adam had been pleased that he was interested in Dr. Courtney's daughter—though of course he never intimated such a thing. And it was only due to his admiration for the doctor: Riverton's other man of—the word he guessed was *chivalry*, if there was such a thing. Adam was so old-fashioned. Certainly in the beginning Adam's attitude had influenced his own. How could you abstract it, however, from dragging the river for David's body? From the whole set of circumstances that staked and staved his falling in love with Judy—staked and staved their sad romance?

He shrugged, and slipped down on the bench.

Had Adam's feeling for Dr. Courtney been a sentimental thing at all? Hadn't the high-toned doctor shown a singular devotion to the Negroes of the countryside over which he practiced?

It wasn't that Judy didn't have charm—a dark, graceful Indian beauty. In high school she had been picked to play in the Hiawatha pageant. She had a low musical voice, and sang sweetly, too. And she had a fine, straight bearing. Though she did stand an inch taller than he. Not clever, but even-tempered; and, yes, there was a breath of chivalry about her, too. And their affair was—in this, and in the fact that he, too, was a virgin—a late-Victorian thing, even to the Freudian undertones. For back in the icebox of his mind, and certainly repressed, was one of those befalls of boyhood that everyone experiences and forgets, or if occasionally remembered, merely as a fragment.

He and Judy had been classmates in grammar school, before her precocity and age (she was actually only three months older than he was) had enabled her to jump a grade and get ahead of him. But before that—they were so small that they stood on a platform to reach the blackboard (all put in the same height at Riverton School)—this thing happened. And, incidentally, the platform—two feet wide, extending along the walls below the blackboards and made of two wide planks—provided the stage property of complication. Marcellus, then a runty barefoot boy, very curious about but not altogether friendly with girls, was detailed by the teacher to gather up the chalk that had fallen on the floor beneath the raised walkway—a bit of schoolroom routine.

Inevitably, as he squirmed under the walk, he was drawn to look up through the crack between the boards, if there happened to be a girl above him. Unaccountably he was rewarded with the (even then) beautiful Judy above. And again by coincidence or whatever, on this morning, Judy's fresh, starched white pantlets beneath her most modest blue gingham dress happened to have a large rent in them.

It was nine o'clock at night, and the supper on the table in the Ransom dining room had dried up on the stove, in the long and uncertain wait. Of the silent family group there, only Carruthers and Marcellus, still in their wool shirts, were eating.

Carruthers' wife, Rebecca, standing behind his chair attentively and facing Marcellus, might have been the statue of a child, a gentle, fair, blue-eyed child, a little large for her age. But when Carruthers glanced up from his plate, she darted toward the covered dish, a little way down the linen plain. This action destroyed the illusion, bringing her shapely but pronounced nose into profile, swaying the mass of blonde hair piled on top of her head, and jerking an apologetic murmuring from her sharpened lips. She took the lid off the dish, disclosing that it was filled with sweet potatoes baked in their jackets.

Carruthers sniffed and turned to the small tow-haired Mona leaning against the table beside him—her big dark eyes upon him. He smiled down at her in mock disappointment, saying, "And 'tain't nothin' but taters."

Standing at the foot of the table, Judy Courtney, her slightly protruding mouth first tightening, gave way to laughter. "I put 'em in the covered dish to try to keep 'em warm," she explained.

Marcellus broke his silence with a thrusting hand. "Hand 'em here! The only thing better than a cold sweet potato is a warm one—hand 'em here!"

They laughed. But their mouths fell away from it, their levity being an effort and the cause slight, and glumness, like the lavender shadows from the room's high ceiling, dropped down on them again.

Men had been dragging the bottom of the Oconee River for a week: two boats, each with a paddler and a man on the drag hooks, twenty volunteers a day, daylight to dark in the freezing weather, under the direction of Carruthers and the mayor. Systematically. Marcellus thought of that first cold afternoon over the willow hole, which Dunk and Buck had just pointed out. He had tied a bandanna about his face against the wind. But the pile of muddy water over the drag bar didn't seem unusual then. He thought he knew how to drag bottom then. Marcellus shook a numb skull on a stiff neck. It was like looking for your lost memory in another man's mind. Tonight he could hear the muddy Oconee laughing. It was windy cold laugher. That ever-moving, deceptively-yielding yellow back, three hundred yards wide and thirty feet deep—yielding nothing! He was still riding it: every time he shut his eyes he got dizzy.

Today they tried dynamite in the hole and two other places, to no effect. They had found out no more about the location of David's body than they knew on the day they questioned Buck Fykes and Dunk Slitcher about it. Unless it was that his body was *not* in the deep hole under the willows. It didn't seem possible that it could be there, however muddy and deep the water and devious the bottom. Adam was sure it wasn't there. And never had been there or anywhere near it. But the sheriff had moved both Fykes and Slitcher away to Savannah jail now, and men from Riverton couldn't get to them.

Carruthers and Marcellus ate with appetite but without relish, and they ceased together abruptly, as if at some soundless signal. "Where're the boys?" Carruthers asked casually, pushing away from his plate.

Rebecca let herself into a chair on the other side of her husband, glancing off at the pendulum clock on the mantel. They were in their room studying, but she was sure they would be in bed asleep by this time. Mona confirmed this with a nod, saying: "I went by to tell 'em good night and they were covered up 'sleep."

Carruthers retorted, in a mincing manner, though without zest for it, "And you didn't get to tuck 'em in and kiss 'em good night?"

"Oo! Yes, I did!" Mona said. Then, taken aback by her impulsive contradiction, she blushed and ducked her head and joined in the laughter that went around the table.

The lift was short-lived. Marcellus, his eye on the clock's incessant brass disk, heard Judy seating herself at the foot of the table with a sense of heaviness. The mahogany painted mantel was harsh in the glare from the hearth, where a revived fire gave out brightness, without cheer and, he could almost believe at his distance from it, without heat. He was weary, weary, but tight at the scruff of the neck, and did not want to talk. What good would it do! On Sunday his mother had called him from Philadelphia to ask about the search, and he had broken down over the telephone. And since then he had been in flight from any chance of being unmanned again.

Carruthers spoke to Mona. "Bed's where you ought to be, too," he said. "It's past your bedtime."

Marcellus had been about to rise, but he checked himself and leaned back in his chair now to smile at Mona and say an adequate good night. He beamed hard upon her soft, pale, still-eyed face, exacting a smile of her, but breaking it off quickly by getting to his feet. She was not as good-looking as David had been, but she had his eyes exactly. Marcellus just couldn't take it sitting down.

He walked halfway to the hall door with her and would have gone on, but "Aunt" Rebecca called him back. She had something to tell him. The tone of her voice made him apprehensive. He always found Rebecca's confidences difficult. It was her feckless dramatics, in her soft playroom voice with the suggestion of a lisp in it, and her sentimentality. He sat down in Mona's chair so that Carruthers would be between them. At least, Carruthers was an antidote for his wife.

Rebecca remained half turned toward the door, with her attention on it fixedly until Mona had released the doorknob from the other side. Then, shaking her head, she adjusted herself, lifting her nose a little to say, in a histrionic half-whisper, "That child is frightening! Do you know what she asked me today? . . . She asked me, 'Aunt Rebecca, why did God have to take away David, too?' "

Later that evening Marcellus and Judy stopped under the big arc light at the street corner that once had been his corner, when his family lived in Riverton, to get a better look at each other. He was taking her home on foot. His truck was broken down and Paul had Carruthers' car, and anyhow she lived less than a mile away. Besides, they wanted to walk. It wasn't desperately cold and they needed air—at least, Marcellus did. Coming along in the dark they had been saying things to each other, and now they wanted to see just what they had meant by them.

Marcellus had been going with Judy ever since they both got back to Riverton a little before Christmas. But is had been only for fun. He had to go back to college, and she had to go back to New York and her singing lessons, as soon as the depression let up. It was fine to get to see more of her, now that she was helping hold things together at Ransoms', because Rebecca had her own baby, as well as the four remaining orphans on her hands, and greatly needed Judy. It had been fine for them, though neither one of them had realized it until tonight. They had been too busy—too much involved even to give it a thought before.

But coming along on the dim footpath, Marcellus had been saying that it was hard enough for him to face Mona, without "Aunt" Rebecca giving it to him, like that. He wasn't going to be able to stay on there. He couldn't take it. Sure, God may have taken the Ransom children's father and mother, but why *God* it? Why should he, Marcellus, have to send his best friend into peril that should have been his own? And why should he unwittingly put him in the hands of his murderers? Why should he have caused the hostility with the swamp rats that David fell victim to, in the first place? Yes, why? But why God about it?

She had said, *Stop it.* Stop it! He was too big to talk that way. What good did it do to ask those questions? Yet there had been commiseration in her voice.

And now he looked at her. He had rounded the fence corner and turned back, drawing his hands from his leather jacket to take hold of her pickets. In the wash of the electric light, a pale blue moon, in a swing, she seemed a little afraid of him and lowered her eyes to take hold of the pickets on her side. He sent up his moan again, his now visible breath like smoke signals, "But you know yourself, Judy, that Mona was completely wrapped up in David."

Emotion twisted her features, now pale and shadow-lined. Then her short nose and her wide lips stiffened and brought her face under control. And after a pause, she reached out, without looking up, and covered his nearer hand with her own.

Marcellus looked at their hands in astonishment. The gesture was one of comradely sympathy, but it was more. And Judy had never touched him before, in this way. He felt a thrill. And he felt honored. (Well, anything wrong with that?)

"I know, I know!" she was saying, low, still not looking up. "It's a terrible responsibility. We never know. We can't choose." She increased the pressure on his hand. "But we can't run away—can't."

He felt buzzing wonderment in his head, and a sense of the unreality of the scene, but he managed to say, "I guess you're right."

She nodded vigorously, her head still lowered, going on. "But—but *I'm* here, Shorty." Then she met his gaze, her eyes brimming full; though before he could decide what was in them, they retreated into the shadow. "I think I know a little about how you feel." Then she murmured, as if she were asking a privilege, "I love the Ransoms, too: I want to share responsibility for Mona."

As he stared on at her, Marcellus felt the egg in his chest break. Finally he said feelingly, but with a proper gloominess, "Thank you, Judy!" And she took her hand off his hand.

But when they had resumed their way, this all began to seem mawkish to him, like "Aunt" Rebecca, and he exploded in fresh pain, "But what in hell can we do?" Yet walking on, there came into his head oddly: *An orphan's curse would damn to hell a spirit from on high.* And he sensed that his suffering wasn't a wholly unrecognizable anguish. (Coleridge had given him a hand!)

During the unutterable weeks of futile river dragging, Marcellus and Judy did occupy themselves with one thing for Mona. She asked if they knew where David's college fraternity pin, his badge, was. They made a quest of it, ransacking bureau drawers and clothes closets, with Marcellus finally writing a letter to his chapter house. For all their to-do over it, however, they were unable to turn it up. And Marcellus decided that though David didn't usually wear it to the woods, he must have had it on that day.

It was a little thing, but a part of the intransigence and mystery of the river—intransigence and mystery of the murder, too. For though

Carruthers and Marcellus and the sheriff made still another trip to Savannah to see again the men charged with the crime, they could get nothing from them that helped. It was still their story (though each laid it on the other still, and it was their only point of agreement) that David's body had been weighted down with an iron pot filled with sand, the handle caught under his belt; still their story that it was sunk in the hole under the willows.

A pot of sand would have held him on the bottom, no doubt, but the body was not in that hole, Carruthers told them. They suggested that it might have drifted, but they would take no further responsibility for explaining about the body. They knew they were in the Savannah jail now.

So dragging and dynamiting went on, on all the way down to Devil's Elbow, two miles below Hightower's Landing. And though the volunteers thinned out, there was a hard core of two or three dozen who kept coming to the Landing regularly. The last of the fourth week there was a freshet in the Oconee, and the river got out of its banks and into the swamp, and dragging had to be suspended for three days.

But the rivermen were hopeful that this would bring the body up. The big swift-moving head of water might loose it from its weights or even wash the whole business up on some point where it would be uncovered when the water went down again. The word was sent from point to point, down-river, for raftsmen and boaters to be on the lookout for a floating body, and a dozen men in launches and bateaux held watch at the mouth of the Oconee.

But the freshet subsided without bringing David's body to light, and the dragging and dynamiting were resumed.

If the days on the river were cold and discouraging for Marcellus, his evenings at the Ransom house he found almost unbearable. He couldn't have stuck it out, except for Judy. Marcellus couldn't have kept on telling Mona that he was sure they would find David's body. He wasn't sure anymore, and he lived in fear that it would show in his face. It would have shown, but for Judy—Judy: even-tempered and unruffled, yet cheerful and always the same. That *same* was a steady eye and the quiet vibrance in her voice. The body would rise. She somehow knew it would rise. It might be stupid but her insistence reassured him. He even believed her while it was going on.

Judy engaged in such talk for good reason. But this sort of buoyancy was getting them off solid ground—let alone river bottom—and the air grew strained. That is, until a thing happened on Tuesday of the fifth week to bring them down to earth in comic relief, if nothing more. Though there was more to it.

Indeed, desperation had made everybody softheaded by the time the fortune-tellers showed up—two marble-eyed men with a matter-of-fact way about them, one of them fingering a bottle of quicksilver portentously. They had had good results floating a loaf of light bread with a mercury ball in it to find bodies, they told Mr. Robert. He lifted his eyebrows, but after a shrug his bottom lip went bland and he said to Carruthers, "Well, hell, they can't do any worse than we've done."

This started a descent of water witches and soothsayers and diviners upon the Landing. Bread and bundles of fodder and whatnot were tried out on the river. And finally a table talker appeared on the scene, dressed in a rusty wool suit, vest, watch and chain and shark's-tooth watch charm. Whether this was the mark of his trade Marcellus wouldn't know, but it did give him distinction in a community almost wholly in overalls. He brought no tool of his craft and asked only for a table—any table with four legs. He did have with him, however, a half-grown albino mute, who seemed to hear even if he didn't talk.

There was a sizable crowd at the bluff, hugging a couple of bonfires, though it wasn't very cold. There were always more loafers than workers at the Landing, and their number greatly increased with the coming of witchcraft. Among them Marcellus noted Big Sam Crews, the slow-witted teamster who looked like a comic stand-in for General von Hindenberg, wearing his secondhand officer's overcoat with black braid still on the sleeves.

The crowd was divided between those who believed and those who didn't believe in the occult powers of the table talker. There were, too, a few who would wait and see. But discussion went on volubly, as Mr. Robert and Marcellus tried to prepare the shack for his use. There was in the place a homemade plank table that would have taxed the powers of a weight lifter to manipulate, let alone a table talker, occult or otherwise. And the rough uneven floor didn't lend itself to sleight of hand.

But the sallow dish-faced stranger nodded at these things with a cold-mouthed self-confidence that amounted almost to indifference. He said now to get him eleven men to sit around the table with him. They didn't have to be believers, just so they had enough sense to *concentrate,* when he told them to concentrate. Mr. Roberts got them together for him and retired, for the shack was too small for spectators within. A little later, however, members of the crowd pulled a plank off one side, about two feet aboveground, to be able to watch the performing table.

Before the table talker began his séance inside the shack, he appeared at the doorway dimly for a word to the crowd. He spoke with a detachment that amounted to contempt. He said that the twelve (including the albino boy) would sit around the plank tabletop with him, touching fingers and concentrating until the "spur't" came among them. He said that he would then ask the spirit questions, and the spirit would answer by causing the table to lift up a leg and knock on the floor—one time for *no,* and three times for *yes*. The only thing he wanted out of the crowd was quiet.

He needn't have bothered; because when the finger chain in the shack got locked in thought and he intoned to the spirit, everybody there was in a squat, staring at those two-by-four table legs so hard they could barely breathe, let alone talk.

That is, everybody but Big Sam Crews. Big Sam was one of the loud disbelievers. Marcellus, as he watched him still rearing around, pulling his red whiskers, after the others had quieted down, wondered about him. Big Sam seemed personally affronted, bowing his neck and barking, "Hell, that 'ere table kain't talk!" Somebody shushed him, and he came to a half-squat but kept mumbling.

Yet the séance went on, and finally the table talker confronted the spirit with the question direct: *Is young Ransom's body in the Oconee River?*

This silenced even Big Sam into a full squat, his overcoat skirts descending to the ground like a hen coop. A long and growing tension fixed the clump of spectators, in tableau, on the muddy bluff above the river, in the clear noon sunlight. Then, slowly, the heavy table tilted, the nearest leg coming up from the floor a distance of a couple of inches. It dropped with an audible knock.

"One," called the table talker.

But even as he spoke, it was drowned in an abdominal earthquake. From the shaking ground Marcellus looked up to see the braided overcoat ballooning out behind Crews as he tore massively through the moss and underbrush beyond the shack. The crowd broke into a laugh as Big Sam disappeared into the swamp, headed toward the hill.

Marcellus was still laughing when he told Judy and Mona about it that evening at Ransoms'. Mona laughed too—out of contagion. But she broke into his enlarging on the tale to ask what the table talker had finally told them about David's body. Judy gave Marcellus an impatient stare, and he dried up. But it seemed to him that Judy had been over-earnest. When he took her home that night, he began teasing her about it. Along the dark footpath he took to calling her "ju-believe-it Judy." In retort, she pushed him into the drainage ditch.

At the lighted corner their boisterous play grew into a wrestling, a wrestling that came to an abrupt pause, with Marcellus' hand covering Judy's right breast. It wasn't premeditated, but his hand having got there, he seemed powerless to remove it.

She grew still, and their eyes met in the thin blue light, as she brought her hand up to cover his. And he saw, in the dark of her eyes, that she wouldn't jerk his hand away. A muscular seizure took him, then, with a lightning glimpse of throwing her down in the drainage ditch and tearing off her clothes to get at her. Her. He knew he could not control himself if he got started, and he suspected she saw this in his face, too. It broke him out in a cold sweat. Then, sucking in his breath, he shouted at her derisively, "Big Sam!" and snatching his hand away, broke into a run. The chase continued the rest of the way to her house, but it did not turn into wrestling again. He was never meant for a caveman.

Chapter 7

THE TABLE TALKER had provided his moment, but the river dragging went on. On, into its sixth week; on, beneath the flat rust-colored surface of the Oconee, from the Landing to the Elbow, stretching like an elongated question mark, its edges embroidered by a tangle of moss and vine and tree, gray and ever green.

Only a few came to the Landing now to give Carruthers and Mr. Robert, Marcellus and Adam, a hand. Andrew Ransom was there when he could be; but, as he said, he was not his own boss and couldn't just abandon his business. Paul, David's older brother, had long hours at his drugstore job, but he was so erratic that even at this time nobody urged him to join in.

The hardest-headed men in the lot were having trouble holding onto a level view of things now. Carruthers grew more and more suspicious of Grip Jackson, kept talking about his not telling all he knew, got so worked up about it that you would have thought he wanted to organize a mob to call on Grip. Marcellus made no brief for him and surely he wouldn't defend him. But Carruthers didn't report anything new to implicate Grip. And after all he was kin to Marcellus, and it finally made him feel sensitive. But what was worse was that one day Carruthers asked him why Adam was so sure that David's body wasn't anywhere about the Landing. What did Adam *know?*

Mr. Robert did something to clear the air, then. He added to the reward for finding the body. Originally Carruthers had put up two hundred and fifty dollars, and Mr. Robert, in the name of the town, had put up two hundred. Marcellus had added fifty, it being all he could afford. Now, by action of the mayor and council, the town had added another five hundred to make a total of a thousand dollars.

The town had acted only on a general principle, and privately Marcellus couldn't see that increasing the reward would do any good. Dunk and Buck weren't going to squeal on themselves. It couldn't have anything to do with Judy's dreaming that old Buck told her the body would soon be found in an unexpected way. Or with Carruthers' and Mr. Robert's absence from the Landing that Wednesday. (Six years afterward, on the train bearing him back to Riverton, his vision of the events that followed still seemed mysterious to him, and nothing more mysterious than his own actions.) On the day in question he was standing on the porch of the commissary at Adair, where he'd gone to get groceries for his hands, smoking his pipe, wondering whether to go back to the river or not, when, as he saw it still, Fate beckoned to him.

Fate's tools were an old bachelor uncle and a cousin, in a mule and buggy, His uncle, John Hightower, whom he liked despite his mother's label of "good-for-nothing," and Cousin David Bright, were a pleasant sight for him. They urged him to go home with them (to the Bright's farm) to eat dinner and help them fish their shad nets afterward.

In his depressed state, this frivolity had an astonishing appeal. The thought of going back to the Landing that afternoon suddenly became unbearably futile. Before he could argue with himself, he had crawled in the buggy with his old playfellows. He went with such compulsion and lack of forethought that he could never regard it as entirely his own doing.

Then when they had fished the nets that afternoon and were about to retrace the two miles to the house with a poor catch, it was he, Marcellus, who said, "Why not hang around awhile and fish the nets again? The shad are running." And they turned back to the river. It was his Uncle John who, to fill in their time, suggested that they go over to the island and walk up a coon, because they couldn't get off at the high stage of the river. And John had his .22 rifle with him. But when they had paddled across the cut and hunted over the lower side of the island to find nothing, and John, discouraged, had turned back toward their boat, it was he, Marcellus, who said, "Hell, don't' give up yet!"

He was leading the way, picking about through the underbrush and drift logs, still scanning the bare trees for a coon, and yelling back at them some foolishness, when the thing flagged the tail of his eye. It was khaki-colored. He looked again through the washup of logs and brush on ahead of him at the point of the island, and saw extended crookedly the sleeve of a khaki shirt. His throat went dry, and his breath began to pop out of his mouth as if pistoned by a pump. And before he knew what he was doing, he was leaping over logs, running as fast as shaking legs could carry him, and—he realized after a time—yelling. He never knew what. But they got the alarm.

In his scramble he lost his hat and almost tore his jacket off him, but at last he leaped upon a log that allowed him to look down on the khaki shirt—to look down on khaki breeches and woods boots, too, covering a blackened and rotting corpse, hung under a freshet-swept sparkleberry bush, face upward.

It was featureless, except for bared teeth. But he identified it instantly: the boots, the breeches, the shirt, the teeth—it couldn't be anybody but David Ransom! But here! How? Almost five miles above the Landing! His pounding, swollen head whirled.

Then his kinsmen were there with him, their faces squinted tight, their eyelids bulging, as they looked furtively down at the grisly cadaver that had been a man.

They spoke together after a time, spoke in whispers. On foot, they couldn't transport it. And probably shouldn't move it until the sheriff saw it, anyhow. Who would go to the telephone at Brights'?

Marcellus didn't know why his uncle had to go along with David Bright to call Riverton, but it didn't make any difference to him at the time. He expected to stay there, wanted to stay. He just wondered fleetingly at the old man's being scared. To be sure, the sun was down and it was growing dusk.

He himself was in a strange, a shrill-breathed, a never-before-experienced state of excitement. His mind seemed preternaturally alert and clear and detached. Yet his movements had a floating, a dream quality. Although the cadaver was resting conveniently on its right side, the rigid left arm drawn out and upward, in an L, he had turned it even more to examine patches of blond hair remaining on the back of the black skull, just to confirm the other identification. And he remembered about the fraternity pin that little Mona had wanted, and instantly, it seemed, he was at the body, going over the shirtfront in search of it, thinking that since the pin's catch had a lock on it, possibly it might be there, though of course it wasn't. From the tops of the socks, above the boots, he saw that they were a pair he had given David.

But he did all this under an awful suspension of feeling, of realization, of being, almost—except for a hot spot at the back of his skull. And then the dusk had grown so thick he could scarcely see at all, and he fell over a log and came to a halt. And as he sat there on the log, still, in the gray lack-light, it came to him. It came over him what this precipitously, perilously, horribly suspended thing was. It was an odor. The sickeningly sweet, ghostly thin, insidiously penetrating smell of rotting human flesh. He had never known it before, but there was no denying it now, for he was saturated with it, from nose to bung. It seeped into the marrow of his bones. His eyes watered of it.

He did not feel fright; he felt an overwhelming horror. David's voice, David's smile, David's eyes; their joking, their fighting, their laughter, their sweat, their whole past, all was consumed in that evil, ineffable smell. It appalled, almost bemused, him.

Now he knew why his companions were so eager to leave. But at that moment he heard his name called from the riverbank—the first syllable barked out and the *ll*'s a kind of echo, so familiar! And warming! He got to his feet and shouted: "There's a boat chained to that leaning forked gum, Adam. Come on over!

That evening Riverton's two physicians—Dr. Courtney and a young Dr. Johns—performed an autopsy on David's body to determine, if possible, how he had met his death. There were no trained nurses in Riverton, and there, in the crowded drugstore, just after they had deposited their tarpaulin-wrapped burden in his office in the back, Dr. Courtney asked Marcellus to attend them.

Afterward he wondered why Dr. Courtney had asked this of him, David's most intimate friend. Of course, the whole town knew David intimately, and Dr. Courtney knew that Marcellus had helped in operations before and didn't faint. Doctors grow callous about such things. But when the polished gray doctor, with his gracious nod, said to him, "This is going to be trying for you, Shorty, but I don't see anybody else in here whom I know can take it"—why, there wasn't anything else Marcellus could do. He had unquestioned confidence in Dr. Courtney. Moreover, he was Judy's father.

But there was more still. It was probably only an obscure possessiveness, but he saw it then as an act of devotion to David—going the last mile. After all, what else could he do for him? Not that he had to prove anything to David. He was proud to be asked, would have been hurt if he hadn't been. Then, too, even after what he had encountered on the island, he was still ignorant of what was in store for him.

Along with themselves, the doctors equipped Marcellus with a mask for his nose and mouth that was saturated in some chemical.

The faceless cadaver, the crooked arm still rigid above the head in final protest or appeal, lay dark upon the white operating table. It might have been black mud, pressed into muddy shirt and breeches and sculptured by the effacing flow of the muddy river. The doctors began with a methodical removal of the shirt, cutting with flat-jawed surgical scissors, a little awkwardly in their rubber gloves. The back presented a slick, burnt-cork counterfeit of human form, shoulders, shoulder blades, and curving spine.

Marcellus' insides were in a hard, almost anesthetized knot; moving about quickly to the doctors' look and beckoning, he managed to keep his grip on them. It was easier for him when they had scraped off what was once skin, and cut and laid open what was once muscle to see that the back was no longer recognizable even as a back.

After a while they shook their heads and turned the cadaver over. There was the modeled black mass of a chest. But below the barrel of the ribs, there was no abdomen, only mud filling with seething, slick maggots. Marcellus' hand shot up, like a referee's. For the first time he had to ask for time out. He went into the water closet and tried to bring up something more from his writhing entrails. After a little while, he rubbed his face with crushed ice, took a swallow of lemon juice, put on his mask again, and went back into the dissecting room.

He lasted out the autopsy with the two doctors. But when the cadaver on the enameled table was only a ragged, muddy heap of rifled refuse, with nothing remotely resembling a man about it, the doctors still did not know how David Ransom met his death. There was no evidence of gunshot wound or knife stab or slash or broken bones. There was no water in his lungs (what was left of them). The only violence to David they could deduce from the corpse, as finally relinquished by the river, lay in the rigid upraised arm. A paralytic blow on the right side of his head, would, they said, have drawn up his left in that position.

Marcellus had got through the autopsy. The thing was that he could not get rid of the smell. The memory of the operating table stayed with him, of course, both awake and sleeping. But awake he was able to keep in motion during these days to push it out of his head. And before going to bed he would stop by his friend Aztec Smith's office in Riverton and take on a couple slugs of corn liquor. This would keep off nightmares till daybreak. But the odor was unaccountable. It would hit him anywhere or anytime, like an angry swarm of bees. And his stomach would act by reflex: up would come his last meal. It made him avoid people, even Judy.

He didn't see her again until the day of the funeral, Friday. Marcellus had gone to his crosstie woods. There was no emergency. But the Ransoms had plenty of kin and close friends to help with the arrangements, and he couldn't trust himself around the house or the church. Judy overtook him in the Ransoms' back hall that morning, and he was uneasy the whole time she was talking to him.

What she told him, however, rather took his mind off his stomach. She'd picked up the rumor that a girl named Agnes Hooker, who lived on the wrong side of the river, had David's fraternity pin and was coming to the funeral. It jarred Marcellus. This girl was a *dark,* all right. And she once had had a date with David. It was a double date, and he, Marcellus, had gone along, the Saturday night after New Year's. But they never went back. And he hooted at the idea of David's giving her his fraternity pin, and it his badge, too! As Judy knew, the Methodist preacher's daughter was wearing his jewel pin, and he wasn't supposed to give his badge to anybody. This Agnes Hooker was *common*—to be sure, she might come to the funeral.

It was only later he realized that he hadn't even been queasy while they were together; the odor hadn't come near him! But at the time he laid it to the shock of her bad news.

The funeral was big; and, in the preacher's rhetoric, boastful before Death, in the usual way. And hard to take. But David's remains were sealed in copper, and the sightseers, at least, couldn't trip down to the coffin to view them. Agnes Hooker was there, in the back of the church, Marcellus was told. But nobody saw a fraternity pin on her, and the place was so crowded it wouldn't have made any difference, anyhow.

He and Judy both sat with the family. And he had been able to hold out. But when they got back from the long trip to Riverside Cemetery, back all the way to Ransoms', to the shadowy blank-windowed house, after sundown, he was due to duck. He had been fighting his insides all the way: church and graveyard back, and he thought he couldn't go another minute. But as he was coming up the front steps to the porch—Carruthers, Rebecca, and the boys had gone on inside—holding Mona by the arm, she, without a sound, collapsed. He thought for a moment he was gone, too.

But Judy came quickly and helped him pick her up. She held the child to her for awhile. Then they started walking. They walked, one on either side of Mona, with an arm about her shoulders, walked around the long porch, in the twilight and back. Again and again. They didn't talk or exchange a look, Judy's arm lying alongside his. Hell, there wasn't anything to say. But Marcellus forgot that he even had a stomach.

On the next day, like Carruthers, Mr. Robert, all the rest of Riverton, Marcellus fell to at making a living again. It had been two months since his first unhappily timed venture on the road, as a buyer. And he had been carrying on his crosstie camp with only one hand, and not very well. He spent Saturday in the woods, and on Sunday night he boarded the midnight train to make the connection to the place where he hoped to buy oak crossties on Monday. During the next five weeks he was either at his camp or on the road buying, both day and night, spending no more than a half-dozen nights with the Ransoms, and seeing Judy only once. He had been about to go broke, and he made a comeback, marketing ten thousand 'ties and a hundred pilings.

But before the fifth week was out, both his fright and his zest had spent themselves. It wasn't that he didn't like the timber business; and his immersion in it had helped him get away from the autopsy and even the "wild bees," as he had come to call the pursuing odor.

And he got a kick out of making money. But somehow it grew less absorbing, and he was surprised at the alacrity with which he rearranged his business to be able to attend the trial of Buck Fykes, the third week in April.

Marcellus, Carruthers, Mr. Robert, and a dozen others from Riverton were witnesses, and drove over to the county seat every day to sit seven or eight hours in the courtroom for a week. They heard a lot of testimony and did a lot of talking about it, before and after. And it was very dramatic and exciting to recast the whole thing there, as a trial, before a judge and jury. But it wasn't the actual thing on the river! Already it was beginning to be transformed and disconnected from first feelings. And in the end, somehow, it seemed to blur a little.

The Slitchers had got a real crafty lawyer to represent Dunk, and he got a severance for him, ahead of the trial. Old Buck had to go it alone and he was scared he was going to swing. He all but pleaded guilty, not taking the witness stand in his own behalf, and when the jury gave him life he thanked them and told the judge he didn't want a new trial. Though Adam still contended, privately to Marcellus, that he believed Dunk had done it.

But the trial brought things into relief for Marcellus and Judy. With the court action they came to see that the involvement itself was over, and to get a little perspective on it. They talked about this a week after the verdict came, at a little party the Courtneys gave for Judy—the first time since David's death. There was another discovery for him that evening, too. This came first, however, and they didn't quite have words for what they perceived. It was really what they knew now, what they saw in each other's faces, there in the porch swing, before the others got there. Judy, smiling—her purplish lips like the flesh of an Indian River orange, he suddenly saw—saying, yet firmed to make small of it, "I've missed you these last five weeks, Shorty." He barely got down his swallow, and didn't speak before she added, "More than I ever thought I would—" then her lips forming the word without sound and smiling, and saying it with her little heaving shrug. And what were words anyhow?

He had cut in, grinning: "I know, Judy. Me, too! More than *anybody* ever missed anybody before!" They ended up, giving each other dog eyes.

Later, when they played the game The Long Way Home, and he and Judy strolled the quarter mile, around the Elbow, through the pines, in the moonlight, it seemed wonderful to be beyond the involvement and to have brought this, this that they knew now, that they were, away with them. And it suddenly came to him then that the wild bees had never hit him while he was with Judy!

He didn't tell her. But he took her arm through his and held on to her fingers (unconsciously, as he used to do with his mother) as they walked in the dappled shade. He talked of a time when she would be back from New York and even the concert stage and he would be out of college. He would reclaim his grandfather's house for them to live in. Though what he really wanted to do, he felt like then, was to walk always under the pines, in the moonlight, and hold her hand.

In a quite low voice she sang a verse from a song: "Santa Lucia."

Chapter 8

WHAT WERE WORDS, ANYHOW? Marcellus bounced up from his bench in the smoker, out of the nonsense rhythm of the train. And into the latrine again. Looking down the windy sewer at the bunghole to enveloping night, he reflected that there had been no such thing as irony for him then. He laughed brusquely and spat after his last drops. As he turned away, he muttered, "Saint Lucy." He backed out of the door, telling himself that Judy had been unconscious of his mother's name and the irony of her song, perhaps. But not for long, not for long.

His mouth was bitter, his tongue tobacco-bitten. He felt an irritable aching in his belly, and suddenly it was very empty, too. The blackness at the windowpane, he saw, was leaching out to mud color. The ceiling lamp looked tired. He wondered if he might dig up the butcher boy somewhere, but decided that his stomach was too queasy for food or soda pop. His consciousness of the pint of smuggled Scotch whiskey in his suitcase grew itchy on him again. He hadn't intended to get into it yet. But his present condition surely met the terms of medical need.

Without reconnoiter, he entered the dimness of the day-coach, stealthily picking his way through the human wreckage of slumber to his seat, and lifted down his luggage from the rack above it. He took two swigs of his liquor neat and brusquely restored the bottle. He would go back to the smoker. He didn't want to be tempted to nip on it again. And the scene about him was a morgue. Besides, where he broke off was the beginning, not the end of his flunkaroo with Judioo.

He made his way back along the cold gray aisle. Bent by the weighty mail of his emotional grimness, he stared out a window to the graying east to glimpse, to gulp helplessly at, a dimpled, distant smiling face.

The Victorian pedestal on which he had put Judy during that summer of 1921 turned into a mushroom, a deadly amanita.

Though they had formerly ended their involvement in David's tragedy with the funeral, their exhausting experience had left them in a somber mood. They were under its spell, together with a sense of the deadly monotony of existence, when they arrived at Lingering Bluff. People of the Flatwoods, with its scrub pine, burnt stump and gallberry bush, always get excited over the coast. For Judy and him that June it came on the wings of an angel—an angel, although before their idyll was over it would turn into an amanita for him.

How remote that day seemed now! Although it was still with him vividly, he and Judy in navy-blue bathing suits, in the green Crow's Nest, among the "affable" limbs of a live oak, gazing with intoxication beyond the river at the green sunswept plain of marsh grass—marsh grass as far as the eye could see almost—and quoting poetry. Judy said, " 'Free/ By a world of marsh that borders a world of sea.' " He had been thinking of her as regal or Amazon, but he gave her a sidelong glance then: standing there, balanced, legs apart, at her full shapely height—and he decided that the word for her was "free."

Yet he had an immature sense of his own bonds. The nearest he could come was a sneaking feeling of awkwardness, nudging him like a familiar puppy at his feet—awkwardness that he (five feet seven) might find in trying to hold her (five feet nine) in his lap. Moreover, when he took up the poem . . . " ' the beach lines linger and curl/ As a silver wrought garment that clings to and follows the firm sweet limbs' " . . . and Judy turned and ran down the steps, perhaps to keep her stomach from turning, he only gazed after her flying feet with a sense of mystification.

She was yelling to Mark Donelson, their host, standing up in a rowboat, whirling a drawnet like a lariat, which he let fly into water. He was casting for shrimp, and she said she wanted him to show her how, too—though, in decency, she had yelled back over her shoulder, "Come on, Shorty!"

The place belonged to Mark's father, and Mark was giving the house party to advance his cause with Eleanor Wimberly, a Riverton girl, who with her younger sister, Edith, and another Riverton boy and Mark's aunt, as a chaperone, made up the crowd. And before their shrimping was over the three Dupré boys had come along, on the excuse of borrowing a Stillson wrench, and had been introduced, as neighbors from down the Bluff: the oldest, who must have been in his upper twenties, fair and plump; the middle one, dark and handsome—Marcellus thought like an Arrow collar ad—and the leggy, coltish youngest. Whatever else the absence of the male pattern from his childhood had robbed Marcellus of, he had no suspicion of competition—it was all Marquis of Queensberry for him then. Even when Judy made known her interest in the Dupré boys, he had too little sense of their threat to see them any differently. Judy professed to speak in Edith's behalf, asking his help, to get the dark middle one for Edith, whose partner didn't dance. And he actually agreed to try it.

But the Coast held them both in a deadly Victorian daze. Willingly Judy went back with him to the Crow's Nest to watch the wind and the cloud shadows ride the sweep of marsh grass, hold hands, and to squeeze as they glimpsed the bright flecks on the faraway blue ocean that were whitecaps in the sun.

The craze was common. In the afternoon they all went upriver by motor launch to visit the Twenty Oaks. These grand gray old trees had been bequeathed to themselves, with the ground they stood on and an endowment for their care, by the will of the woman who had owned and loved them. Although oaks, pines, palmetto palms, and dripping Spanish moss were everywhere along the way, they must, to be sure, visit this Druid temple to drink the soul of the oak. A picnic supper over on Saint Simons Island in the evening brought their youthful sight-seeing orgy to a climax. There was a spring tide running; and after they had bathed in the surf, and eaten, they scattered to stroll the beach in the moonlight.

The moon was full and rode high in the sky, spreading its spell over tree and bush, sand and sea. Marcellus and Judy rambled far up the island, heading for the seawall in front of a new resort hotel where the breakers were highest. When they had finally reached the wall, climbed its embankment, and stood up to face the scene beyond, they felt wobbly on their feet before the glittering high, roaring surf. The tide was almost full, but still tumultuous, and seemed to make the whole world rock. And moonlight played on the sea along a wide path from the foaming breakers to the horizon. Luminous white waves rolled in to shatter at their feet.

It took their breath away. Took their speech. They stood still, in wonder and awe.

When the waves had become only the light, fleeing and returning, and Marcellus began to inch toward the brink of the wall, muttering, she had grabbed him by the shoulders to hold him back. He was trembling from head to foot, and put his arms about her, and they stood there, holding to each other. Then she had been moved to touch her lips to his cheek. But he did not seem to notice it. . . .

That night he had been struck dumb, but the next morning, and afterward, he talked about it a great deal. He was deeply stirred by it, and mystified. Under the hold of that day he had sought a special meaning in it, and he struggled for definition and, awkwardly, even for art. It was the moment of moments. In fact, out of Time altogether. He had to impale it, to re-create it for Judy. He grew fairly hollow-eyed in the attempt, but triumphant, on Friday evening, as they sat on the front steps of the big cottage in the twilight, he gave Judy his creation—gave it, without a tremor for its out-size rhetoric. He couldn't get rid of his stage fright, however, and began haltingly:

"Spring, night, the sea wall and our surprise:
High tide—under moon-touched, tensing skies—
Roaring, roaring, roaring an imponderable thunder,
To drink us down in awe and wonder:
Bounding, boundless mirror sea
Unearthing murder's mystery."

On the final verse, naught for its incoherence, he had managed to lose self-consciousness and self-restraint, too:

“Waves staring, staring, staring ecstasy and pain:
Our grasping, gleaming, fleeing to form again—
Whirling drowned galling gallantries ‘gainst our wall:
White, dashing a black body, a fleeting music, they fall, fall.
But out yonder, yonder, beyond seen joy and sorrow,
Zigzags the reenactment of our tomorrow.
Vanishing waves leave thought lightning, lightning enduing us,
With pure love, pure love pursuing us:
Eternal yearning toward Eternal Light.”

(Goddamn, What his city editor would do to that! Marcellus snorted, bouncing on his leather lounge, in the smoker. Yet, somehow, the words still gave him a harrowing experience. What did they mean? He didn’t know—if they meant anything. He had never tried to work it over, never had the nerve to show it to Red Lull. He’d rather forget it!)

That evening—when he finished speaking on the steps, in the twilight—his voice exhausted with the weight of his words, after a moment’s settling silence, Judy leaned forward and took his hand and pressed it. “Oh, that’s nice, Shorty!” she said, a little stiffly. “Really quite good, I think!” Then she sat back.

He’d sat lumped there, blinking his small red eyes. Even in his state the politeness in her voice couldn’t escape him. He shrugged and swallowed and pulled his ear, staring at her hungrily. He knew he should grin in deprecation and say something ironic. But he couldn’t muster the gristle for it. And before he could halt himself, he was handing her a written copy of his verses—without her asking for them. Though she took his hand again and said they were nice.

Feeling as if he had shrieked himself hoarse and hadn’t been heard—and without suspecting that he might have deafened Judy—

he made an excuse, saying he had to run an errand for Mark, and backed down the steps, heading for the boy's cottage. He didn't know what he had expected, but not this, to be sure—not this!

Thinking about it later that night, he rationalized Judy's attitude. She just hadn't altogether got it. And, sure, that was to be expected, was really all right, he solemnly agreed. For actually he didn't fully understand it himself! He felt that although his—his whatever it was had got it into words, spoke truth, he really didn't quite know what it meant.

He was to find, on the following day, other sides to his artesian genius that went unappreciated. Judy and Edith showed up at swim time, in the afternoon, with the two older Dupré boys. He was astonished at this—that is, astonished at Judy. But he took it that she was helping Edith out.

And on the following afternoon Judy supposedly stayed with Aunt Maria, who had a headache, and didn't go on the reconnoiter of Black Beard Island. And when they got back, he found her, not with Aunt Maria, but in the rope hammock, while the plump Dupré boy stood by, swinging her and talking. He was winning a sailboat race for her, and Judy's glib laugh struck Marcellus right between the shoulder blades. But he reasoned, ha ha! that, after all, *he* hadn't been there and Judy couldn't do any better. That evening, however, when Judy disappeared along with Edith while he and Bob were out at the store getting cigarettes and they didn't show up again until eleven o'clock, and then with those two damned Dupré boys hanging on to them—why, why he found this impossible to explain away. And without intending to, or even knowing that he was going to say it, he blurted out, "Judy, I think this is very strange of you!"

And when she retorted—for that was what it was, and a stiff one—"Thank you—Shorty!" he had strode indignantly out of the living room and down the Bluff to the boys' cottage.

After he had cooled down, lying awake in his bed that night, turning everything over and over in his mind, he had to admit to himself finally that Judy actually had never promised him anything. Really, they had never put anything between them into words. It had never seemed necessary. It had seemed better not to. To put it into words would only, well, diminish it—make it like other love affairs, maybe. And it wasn't, of course. At least he had always thought it wasn't, until then. Suddenly he had felt profoundly ill-informed and insecure.

Saturday afternoon came, and they were all supposed to go to Savannah to see a play, a New York road show, and have supper afterward. Mark had planned it from the beginning. It wasn't a jumped-up affair. They were going to eat an early snack and leave at five thirty, for they had a seventy-mile drive.

When mealtime came, Judy didn't come to the table, but lay on the couch in the living room, saying she had a headache. Marcellus would have run to the store to get her some aspirin, but Aunt Marie produced two tablets. Judy, however, said she had never taken aspirin, and would wait to see if her head wouldn't get better by the time they were to go. But it didn't. He offered to stay with her, but Judy wouldn't hear of it—after all, Mark's Uncle Rodney would be on the Bluff. And the long-planned trip was to be a big *do*. Marcellus decided then to go, even though he *was* disturbed. He didn't admit it to himself, but there was something in Judy's insistence that he *not* stay, something in her tone of voice, that sent him on, more disturbed than ever.

They left Judy lying on the couch, with a towel over her eyes and an ice pack on her head. And the fresh feeling of insecurity riding him.

They were late getting away because of Judy's headache, and had a puncture on the way and missed part of the first act. And Marcellus never did really get into the play. Though not from anything they missed. Indeed, Judy's absence and their mishap on the road seemed to dampen everybody's spirits. Afterward, at supper (which was at a fish house, and excellent), Eleanor succeeded in rallying them a little by giving a rakish imitation of passages from the love scenes. And, happily, they didn't have another puncture on the way home. But at that, it was almost two o'clock in the morning when they got there.

Marcellus was the first one out of the car, when it came to a halt. And he didn't head for the boys' cottage, but trotted over to the big house. He had seen the lamp turned low in the living room and he thought (not very rationally) that Judy might be asleep on the couch. When his feet hit the front steps, however, he heard a noise, under the trees behind him, a noise like something flushed in the brush. He whirled about in time to see, below portieres of Spanish moss, against a pale indigo sky, two heads coming up together from one dark mass, in the hammock. A moment later Judy and Clyde Dupré were walking toward him. "Y'all back already!" Judy said.

It had been an awful moment for his innocence, though the night had covered Marcellus' confusion somewhat. For which he was grateful. And though he remained speechless, the others came on from the car in time to keep it from being calamitous. He had even succeeded in getting away, a charitable darkness shrouding his manifest shame.

If he could only have bowed out then, he thought. If he could have got back into the car and driven away into another world, out of reach of this—into the depths of the Hightower swamp or, better still, the Okefeenokee. But he didn't—he couldn't in decency, he told himself. He lay awake, writhing and turning on his mattress the rest of that dark morning, successively cursing Dupré, Judy, and himself. And came, pale as the bottom side of a flounder, at ten o'clock to breakfast.

Or if the house party had just broken up there, that morning, as it should have—if Mark hadn't prevailed on them to stay on through Sunday to go to an oyster roast at his sister's, on Saint Simons, he wouldn't have betrayed himself so ignominiously.

It happened on the beach, behind an oleander bush, after they had swum in the surf and eaten oysters—that is, the others had eaten them, two whole croker sacks full, with drawn butter. All afternoon and into the evening, he had kept his mouth shut. Likely, his silence seemed glumness, but he had, he hoped, kept the dying-calf look off his face. If Judy hadn't relented (if that was what she did) after moonrise and gone down the beach with him, he might have made it. But she did. She sat down on a sand dune, behind the oleander bush, looking up at him, giving him the brimful eyes, her lips softening.

He didn't know it was pity, then. But he wasn't sure he could have kept from being grateful, even if he had. He came to his knees. The blinding thing in him was that he just couldn't believe it possible that she didn't' feel about him the way he felt about her. Though he had a rudimentary sense of the situation being out of control, and he tried to get a headlock on himself—was trying when it happened. It came on its own, against his will. Actually, it seemed to be another man talking. Out of his appalled mouth sounded the shrill voice of Mickey Mouse: "You are the beautiful princess. I guess you can't love . . ."

The recollection of it still made Marcellus wince. His maudlin words had kept coming in spite of his shame.

She was wincing, shaking her head. "Stop it, Shorty. Stop it!"

Though he wanted to stop it far more than she could want it, the treble voice had gone on. About pearls rolled down the plank to him. And he couldn't give them up. The toadstool, in all its deliquescent bloom.

Judy was on her feet by that time. "No, Shorty! No. I'm sorry, Shorty! You've been wrong about me all along." He had remained on his knees, and she had knelt beside him, like a doctor, and spoke in a forced kind voice. "I'm not at all what you think I am. I'm not noble or highminded, like you think—and like *you* are." She couldn't stick it, and came to her feet again. "Forget me, Shorty!" She had said this firmly and turned away and walked back by herself toward the distant bonfire up the beach.

He stared after her, not rising, but hugging his ribs against his shuddering, and watching her walk away. She was almost back at the fire before he got hold of his own voice again. It was hoarse, but natural now. "You sniveling son of a bitch!" he said. "Hightower, you sniveling son of a bitch!"

Chapter 9

MARCELLUS BALANCED himself introspectively on the stool at the lunch counter, in the Terminal Station in Atlanta, suitcase at his feet. He had hiked over from the other station, toting his luggage, and had worked up a light sweat and an appetite. He sought to damp both with a cigarette now, as he awaited his usual workaday breakfast of coffee and doughnuts—when the waitress would discover him. Last man in a row of six along the marble top, and partly hidden by the tall nickel-plated coffee urn at its corner, he swiveled to and fro, inhaling his smoke against the edge of hunger. There was thirty minutes to kill before boarding the train for Riverton.

He paused to examine his reflection in the urn. The face was Mongoloid, and the hand holding his cigarette, extending from a midget's arm, was that of a giant. He knew this unlucky oaf well, he told himself. Seated, as he was, on his fated, his usual, love seat: a deliquescent deadly amanita! Yes. He had been imagining that he was off it, since he met Melanie. But was he? He stared searchingly into the background of his wonderland mirror, without being able to pick her up anywhere. After a long drag at his smoke that finally subdued the flesh, he dropped it into a spittoon near his foot. She was hiding out on him, fearful of the photomontage!

She had said a thing that put him off, in her sorority house parlor, on that second date. Giving him that cynically twisted dimple, she had said, "I chewed a round of your sugarcane—don't you remember?"

He had been so uncertain of how to take this that he couldn't remember at all. Now it came back to him: it *was* his sugarcane, but David gave it to her. Comedy of errors, his errors. The jaundice in his eyes was virginity—his.

The thing was that David, in that last fateful autumn, had got ahead of him again: he had been initiated. His sexual favor had come of a colored girl on the place. And actually it had nothing to do with Melanie Crosby. David's girl was one of Aunt Mary's granddaughters, and almost white and seventeen at the time. Her name—would you believe it, was Venorial—Vanie for short. Marcellus had color scruples and was mutely censorious of David for this promiscuousness, but his feelings were not unmixed with envy. It gave David a mysterious advantage over him. And he couldn't keep Venorial off his mind.

It was only her back—the middy blouse and the pleated skirt switching from her little behind—that he saw disappearing through the doorway, into the "company" bedroom at Ransom's that day. He could not have said who the girl was. It just happened to be Venorial who came to mind. Melanie was not as tall as Venorial, nor as fully developed, though she was conspicuous for her age. Moreover, he scarcely knew her name and didn't know she was in the house. He was merely passing through the back hall on his way to the barn lot where sugarcane grinding was going on, and he didn't think anything of what he had seen at the time. It was not until he had filled up on cane juice from the mill and had picked himself out a stalk of green cane to chew that he got around to asking where David was and learned he was taking a nap in the "company" room for quiet. Only then did he reflect on the disappearing behind that he had seen, and assume it was the Negro girl's. And this delusion, of course, colored what he did see a few minutes later.

As Marcellus came across the back porch to enter the hall, David and Melanie were coming into it from the other end, out of the guest room. David had an arm about her shoulders. And Marcellus could swear, could almost swear that he was playing with one of her breasts—of which she was so proud. But by the time Marcellus got through the screen door, they had separated. Indeed, he was sure David jerked his arm away, when Marcellus took hold of the latch.

With unruffled poise David held out a hand for a round of the sugar cane he was chewing, and gave a quarter of it to Melanie.

It was no more than that. Indeed, when Marcellus saw that the girl was *not* Venorial he dismissed any idea of wrong-doing between them. At first. It was only after he was in bed in the night that the thing began to gnaw on him. Though at the time his concern about Melanie was categorical. He bore her no feeling except a vague annoyance, annoyance at her being around—and being the cause of David's ungentlemanly conduct, as he suspected. He didn't know about the Violation of the Age of Consent Law then, but he was sure that Melanie Crosby had gone into the guest room to get violated. He decided, uneasily aware of those insistent breasts, that David would not have been able to resist her seductions, once she got in the bed with him.

In all his self-righteous virginity Marcellus accused David of violating the age of consent. But there had been more envy than contempt in the boy who squirmed between his bed sheets.

Maybe there still was? Marcellus resumed his musing after he was again ensconced in a day-coach chair on another train, moving in a winter sunrise blaze toward Riverton. In his hard hurry to be rid of the curse of his petticoat upbringing, in the fall following that house party on the coast, he had resorted to piney-woods whores. To be sure, there was more than envy of David in it, or even hunger for experience. He could remember the fever of his lust. But it couldn't have been the attractions of those anonymous women in the big town of Albany. For he had never seen a white prostitute then. Fever? An erection was about to embarrass him now. Marcellus came out of his seat and moved toward the water cooler.

Incredibly: it had been little Melanie's breasts. And still was. My God, he had seen, must have seen, nipples before Melanie's? Moreover, Melanie's hadn't been uncovered. Puberty's earthquakes. Marcellus held the inadequate paper cup under the uncertain spigot and tossed off the contents, gulping down more air than water. He backed away to blink for a moment longer at the round, pasty-faced woman with protruding eyes in a nearby seat. But he did not wait to see the effect of his affront. Moving off along the aisle, he wagged his head.

Ah, but he had uncovered them; and how many times! Sweet torture! The whores of Albany hadn't tarnished, had not been able to touch, this fugitive wanton. Indeed, all he had come away from Albany with was a liquor-swollen head and the nausea of a stale fish sandwich in his nostrils—they had eaten them on the way home, an unctuous gesture, he would say. He had uncovered Melanie's breasts and he had substituted his hand for David's, playfully, over her left shoulder, in the Ransom back hall.

To be sure, almond-eyed Hulda, the Piney-ridge banker's luscious daughter, hadn't needed Melanie's breasts. Yet Melanie and David had been in conspiracy against him in this first encounter of his sexual unshackling. They, as it were, egged him on with a smile of superiority.

To his astonishment Hulda abided his rashness. Before his reaction could harden into an intention, however—he was but exploring, exploring the hidden continent, there on the parlor sofa—she, with only becoming resistance, opened her ivory-white thighs to him.

He had been taken aback, really thunderstruck. Yet neither amazement nor petticoat upbringing had stayed him—nor, he would guess, did the knowing smile send him on. For the world faded smokily, and he reared up on his haunches, stud horse. Stud horse, but at the last possible moment he heard the front door rattle, come open, and her father come striding down the hall. Only some handy sofa cushions saved them from embarrassment.

Afterward, he wished he had just gone ahead and got shot in the arse. It would have been less painful. For, adding to his surprise, he got from Hulda mutely that she was as much taken aback at what she was doing as he was, that she was *gone* on him. His conscience came alive. With a swirl of Victorian skirts, Conscience had turned a pointed nose, a palisade of forehead and glittering pince-nez glasses on him, and leveled at him steadfastly. He shrugged and shook his head, but he had no further doubt as to what his moral responsibility was. The wanton he had been pursuing quit the game.

In the days that followed, he suffered but found no way out. He knew that he was not led by any *serious intention* toward Hulda. But this first sense of possession, sense of power over her, overwhelmed him. There was a little while when he wondered if he couldn't be falling in love with her. He had to confess to himself, however, it wasn't love—he was unencumbered in the head.

But whatever it *was,* he was in a fever of desire by day and ached with lust by night. He had to put a water pitcher by his bed, he recalled. Her family were pretty straitlaced, and believed in a lot of chaperonage. He could have evaded it, to be sure. Hulda would have connived with him. But under the stern eye of Conscience he had submitted. It was the safer way.

Yet the Issue was with them to the very last moment. The final night of Commencement they drove one of the children in the play home late at night, into the back country, unchaperoned. She was driving her own car, lingering and trembling over the crooked sandy road back, with its accessible shelter of oaks and pines. But he knew now—they both knew—that she was no longer a free piece. To be sure, he could have her. But his Conscience, armed with obligations, sat between them then, as palpable a chaperone as her mother would have been.

However, when tempted to pursue the fugitive wanton again the following fall in nearby Athens, where he had resumed his education at the University of Georgia, he had made a different response. His determination to throw off the petticoat upbringing had redoubled. And, to be sure, he was already moving into the new postwar moral country. Though, God forgive us, not fast or far enough. Marcellus grimaced unconsciously. For he had been caught between—*they* had been caught between. From which consequences still flowed.

But the circumstances had been different at Georgia. Blossom Jay, the coed in his Shakespeare and French classes who took his eye, was a finespun thing, and smart as she could be. Coeds were still a little short of the social swing. But Blossom was unusual: a girl of natural loveliness with a keen mind, unlike all others, he thought then. She might have been, he fancied, a silver doe, with wholly intelligent green eyes. Though actually her slim oval face was a light brown with a gray undershading. And her fine longish nose and full lips made her chin seem almost timid. She led French class and was at the top in Shakespeare, too.

They had swapped confidences on their Shakespeare teacher: both found him a bureaucrat who wanted only your admiration and his notes back on examination. This had proved a beginning for them. He had thought he was falling in love with her, too. That is, it got more mixed up in his mind after the final football game, Georgia and Auburn, in Atlanta.

The trip to the game set the stage, and two kinks accomplished their assignation. While he was "tittybumming" his way over with the band, he got chased out of the special car by the train crew into the coeds' Pullman, where Blossom, gown and jacket over her slip, hid him behind her in her berth, while the conductor came by. Two weeks before, and before he had known Blossom was going, he had—on a peach-brandy impulse—made a date with his old girl Judy for the game and the dance, which now threatened to queer him. Then things misfired with Judy in time for him to try for a date with Blossom after the game (he'd sent his tickets to Judy). Blossom said, "Why after the game?" and they let football go by.

The meter in their taxicab became distracting to their lovemaking, and they transferred to a divan in a corner of the mezzanine of his hotel. But the bell captain, in the lobby, kept spying on them. And, by then, the key in Marcellus' pants pocket was burning his leg. As they broke out of a clinch under the supposed scrutiny of the flunky, Blossom whispered, "Oh, can't we go somewhere else?" And Marcellus knew by the hot snow in her voice—his fear of lying to her, or himself, had grown irrelevant. "Hell!" he said, gripping her by the arm, "hell!" Abruptly he pulled the key from his pocket and held it up between them.

She stared at it for a long electric moment, her face going gray and perspiration beading her upper lip. Then she met his gaze, eyes black and whites glistening, bending limberly toward him. They got up together, joined by the eye, and moved to the elevator.

That night, after the dance, Marcellus got back to Athens for fifty cents with a bunch of boys in a cut-down Ford. He alternated with another man, between the gas tank on the back and the seat. There were times, astride the bucking tank, when he thought he as a goner. It made the springless seat positively luxurious. But the ride was mixed for more reasons than one.

Luxurious? On their blind bed he had known a scary half-second, then—so unlike the time with the whores—a drowning. They were drowned together. And afterward, a long time afterward, he had awakened to Blossom, not a delirium now, but the *captive* beside him—her breasts against his chest, he thought, like hummingbird's wings. Glancing down on the modeled amber of her back, he knew the luxury of possession. . . . The image made him ache and stiffen in the reclining car seat. But on through the night, the bucking gas tank plunged him toward the question he couldn't word. Did he find it? Was he committed? Why was he doubtful?

On Monday morning, still a little sleepy and stove up from his trip, Marcellus glanced at the seat to his left in his eight-o'clock class with a sense of relief. He did not consider why he felt so. And he did not come anywhere near asking himself why Blossom wasn't in it. He was too thankful then not to have to face her in the quick. Though thoughts of the trip browsed in his mind. He had had a famous time at the dance. And he thought Blossom did, too. They had been high (less from liquor than the way they just felt) and were openly gone on each other, without trying to hide it. His brothers had made a thing of it by lining up to break on them. In the vastness of his sense of possession he didn't mind. And, to be sure, Blossom found it flattering.

Judy had been there, too, with a blond-headed bean pole of an engineer, for whom she had broken their date for the dance. Marcellus lifted his gaze to the dim, moving scene in the ballroom at the Atlanta Biltmore Hotel, seeing Judy's vivid image—a tide of poetic tortures brimming in her dark eyes. But he had moved upon them without damage—indeed, he had felt as if he wore a bulletproof vest.

Judy had been friendly, and confessed to being hurt at his having stood her up for the game, even if it was tit for tat! He had offered no further explanation, had kept his distance, though he was friendly, too. He had danced with her twice. On the second dance, she had asked him if he was in love with *his girl*—talk must already have been going around, or maybe it was the way they had been looking at each other. He had laughed and said, "Sure thing."

Then she had drawn her arm closer about his neck and looked into his face and put the question again, "Are you really in love with her, Shorty?

Some man was touching her arm to break, and he allowed the break, repeating his laugh and saying, enigmatically he hoped, "What is real?"

Marcellus turned his attention to the French novel on the arm of his chair, in the classroom. He was in no state of mind to try to answer his question. He kept away from it. Indeed, he didn't think about it again until Blossom reappeared at his side in the French class on Friday. He saw by her paleness and quiet that she had been through something stiff. He winced. Suddenly he felt like a bull in a china shop—or rather, an ex-bull. Gritting his teeth and dropping his eyes to lessen his breathing, he turned to her. "Why wouldn't you answer my phone calls?" he lied, adding in a hoarse whisper, "I think you've treated me hideously."

"There wasn't any call before Wednesday afternoon," she said, the green eyes of intelligence on him, "before I went to the infirmary."

Marcellus gagged, flushing hotly. But he finally got out, "Forgive me for living, honey. Forgi'me. But I've had my—my hospitals, too."

They had been then just about ready to break off everything, altogether. But they didn't. And the upshot of it was that, in the midst of his private doubts and her misgivings, they had sexual intercourse again—in her bedroom (her roommate had gone home for the weekend), Blossom helping him through a back window. This relationship went on as inevitably and unevenly in its extremes, as young nature is liable to—on after Christmas, on through the winter and into the spring. She had his fraternity pin, of course, but he brought himself to mention marriage only once, and that in a negative tone of voice. "Do you believe in getting married in college?" he said. To which she could only reply agreeably in the negative. But, be it said, she did so without hesitation.

Then in April something else, almost inevitable, happened. There were, to be sure, contributory circumstances. Blossom's boardinghouse was in one of those converted antebellum, white-columned, southern colonial mansions that have detached kitchens—so prevalent in Athens. And this small house, ten steps from the main dwelling, housed the apartment she shared with another coed. Moreover, after Christmas, Marcellus had begun taking his meals at her boardinghouse, and thus came more casually to hand. And so it happened on that wet April Sunday morning that Mrs. Stalkup, the boardinghouse keeper, at the breakfast table, as Marcellus was getting up to leave it, casually said: "Won't you beat on Miss Jay's door as you go out through the backyard? She told me to be sure to get her up for breakfast." Contributory also was it that he didn't know the roommate was going away for the weekend, nor did he—after he had beat on the door without response and tried the knob—expect to find the door unlocked.

Then he stuck his head inside, to get it out of the cold rain, and after a moment Blossom stirred among the pillows to groan, "Shut the door; that wind's freezing me!" He did, with himself inside, though his intention still was only monitory. He approached the bed not yet quite sure that Bettie, her roommate, wasn't there too, and, it must be admitted, naively unwary of the conditioned reflexes of established sexual intimacy. Indeed, he thought Blossom's eyes looked puffy and the pink-trimmed flannel nightgown she had on repulsive.

As he stood over her, about to deliver Mrs. Stalkup's words, however, she smiled up at him and stretched voluptuously, inadvertently pushing the covers back. Somewhere in him the low spark flared; there was the slight swinging within the viscera, blood pressed his skin, and the train of his thinking snapped. Then they stared at each other, stared at each other with him pulling down the bedclothes, and their complementary image might have been focused in one pair of eyes.

A thought tugged at the back of Marcellus' brain, but it did not get through to him until too late, much too late.

They were abysmally ignorant, they discovered, and they did not get stirred up to the seriousness of the situation until Blossom was far into her second month of pregnancy. Marcellus wrote a fraternity brother in medical school for advice, and the response jolted him. But as her time of the curse approached again they tried—that is, he prescribed and she tried—all the household remedies, without helpful results. The days continued to pass, grimly uneventful. Marcellus looked up a boy from Riverton there who he knew was something of a reprobate, and this boy took him to see his doctor—the doctor who had treated him for gonorrhea. But this medico of cold blue eyes, bristling blond pompadour, and narrow antiseptic moustache seemed to specialize only in ruthlessness. What Marcellus clumsily hinted at was not merely unethical but against the law. The only thing the doctor could suggest was that he marry the girl.

Marcellus batted his eyes painfully, in a face stiffening and sagging both, as he sat in the doctor's inner office. That had not been mentioned before! Blossom certainly hadn't hinted at such a thing. And while the thought had, like a wild dog beyond the fence, threatened him a time or two, it had not actually crossed his mind as a realistic possibility. Each had another year in college. And it was just about as embarrassing to *have* to get married as—as—

But at this point his appearance had grown so woe-begone that the young specialist's ruthlessness was affected, and when Marcellus fumbled his way from the inner office, the fellow followed him outside to say to him: "Look, I'm still young enough to have some sympathy for you in the spot you're in. What I'm about to suggest is not as a doctor, but man to man. There are one or two disreputable men around here who will perform an abortion, if the girl is willing. Though I can't tell you who they are."

Marcellus' favorite cabdriver-bootlegger supplied the name and address of one of the disreputables.

But he was alarmed by what he met. The half of the room for waiting, with its two skint-up chairs and a broken-down couch, outside the dust-gray osnaburg curtain, seemed as dirty and derelict as quarters abandoned by squatters, and as irrelevant. From behind the curtain, the faded fat man, bloated face of a disinterred corpse, given a macabre quaintness by the weather-stained derby on his head, dragged toward Marcellus to appall him. The man never mentioned the operation he would perform on Marcellus' wife, as he insisted on referring to her, but only the price—twenty-five dollars—part payable in advance. And Marcellus, if he had been less distraught, would have broken off the thing then, but he agreed to an appointment two weeks off and left a five-dollar deposit, fully determined that they would not keep it.

When he made his grisly report to Blossom, he did propose marriage seriously. Indeed, he told Blossom they must get married. But she only laughed and said she wouldn't marry at gunpoint. She said she wasn't afraid.

However, she shuddered, too, when she looked into those red-threaded china-blue eyes with the pus bags beneath them. For her he took off his discolored derby, uncovering dirty yellowish-white curls parted in the middle, and bent over her hand as if he would kiss it. He led them behind the curtain, where a tiny electric bulb depended over a scarred operating table, the only object visible besides his pallid face, which seemed to glow phosphorescently in the semidarkness.

Blossom asked only that Marcellus be allowed to stay and hold her hand. It was only a matter of seconds by the clock. Marcellus, before turning away, glimpsed a long instrument like a letter opener with a curved point in the hands of the doctor at the foot of the table. Slowly, her grip tightened on his fingers, her lips becoming a straight scar. She writhed briefly, her eyes distending, and cried out. Then there was a purring murmur from the foot of the table; it was over and her grip relaxed. Two big tears stood in her eyes.

Final examinations at the university were already over, and the next morning their sad mishap seemed just about a memory. Blossom would stop over at a small infirmary in Atlanta for a couple of days to be sure. And he would remain at school to make up some work and await word from her. They were still friends, at all events; and they parted with hardy good cheer.

The oaf on the toadstool did not suspect that Fate was making a feint! The be-derbied derelict had to perform his operation on Blossom three more times. And they moved their place of hiding from an anonymous back-street hotel—after he had failed there—to a rest home, arranged for by the doctor, run by a bigmouthed, red-faced Irish woman with an imbecile bastard boy, on the outskirts of the black section of town. *Yes, Jesus,* she operated a *respectable place,* as the other patient, a gold-toothed streetwalker there at the time, agreed. Marcellus suspected that this was where the doctor ducked out on his mistakes, but he said nothing. The thing had them surrounded, and showed no trace for retreat. They knew they had to go through with it now.

Their calendar was measured by *his* visits—an hour, a day, three days. A fourth day passed in gray rain, though this could add little gloom to its uneventfulness. He and Blossom rose and dressed and hung up their nightclothes and made up the bed and tidied the room, like inmates of a mental institution. There were no events before. The world had ceased to exist. Neither of them had even thought of writing home. Life held only one contingency—its core, its quick wrapped in gray, endless dread.

Even so, there had been one lifting moment. The afternoon sun broke through the clouds. He and Blossom followed a spangle out of the house and into a scrub apple orchard behind it. They stood there under the old trees, where new green leaves were coming and a few blooms held on. Suddenly a scampering wind set the boughs dancing, and sprinkled pink and white petals down on them. Petals fell on Blossom's nose and cheeks and embroidered her crisp brown hair. They grinned at each other, and Marcellus grabbed her hand and they ran down the avenue of trees until she fell, laughing and gasping for breath.

Then they turned back. Their calendar, with another visit by the abortionist, began its narrow circuit again. Yet it wasn't to be completed this time. Late the next afternoon, Marcellus looked up from the pages of *The House of the Seven Gables,* which he had dug out of the attic and was reading to Blossom, to discover that she was flushed with fever and moaning incoherently. He called in their hostess, Nora, to sit with her, and went to the nearest telephone, a quarter of a mile down the road at a Negro's house. An hour later, he held Blossom, wrapped in a blanket, in his arms on the back seat of an automobile the bristling blond urologist was driving toward a hospital.

As the car wheeled into the ambulance entrance of their gray-stone oak-framed asylum where white-clad Negro orderlies swung open the doors welcomely, Marcellus looked on the scene with a loosening relief—how long and twisted the way to it!

Yet, again, his sense of security was premature. He felt like a dug-up mole in the light-bathed glittering corridor, where he had been halted at the operating-room door, about him gliding antiseptically white ants, whom he hoped were too busy to be interested in why he was here. But a few moments later he was given something more serious to concern himself about. The white-gowned urologist led him into a room where two other aproned and gloved doctors lined up to form a phalanx of professional gravity.

A case of this nature required consultation. The patient has acute inflammation of the parietal peritoneum. The senior surgeon advises an effort be made to check the infection before operating. The patient has about one chance in seven to recover.

Marcellus couldn't move until the urologist, Dr. Spate, had put a hand on his shoulder to limber him up; then he shrugged and muttered numbly, "A crap-shooting chance!" But what was on his mind was how often he crapped out.

He found Blossom in a darkened room, fettered with white bandages and sheets, stretched out on a racklike bed, the foot of which was elevated. She answered him but her voice wandered off into a quavering cry for *Water*. The nurses on the hall gave him a glassful for her, but she didn't drink it. This became the ritual of his night's vigil. When she seemed lucid, he tried to talk to her, held her hand, stroked her arm. But she always went off. "I'm burning up!" He pressed the nurses for ice packs and more water. Once she seemed to sleep fitfully, and he went out into the hall to stretch his legs. She cried out. She was on fire, couldn't stand the pain. He hounded a nurse into giving her a white tablet, but it did no good. He wound up holding her hand, gripping it tighter and tighter, muttering, "Hold on, hold on, hold on." . . . At last she fell into a troubled sleep. When the morning nurse found him walking the hall, however, and wanted him to bed down awhile in one of the empty rooms, he gruffly retreated to Blossom's bedside again, and inadvertently woke her up. The night wouldn't end. She was conscious now, and her ragged cries and rigor were harder to bear than her delirium. Again he dragged a protesting nurse (threatening to put him out of the hospital) to her bed, and another white tablet was administered. Blossom's cries went on, nevertheless, rising—a needle piercing his eardrums.

Then, miraculously, the darkness was broken by a gray loop of light, an opalescent fan flaring open, a soundless bugle to end their wake: it was daybreak! Both he and Blossom turned toward the brightening window and took a new grip on things. At eight o'clock she was wheeled back into the operating room. At ten she was returned to her bed, weak and wretchedly nauseated, but conscious and safely through the operation. She smiled at him wanly.

He bent over her. "One chance in seven, the doctors said. Beginner's luck!" Her face was wet with his tears.

Blossom left the hospital three days later, and went home. Marcellus stayed on in Athens. His mother and sisters were still in Philadelphia. Besides, he did have a term of college algebra to make up. They had used summer school as an excuse for their being here. And he had actually matriculated while he awaited Blossom's return. Now he was glad to get down to studying—even algebra. And to be alone. Though he did move back to the fraternity house, for he now found male companionship unexacting and restful. He and Blossom exchanged only two letters during the month of July. And they were brief and noncommittal, positive only in what they didn't say. And that was that maybe they'd better leave each other alone.

Marcellus might have been willing to let it rest there. But at the beginning of the second term, Blossom suddenly reappeared in Athens and on the campus. She had not written Marcellus that she was coming, nor did she look him up. They encountered each other casually (insofar as he was concerned certainly) on the mall. He was standing in the shade just outside the Administration Building, lighting a cigarette, when she walked by. His astonishment was complete. And he found the sight of her a mixed pleasure. Not that she didn't seem pretty to him now: he thought she had never looked more taking, in her sleeveless pink checked muslin and flesh-colored stockings and white sandals. And trig. And—and untouched. But the sight of her made him feel strained and sore inside—as if he had charley horses in his head or somewhere.

She said merely that she had sold her parents on the idea of her coming to summer school, and they insisted that she stick to it. He didn't believe this and she didn't ask him to. But it was all she said about it. The charley horses seemed to be mutual. They didn't have a date. But they kept on seeing each other on campus, and now and then sitting out a vacant period on a shady bench here, there, or yonder. Talking about nothing at first, just dumbly drawn together, though she at the outset thanked him for settling the hospital bill. But one afternoon, under their favorite magnolia tree, she looked at him speculatively, her eyes darkening; then a sort of inward rueful smile came into them, and she said, "Remember Nora?"

It was the first mention of their trouble, but his own reaction astonished him. It was as if she had touched his funny bone. His jaws relaxed and saliva flowed in his mouth, and he found himself saying, "She had the biggest heart and the biggest behind I ever saw on a woman."

Then Blossom's mouth crimped as it did to say something risqué, her lower lip looking babyish. "And her poor half-wit boy who couldn't figure out what *you* had come there for!"

They dropped it at that for the time, but it kept coming up. It persisted, although they approached it with reluctance, almost gingerly—or they seemed to. They were not trying to get anywhere in their talk about it. And they took no positive attitude toward it. They were quizzical. It was as if they were asking of Life, *What has happened to us? What does our calamity mean? And is it a calamity, by the way?*

He broke off his triggering with an algebra problem one night in his room, broke off in astonishment, the question facing him firmly. *Why wasn't he in love with Blossom?* This thing of theirs was surely a bond. He knew her now more intimately than he did any other woman in the world. And she had shared the blame with him from the start. Indeed, she had been game in every way throughout. By damn, they could really appreciate each other now, and rely on each other, too!

He got up and went into the bathroom to brush his teeth, as his Athens dentist had prescribed. It couldn't be social! To be sure her father began as an automobile mechanic and still was, though he owned his own shop—the biggest in the town of Edison. True, she didn't get a bid to a sorority until the past year. It was a little weak in her to take it then, perhaps. But there were different ways of looking at that. Her good grades in school meant more to her perhaps than his did to him. But by God, they ought to; they were better. He couldn't believe that any of these things meant anything to him in his feeling toward her, one way or another.

He ran water through the bristles of the brush, then tapped it on the edge of the bowl. Did he fear Blossom with his mother? Would she suspect? Saint Lucy. Would Blossom cut him off from her? Could he explain her to his mother? Why not? His mother admired any girl who was smart. And she didn't want him to marry Judy, at all events. . . . Ah, Judy. Was that real? Was it? Perhaps he had never known any other moment like the one that Judy had shared with him there, as they walked with Mona between them on the Ransom porch. Maybe he had never got as high off the ground again, as he did that evening walking in the moonlight through the pines, holding Judy's hand and talking about their future—their future. Maybe . . . But hell, that was the sugar chiffon of childhood. Just about! To be sure, he'd found finally that Blossom's brain had its limitations, too—but, hell, who would want to marry a woman who he thought was smarter than he was? As he moved back through the bathroom door, he realized mistily that somehow Blossom's face had never washed up out of his emotions into the moonlight and waves, never lightning. But, for God's sake, that wasn't healthy, anyhow. This sort of thing had only queered him with Judy! He sat down at the table again and slammed the algebra book shut. Well, then, what the hell *was* this thing? He shrugged, and wagged his head and got up again. They hadn't got started right, that was all. He was in love with Blossom and just didn't know it.

No syllable of this mental witch hunt came out in Marcellus' talk with Blossom, of course. Though what may have been reflected in some of his quizzical looks he could not know. But one sultry afternoon soon afterward, under the magnolia tree, something seemed to hush their talk like the abrupt stillness that falls upon locusts in a hot dry season. Each lowered his glance for a moment, aimlessly intent, it seemed, upon the half-smoked cigarette Blossom had thrown on the ground. Then they lifted their eyes, and their gaze was joined to lose focus in a wordless passage of emotion. They both got up, still staring and silent, and Blossom hurried away to class.

"Rules, hell!" Marcellus barked into the telephone transmitter late that night, "Be there!" Twenty minutes later, Blossom moved along the mall as if she were headed for New College, the dormitory currently occupied by coeds, veered off behind a hedge, then ran to the dense shadows of the magnolia tree. Her silhouette was plain. He took her hands as she came under the tree, folded her in his arms, and pressed his mouth on hers, without a word. It was as if they had taken up just over the precipice on which, teetering, they had broken off in the afternoon. They stood with their bodies pressed against each other, in passionate embrace, until she broke away to say, "The campus police!"

He looked back over his shoulder, and nodded. They quickly ducked out through the hedge and moved along a row of trees. There were no stars. It was a dark, heavy night, but cooler now. They moved like a shadowy quadruped, a little denser than the dark atmosphere, across lawns, through hedges, over ditches, up lanes, and finally off the campus altogether, into an old vegetable garden. A remote streetlight cast dim reflection about them. Marcellus could make out the silhouette of old collard stalks. They stood on the uneven footing of last year's corn rows. Things at the periphery of consciousness. Their consciousness, joined by and absorbed into pulsing blood. Clinging to each other, throbbing with the same hammer stroke, in the stillness, in the dark, at some signal of the body they crumpled upon the ground. Blossom found that an old corn furrow fitted well into the small of her back. Earth heaved, and Marcellus, melting into it, thought: *It is Nature; it is bigger than us; it is love!* But there was a cold core at the center of his head that didn't melt.

With steam popping off and a gut grinding of iron wheels, the train dribbled to a halt, and Marcellus discovered to his astonishment that they were already in Lancaster. He bolted from the chair and down the aisle to the vestibule and down the day-coach steps to the station plaza to look about. He had not told his sister his travel schedule, but it was late morning and she just might be on hand or passing by. Maybe he could send her word by someone that he would be up to see her in a few days. But he saw no familiar face, and got back on his coach.

A few minutes later the short local train was whipping the rail joints into a fidgety fugue and laying a whistle-moaning dirge behind it, while pine forests whirled past Marcellus' window, like a merry-go-round in a dead march. This flat, burnt-stump, palmetto and piney-woods country always made his chest bone ache. But he could never tell whether it was longing to be in it or out of it. It was as familiar to him as waking up. Or going to sleep—and maybe a bit of both. It was a ghost story, at his mother's knee, in now-I-lay-me. What were David Ransom's last words?

Marcellus couldn't keep his seat, and ranged down the aisle to the smoker. Lighting up his pipe, he told himself it was only that he dumbly resisted reentry into his past. But was anything past that you somehow carried round with you? Buried or unburied. It was like the birthmark on your back. You had to have a look at it once in a while to see that it hadn't turned into a cancer. What is absurd Victorian sentiment, anyhow?

Out the window, in a clump of palmettos swimming in gallberry bushes, he saw Melanie's fleeting face again—a pained look in her eyes, above the twisted smile. He muttered aloud: "The future is only the past, with a new face on it!" *Future? future?* Marcellus' gaze lost focus in the deep, the bone-breaking suspicion that he could never get far away from Devil's Elbow and it surroundings, the birthmark on his back.

Nor was this a superficial hunch. Returning to his past was to become a dominant pattern of Marcellus' future. Hero of many faces and one myth, he would come to the river country three more times yet in search of them.

Again, the train was slowing down, sand on the track, the wheels grinding to a stop. Marcellus leaped out of the smoker and hurried up the aisle to his chair. With a knee on the cushion, he snatched his suitcase off the rack and himself along the passageway, toward the vestibule. But, halfway, he came to an unsteady pause, his face pale and sweating. Abruptly, he lifted the bag above his head and squirmed back up the line of passengers moving out, to his seat again. Panting, he bent over to look out the window at the signboard saying RIVERTON. *What lay out there? What lay in wait for him?*

Chapter 10

MARCELLUS GAZED speculatively at the peach bloom on the soft white cheeks of the gaily attired man nearing middle age across the table from him. Was it rouge? as some of Riverton's gossips said. Perhaps it was. There was surely no blush or softness inside Henry Harrrison. People called him Handsome Harry, but that was for revenge, behind his back. Marcellus shifted his glance to the end of the long, well-molded nose to say, "I have a proposal." The banker did not look at him, but merely indicated by the degree to which he lifted the nose and lowered his eyes—lashes shading his irises with the guardedness of a rabbit's—that he was listening.

Marcellus had put off this meeting as long as he could. The mortgage was due January seventh. And Christmas was only four days away. From their letters he already suspected what was going on in Harrison's mind. But the bank was actually in a tenuous position on this second mortgage, which really the Hightower estate should not have had to pay. He ought to be glad to take what he could get. The thing was, Marcellus didn't want any deal that would bring him back to Riverton. He was just getting established on the paper. And having an exciting, a really fabulous time. He got a real kick out of the police-court column they let him do; already he knew his way around Nashville's underworld, and there were Bill Trice and the Bluff. There was another thing, too. However mixed up "Plump" and Squirmie Irmie were in his mind, he wasn't about to give up Melanie. She was keen. And, God, Riverton was so little-town. And shabby.

Marcellus glanced about the blank white plaster walls, his gaze settling on the pensive mauve eyelids again. "The bank is all but out in the cold on that second mortgage with land and timber values like they are," he said, stoutly, modulating his voice a little as he went on. "And you-all don't deserve to get that fifteen hundred dollars anyhow, the way you-all settled the insurance suit on the house that burned. I think you took advantage of my mother there. But I want to shoot square with you." He flushed slightly and paused for a response. Harrison merely swallowed, his Adam's apple appearing momentarily above the edge of his high General Dawes collar, and held to his listening. Marcellus went on: "If the bank will buy Cleve McNale's first mortgage, along with the unpaid interest, and renew for a year on the total amount, that would give me some time to sell the timber. And I'll pay the *whole thing*—including the second mortgage—off when I do."

Harrison spoke in a monotone lowered like his eyes. "The stumpage wouldn't bring enough to cover it."

Marcellus was staring at the rosy spot on the impassive cheek. "How do you know?"

Briefly the eyes lifted. "Oh, we've had it cruised."

He bridled at the temerity of this, but held his tongue. After a moment he said, in a positive manner, "The lumber market's going up."

Harrison for the first time met his gaze. "It may well go down," he said. "Look, Mr. Hightower, I don't know how it is in Tennessee, but these are hard times in South Georgia. This bank can't increase its mortgage loans at all—the bank examiner won't let us." He went on peremptorily: "I've got an offer to make. It's the only offer my committee will let me make."

"Humph!" Marcellus said, and came to his feet impulsively. He knew about what it would be. He strode over to the water cooler against the wall and put the small tumbler under the spigot and turned it on, but nothing came out. Harrison was talking on as if he hadn't moved. Marcellus had done well before. If he would cut the timber himself, moving in a peckerwood sawmill perhaps . . . and his connection with his brother-in-law's lumber company . . . the bank would run him for a year, let him see how much he could pay off over the twelve months, then . . .

Marcellus was back at his chair, and, pausing, stood behind it for a moment, a hand on the spooled upright, with some dim sense of support from the past in this gesture. He meditated the table. Fifteen years before, Adam had stood in this room, behind this chair, as *he* was standing now, facing a banker at the other table end—another banker and a lawyer and landowners—a whole crew of white scoundrels, his would-be murderers. And outfaced them! And he, Marcellus, had been sitting in the chair, pulling for him then.

He shrugged and sighed and slumped into his seat. That was another time, another world. And he reflected uneasily that Adam was not with him—or wouldn't be if he knew of it—in his wanting to stay in Nashville. Adam was somewhere over about the hitching racks behind the stores at this moment, waiting for him to come back from this set-to with the banker. He hadn't told Adam what was in his mind. It was all right for Adam to be concerned about whether they lost the place, because he still rented from them. But not about whether Marcellus came or went, did or didn't return to Riverton. He told himself this. Yes, he had told himself this, but now that he was back here, back in this resounding room again, back into his past, Marcellus knew it wouldn't stick. The desperate chance Adam had taken then (even though the men feared exposure), and the adroitness, the terrible impeccable cunning of the inquisition he had put them through. And it had all been over Hightower land lines, among these same lots of land. He had done it for the land. Marcellus lifted troubled eyes, feeling a twinge at his stomach. He couldn't desert Adam.

But even if he took a year's leave of absence from the paper, he couldn't get out of this hole in a year. Of course, what Adam wanted was for him to stay here and open up the land. What would happen, however, was that he would work himself half to death for three years, turning over every dime above expenses to the bank. And at the end of that time all the timber would be cut off and he wouldn't have any capital left for opening up land. Wasn't opening up the land a thing of the past, anyhow? Marcellus sat, listening to the banker out of his other ear, absently drumming his fist on the table—the same bare table. Then he saw the torn half of a hundred-dollar bill on the unpolished, grit-brown, sweet-gum top, where Adam had tossed it, saying, "I-I d-don't know whose it mought be."

Marcellus shut his eyes with a grimace, sliding his chair back. He got up. "Look, Mr. Harrison, the fifteen-hundred-dollar mortgage is not on *my* back! If you-all are going to take the land away from us, I'd rather you did it now than three years hence." He paused, and glared at him a moment. "If the bank wants to be decent, I'll listen. I know it's big, but take over the McNale mortgage and past-due interest, lump everything together in a new note, due a year from

January and, if you'll run me, I'll come back and cut my timber and try to work out of it—work it out if it takes me three years." He paused, gazing quizzically at Harrison, then glanced down and muttered as he turned away, "If that's your money on the table, pick it up."

The banker, his guarded eyes on the grit-brown top, said he would place the proposal before his committee.

Marcellus looked at the clock as he put on his hat, telling himself that Adam by this time would be at the railroad station with everybody else in Riverton to meet the afternoon train. He hadn't meant to, but he would go too. And see Judy come home.

He made his reentrance at the Courtneys accompanied by Alice and Dan Walker. There was a long and uncertain distance between him and Judy, as they approached each other, there in the living room. They hadn't exchanged a word of any sort in over two years. Judy gave him a quizzical, a queer look, but only for an instant. He said, "I dreamed about Tiger last night!" as they shook hands and everybody laughed. (Tiger had been her pet airedale, and it had bitten him.) They became, then, part of Christmas and the old bunch.

But as they all hunted mistletoe in the river swamp that afternoon, Marcellus encountered more than old times renewed in Judy. Holding her hand, as they scampered like schoolchildren over a lawn to get into the woods, he found that the grip of her fingers and the texture of the skin on them brought back the same special feeling that they used to. And wisps of her dark curly hair against the tight skin above her cheekbones, in the tail of his eye, still affected him in a sexual way. He had to smile at his impulse to show off before her his prowess with the ax. He smiled, but he didn't stop showing off. Judy's laugh was firing his blood.

And before the afternoon was out, he came to himself fifty feet up a willow oak tree, where Judy's protest to their abandoning a bunch of mistletoe they couldn't shoot out of it had sent him. And if he hadn't run into a wide gap in the limbs that he couldn't span—and Judy hadn't kept yelling for him to come down—he would have gone on to the top to hatchet out the golden bough. The old applause was working on him—applause or applesauce: it was working on him, all right.

On the evening before Christmas Eve, the Courtneys had a small eggnog party. They had it because Aunt Janet from Atlanta, who liked eggnog and made it very well, was there. And they kept it small because serving alcoholic things was frowned on in Riverton. Marcellus was the only outsider. And it was all over by eleven o'clock. He had drunk only one cupful (for he abhorred it), but he and Judy had covertly slugged their glasses of grapefruit juice with the corn liquor. And now they sat in the oversized leather chairs in the living room, sipping their drinks. In range at his right was the rosewood grand piano where earlier in the evening Judy had sung the old songs again and all had resounded the Yuletide. In the subsiding quiet Marcellus felt more at ease with her than he had at any time since his return to Riverton.

He shifted to a cater cornered position (the chairs had always been too big for him) and glanced at Judy's graceful posture (her extra inch and a quarter made hers fit her), his eye settling on the sleek, silk calf of her leg to find it still an excitement. She did have a shapely calf, and fine pillared legs. He thought with a sense of irony that he had never fondled them, never touched them really. Did their forbidden, ineffable beauty lie beyond eye, beyond memory? He said, with a shrug, "I remember the first time I ever sat in this chair."

Judy's eyes shimmered. "I do too. You complained about it *then.*" He grinned, and after a pause she went on. "That was just before Christmas, too. I had a visitor, Molly Hopkins, and you and David came together." After a longer interval, she added, a special timbre in her voice, "It was actually only five? six? seven years ago, but—"

"But irrevocable!" he said in a melancholy tone, too familiar to him.

"Yes, but no need to think about *that,*" she said, in her mollifying way.

"But if I just hadn't blindly sent him out to the Hightower—" He broke off, biting his lip. The oft-repeated speech now struck him as banal, and worse. As he recalled what he had been going to say about Fate, it seemed silly.

Sensing that he was displeased with himself, she spoke up impulsively. "But Daddy said you showed more control at the autopsy than anybody he'd ever seen—you know, anybody that had never—you know—"

He shuddered. Shrugging, he thought he'd drop the thing, drop it then, but at that moment the table talker came to mind. He brightened, smiling. "I'll never forget the look on Big Sam Crews' face when that table h'isted its leg!"

They laughed, Judy's contralto voice rippling unhurriedly through him, and over him and under him, like a tide. A fabulous warming tide from the past! He said, as if it were his cue in an old play, "Where is Mona now?"

"She's staying with her Aunt Deborah in Eatonton, going to school." This was news, but after a pause she turned it into ritual. "She's got plump, almost moonfaced. Her eyes don't seem so big"—Judy spoke with restraint, in recognition of the feeling this had once meant for him—"nothing fragile now." At length she added evenly, but in lower register, "She doesn't look so much like David anymore." The sad pain of the memories joining them was plain on her face.

With a recollected sense of height and sweep, Marcellus felt as if they were resuming something, a stride, an adventure—he couldn't have, would not have wished to, name it—but it was taking them again, under Judy's dark, intimate smile, with the legend shimmering out of her eyes. They were ten feet high, and the clouds looked real! Were they? He braced with his elbows on the arms of the wide chair and swung his legs around. "How are you and that skinny Auburn engineer getting along?" he asked.

She laughed. She hadn't seen him since that fall, she said. He was just a junior! Then he asked about Fats Dupré. She countered with inquiry after the little long-nosed coed he had taken up with. They ended on a mutual look of bland indifference. And Marcellus asked with a grin, "Am I still on your snakebit list?"

This produced a flattering change in her. Her eyes dropped as if he'd touched the quick, then opened wide to stare at him feelingly. "Don't say that, Shorty!" she murmured, grasping his hand impulsively and drawing it up to her cheek. "I know I was awful!" she went on, gently playful. "I was young and foolish then. We both were awfully young, Shorty. Milton Dupré taught me how young."

Marcellus said, "But I was younger than you were."

"Yes," she said, now serious.

He looked at her wide lips—grained like the flesh of an orange, but fuchsia in color. He repeated, "Younger, and harder hit."

"Oh," she said, her eyes fastening on his mouth, "I know."

He swallowed. He had gazed at those lips for years. Untouchable. Flags of virginity (his and, he supposed, hers), they had become its color, form, motion. But more. They had become an equation of his being—taboo, moral balance, fought for and against and forgotten, yet re-marked. They were the promise of voluptuous passion. They were denial. But always they had been high and mysterious and desirable and, until now, the bars of a boyhood inhibition. Was he going to kiss her?

He loosed his chair to bring his right hand to her other cheek, but he didn't. Inhibited still? He shrugged, shrugged himself to his feet. "Well, I just wanted to know if I was snakebit," he said. Yet he hovered near her for a moment longer, with a hand on her chair, wondering why he didn't. He turned away without kissing her. . . .

He did kiss her finally. The next morning he went up to Lancaster to spend Christmas Day with his sisters, and stayed there longer than he expected to—indeed, he stayed until he got word from Henry Harrison that the bank committee had turned him down. But by this time, turning it over in his mind—as he lay in bed in the guest room under a comforter, sniffling the frosty air, listening to the fire the colored boy had lighted in the fireplace crackle and roar—life seemed pleasanter hereabouts. And Marcellus decided he should make further effort to save the place. He owed it to his dead father, to his sisters, and to Adam. Moreover, whether he had kissed Judy that night or not, it was obvious that she had had a change of heart toward him. Somehow, sometime. He wondered now if that night at the Auburn-Georgia football dance his face had disclosed something to her that he didn't know about.

So he came back to Riverton and made his proposition to Cleve McNale: if McNale would make a new note, adding the past-due interest to the face of it, and would supply Marcellus out of his general store, Marcellus would cut his timber to pay off. Even with McNale's markup, he thought he could make it in a matter of three years. But McNale was never an impulsive man, and he said he would have to think it over.

Marcellus did not, to be sure, let this hamstring his enjoyment of Judy's company, nor the Yuletide in Riverton. While he waited, he took Judy to a party every afternoon or evening, or both. He was having a fine time. . . . New Year's Day came, however, and he had heard nothing from McNale, and Judy had to go back to her school in West Georgia. Not that he and Judy were dependent on McNale. New Year's is supposed to be a day of decision, and he would rent a car and drive Judy the forty miles to the Atlantic Coast Line train and propose to her on the way.

He waited until they had ferried across the river and were in the swamp on the other side. He drove off the highway a little way on the excuse of looking at the old brickyard—but the place where he stopped was open and visible to passersby. And he didn't suggest that they get out of the car, though it was a mild, sunny afternoon. He had been talking, talking on about their having been through the mill.

He parked the open Model-T on the brink of an abandoned clay hole, beside the fallen wall of an old kiln, and remained under the steering wheel. He began by saying his being a widow's only son, he'd had to find out some things the hard way. But he'd found out. Whether she was and always had been the only woman he'd ever loved, or whether he'd fallen in love with her all over again, came to the same thing. He knew now that it had to be *her,* for him—had to be! He came a little way from under the wheel toward her to take her hand, saying matter-of-factly but not without conviction, "Look, this is it, Judy! You and I both know that we are bound together by invisible things, chains we can't break—and shouldn't want to—that mean more to me, to us, than"—here he had the suspicion that his voice was flat, and tried to raise it—"than *anything* else does!" He paused, clamping shut; then he said briskly, "Let's get married?"

For an instant her eyes kept their inquiring look, as if to see if there were more to come, after which she blinked and leaned toward him assentingly. Yet feeling the tension in her face, and before she could speak, he put her legs across his lap to get himself in a better position to embrace her, in the close quarters of the front seat. At last he confronted the lips. Gazing at her mouth for a fascinated breathtaking moment, he kissed her forcefully, After an instant's hesitation, he swallowed hard and let her go.

She said, as she adjusted herself in the car's restricted space to a more comfortable position (he saw now they should have got out of it), "Yes, Shorty, I guess you're right. They do mean a lot—to me, anyhow. I agree. And I'll marry you."

He started to run his hand up her thigh then, but somehow he didn't, and it annoyed him that he didn't. He almost said *Hell, let's get out of the damned car and begin over again.* But looking into her quiet, quizzical face, he couldn't come up with it. Instead, he said, "When?"

"Ooh, not before the end of the school year!" she returned with more animation than she'd shown up to that point.

And now he managed to pop off, too. "Five months! Why, the hell with that!"

"We've waited for five years," she said. And after thinking this over, he cranked up the car and they drove on.

Dunk Slitcher's case was taken up in Superior Court at Clarkesville on first Monday. Marcellus was there, though he hadn't been summoned as a witness. He had rented a car again and brought along Adam, who was to be a witness. There was no one there from Riverton, except Rup Willis, the marshal. Mr. Robert was in Savannah now, working for a lumber company there. And Carruthers had lost his grocery store within a year after the Buck Fykes trial—and largely because of the expense of the whole thing. He was now running a commissary a few miles out of Clarkesville. Though, of course, he was at the trial.

Times had changed, and so had the atmosphere at the courthouse. There was open talk in the corridors that the charge against Dunk would be reduced to accessory. This somehow shook Marcellus, but he was already depressed. That morning, before he left Riverton, McNale had turned him down. The old skinflint had made him a counterproposal—all he asked was for Marcellus to put himself in peonage. Though Marcellus hadn't yet rejected it. The first day of the trial was taken up with filling the jury box and the reiteration of the State's case, in which there was nothing new.

But the next day brought surprises. Marcellus was deeply shocked. Grip Jackson, his cousin Grip, took the stand for the defense, and testified that, to the best of his knowledge, Dunk Slitcher was not in the boat that day when Buck Fykes and David Ransom paddled him across the river. That would let Dunk out altogether. Grip was a sorry sight to see—the great big fumbling corrupt liquorhead! The defense had bought him for sure.

But Grip did not deliver the knockout blow. This was reserved to Grip's wife, whose identity in itself provided a shock for Marcellus. Marcellus recognized Agnes Hooker—who had been David's date that night they went across the river after Christmas—sitting in the anteroom. She hadn't changed much since then. She was still handsome, with fine dark eyes, both amiable and bold, and something sex-charged about her roughened, muscular face. She told him that she had married Grip soon after his first trial. "Grandpaw Grip?" Marcellus had gibed, and wagged his head to add, 'Well, this *is* ironic!"

It sounded as if it were a *non sequitur,* but she got it. And she didn't like it. Glaring up at him from where she was slumped down in the low seat, she snorted, "It's nothing of the sort. I thought as much of David as anybody did."

"Yeah," he had retorted, standing above her in open contempt, "on the strength of one Saturday-night visit?"

She sniffed. "Well, *one* can be enough," she said, in an insinuating way, and added, "How do you know it was only one?"

Marcellus never knew what he would have said, for at that instant out of the dark came an image like a lantern slide: he and his squarish blonde girl of that evening making molasses candy, Agnes and David disappearing the while and not showing up again until it had been pulled and cut upon a plate. They said they'd gone to get cigarettes. . . . Agnes had been rummaging in her pocketbook, and now she brought forth a small red snap purse and opened it and shook out into her other hand a star-shaped gold and enamel pin, which she held up to his inspection. He saw it and kept on staring, though he did not fail to recognize it. Finally she said challengingly, "Want to see the name on the back of it?"

He wheeled and walked away without a word, feeling weak in the knees. . . .

Marcellus stopped the car by the watering trough in the lane to let Adam out late that afternoon. He had been telling Adam about the McNale proposition, telling him that it would be useless for them to try it. He said McNale wouldn't renew but would keep the mortgage foreclosure around his neck like a noose, while he cut out his timber. The final straw, however, was the thing he had found out overnight: McNale had been trying to buy the second mortgage (at a bargain), which could only mean that he aimed to take the land away from him after he got the timber.

Adam didn't say anything at the time, but he urged Marcellus to get out, have a drink of water, and rest a little. Marcellus said Hell, there was nothing to be gained by fooling around or by talk, but he got out. He swung his feet over the false door of the Ford on his side and stalked around to the other running board, where Adam was resting a foot. He was disgusted and mad and glad to be getting out of this poor piney-woods country, he said. Adam picked up a splinter and whittled on it awhile before he spoke. McNale was a hard man, he allowed, but no more underhanded than usual, and he would do what he promised.

"Yeah, and if you read between the lines, he's promising to cut my throat," Marcellus retorted.

Adam wagged his head. "And you payin' him off, I doubt he'd want to stop you."

Marcellus shook himself in annoyance and threw the cigarette he was smoking on the ground. "Goddamnit, but that's just *part* of it," he said—"Goddamn part of it!" He started walking back and forth. "I've been a softheaded fool all of my life, but I'm getting cured of it, cured of it!"

Adam straightened up, saying dryly, "I don't know as it does any good to G-Goddamn about hit."

"You're right at that," Marcellus barked. "It's just a *word*, just a word. And David Ransom was just an animal, just a *kifing* yak! No different from that dog-assed wench he swapped his fraternity pin to for her tail." He hawked and spat, and added in a lowered voice, "And I guess he's not to be blamed for it—I guess not." He strode to the yard gate and opened it, as if he might be intent on water, but slammed it shut again and turned back. "I've been a fool to come down here at all. I could have let the sheriff sell this place just as easy from Nashville, and a lot cheaper for me. And not wasted the time." He hawked shrilly and spat once more.

Adam's face was straight, his jaw set, his eyes molten black. He spoke in an iron voice without stuttering. "These hard times, Marcellus. Hard bargain goes with it. You got to meet it. And t'aint all sweat: you got to outfigure and outgamble, too."

Marcellus' face fired up, and he blurted, "I ain't *got* to do a damn thing!" But he wheeled about and walked away from Adam to cool down. At a dozen paces, he turned and came slowly back, saying ironically, "But I've *got*—I've got myself engaged to get married." With a snort, he added, "I guess you'd approve of that, though?"

Adam limbered, lowering his chin, putting up his knife, "W-Well, that's the right thing, that's fine."

This put Marcellus in pain again, his face twisting. "The hell it is, the hell it is. I've been kidding myself." He glowered up at the sky, and sneered, in silence: *Pure love, pure love pursuing us.* Moonshine! Saint Lucy! "Both of us," he broke out, stamping about in a circle, "just kidding ourselves— No, I don't believe she's that big a fool!" He threw himself into the front seat. "And Goddamnit, I'm not going to embarrass her by writing—" He choked off his words with a yank at the self-starter under the dashboard. "Good-bye!" he yelled, in an uncertain voice over the door, adding under his breath as he ground the car into low gear, *"old man."* He wheeled around in the lane and made off in a cloud of dust.

SECOND RETURN

*

Melanie

Chapter 11

IN NASHVILLE, back on his police run, by press time each afternoon, Marcellus was able to work himself up into the usual swivet. But by nightfall he was down in the dumps again. He felt like an undertaker who had accidently embalmed himself. He had no doubt that his too old and too honorable affair with Judy was better laid away. And it was just as well that the mortgages were being foreclosed on the homeplace. He must wait a month to be sure that Judy wasn't going to write him; a month, and the sheriff would be selling the land. He was sensible of a detached sadness at the passing of both of them out of his titular possession. But the hell of it was that since his return he hadn't been able to feel anything else. When he left he'd thought he was falling in love with his new girl. The embalming fluid had knocked him out on her, too. Whether out of the past or the future he couldn't tell, but something threw him off.

The only thing he could be sure of, as the third Saturday night approached, was a rising redheaded lust. On Friday evening, from his flat, he called the grass widow who had been sharing such occasions with him during the past year—a little sheepishly, because he hadn't called her in so long; a little diffidently, because he sensed her retributive demands. He had to submit to a new encroachment to get the date, it turned out. He agreed to take her to the Saturday-night fling on the Bluff, which Melanie would be almost sure to attend. He did, and he didn't want to see Melanie; but for sure, he didn't want her to see him with the widow. It wasn't so much that she was a "dark": technically, she wasn't—she came from the right side of the river, and her family was passable. Moreover, she wasn't bad looking, or any older than he was. But grass widows were a bit off color categorically; and she would doubtless somehow publicly assert her claim on him. Worst of all, she was a moron.

Still, Marcellus figured that he could handle it. He would work the early evening shift, getting off at eleven o'clock, to appear at the dance with the widow around midnight, after Melanie would have gone back to campus.

The party was at the Murphy camp, a long log-and-mortar affair, and the dim main room was full to overflowing with dancers when Marcellus and his date got there. The Saturday-night fling was a free-for-all: every man brought his own liquor, and nobody's girl had to pass a committee. Still, he led her in warily. The Victrola was belting out a one-step; the clinging contenders were in a fierce-looking hell-for-breakfast round. Some clodhopper could trample them. Moreover, even if Melanie had gone, he'd just as soon not run head on into Bayless and have to introduce his lame-brain to her.

They had made their way in through a side door, next to a large fireplace that took up that end of the room, then to the blaze, to hold our their hands to it for a moment, though the night was so mild his girl had worn only a fur stole over her maroon satin dress. The room was already too warm. Marcellus used the time to look about, glancing over his shoulder; but he saw few familiar faces. No other coupling, however, could be as anonymous as dancing. "Let's don't waste time," he said, taking Becky by the hand.

She lifted her gay, pointed face to him, and, as usual, he had a touch of giddiness before it. Under those long curved lashes she was cross-eyed. Not too badly. Indeed, when she gave him her smile, her still-soft lips, especially the short upper one, seemed childlike; and her thinnish face was tender; even the popovers under her eyes weren't too noticeable. And there was something helpless and trusting in it all. You wouldn't think she had three children, two of them already in grade school. Her legs were still delightful, too, and she could dance.

"Oh, Marcellus," she breathed in his ear, "I'm so threeled!"

He swung her out into the swaying crowd, suppressing a shudder. If she just wasn't so damned silly.

He grew too warm rapidly. He decided it was because of the mohair vest he was wearing. After fifteen minutes of dancing, he turned Becky over to a slender, immature-looking though graying man who had once been on the paper and whom he could trust her with, since he was a lampshade-maker. Marcellus went out to his rented car to shed the waistcoat, take on a drink, and cool down.

So it was that when he got back to the house, pushed his way through the clutter of onlookers to get to dancing, and stood there blinking and peering at the smoky, undulating, amorphous mass, with Becky's imprint in his eye and saw Melanie glide past—he suffered a brief state of confusion. Automatically, he wheeled about to the stag line: *What the hell was she doing here?*

But he had recognized her partner, too: a Nashville Vanderbilt senior. He had recognized, moreover, that he was pretty drunk. He was probably her date, and she hadn't been able to get him to leave. A moment of swallowing all this down and examining the visceral effect, and Marcellus turned back around. After all, there was nobody standing on his feet, he reflected—not at the moment, at any rate. And there she came again! She probably couldn't say as much for her feet with that drag! Yet from the way she moved she might be floating on air. He gulped and swayed a little. Good God, she was pretty! And now—he shut his eyes tight for a moment to be sure—no shadow. He opened wide to catch sight of her before she disappeared, and rubbed at his dazzlement. That dimple, set in diamonds; and those dark flags to the country of wit and camaraderie!

His gaze roved hurriedly and evasively over the rhythmically heaving, many-headed caterpillar. She was the difference between emancipation and body barter. He glimpsed his widow still in the arms of the lampshade-maker. And how great it was. What in hell had given him buck ague, anyhow? He shook himself. He couldn't remember now, he couldn't for the life of him imagine. Ritually he buttoned the middle button of his navy-blue worsted jacket; his knees limbered and he slithered his way into the human hugger-mugger in pursuit of knowledge.

Thirty minutes later Marcellus sat with Melanie on the wall bench of a summerhouse overhanging the Bluff, and searched for the reflection of a fugitive moon in the gloom of the river, a hundred feet below them. This had been prefaced by his suggesting, after the second dance, when they had gone outside the steamy Murphy camp for fresh air to find the clouds breaking up, that they stroll in the moonlight. They had got chilly. And Marcellus happened to have—he didn't explain how—the key to this gazebo, which along with a nearby camp belonged to a group of his fraternity brothers. Screens had been replaced by glassed windows; and they sat in the red glow of an electric heater at their feet. Melanie's manner of laconic indifference and Marcellus' air of beleaguered resignation had been replaced by a lively, not to say sportive, interest in locating the pale glimmering from the sky in the flowing water.

He had managed telegraphic, and he hoped telepathic, apology for his month's silence. He had had so much jerked out from under him at Christmastime, he said, it had left him in a daze. To begin with, twelve hundred acres of land, to satisfy no more than four thousand dollars in mortgages. You couldn't give a farm away in South Georgia now. Then Dunk Slitcher—she would recall the younger one involved in the murder of David Ransom and the one who *he* believed did the actual killing—was practically turned loose, with a three-year sentence that would let him out in eighteen months. Finally, in a Swinburnean tone of irony, he had given a representation of the obsequies for his too old and too honorable affair with Judy—whom, to his surprise, Melanie couldn't remember ever having met. That it was dead they both had recognized, he said; the problem had been how to bury it. Frankly, the whole business had left him in such a state of feather-legged uncertainty—unsure of what or who was alive or real—that he hadn't had the nerve to look her up yet.

She couldn't, of course, know how incredible she was. And when she stoutly sneered at this, he retorted with such conviction—"Fantastically improbable!"—such fervor that she didn't overly resist letting herself be kissed to establish contrary proof. But she stopped him there, he took it, for some proof on his part. Gesturing beyond a black conical treetop at the watery glimmering that must have got to his brain, he murmured, "The angels brought her to me in the bloomy night." At once he sensed that the line wouldn't do, whatever the impulse behind it, and was sure of it, as he recalled the author.

She said clearly, "Or maybe the *Raggedy Man?*"

He laughed apologetically. "Yep. Raggedity! And still in a funk." He worked out of his side trouser pocket a thin pint flask of corn liquor, and extended it toward her.

She regarded it dubiously for an instant, then took it and, pursing her lips in acknowledgment, said, " 'Only a little, Mr. Flood.' " She swallowed briefly and handed it back.

He held it up and gestured ceremoniously toward the moon, the heavens, chanting, "Well, Mr. Flood, we have the *winter* moon, the winter moon. Let's kick'er with the mule!" He wobbled the bead on the surface of the colorless liquid in the bottle. " *'The bird is on the wing, the poet says. . . . Drink to the bird'!"* He brought it to his lips and let the stuff bobble past his Adam's apple until she caught his arm and pulled it down.

"I don't want"—she panted, in some emotion as she broke him loose, then went on, in mock and tender querulousness—"another drunk on my hands tonight!"

Out of a liquored sense of his effectiveness, he tried a hand on her leg above the knee. She brushed this off, but she let him take her in his arms, and she responded to his kisses. This asseveration of their blood was such then that she offered only initial resistance to his hand on her breasts, breasts within the security of a plaid wool dress, buttoned almost up to her chin.

Their awareness of this barrier grew dynamically. In the half-light of the heater's glow he was conscious of a primordial definition on her face, eyelids impounding the secret, rose-shadowed cheeks, dim nostrils breathing. Earthquakes. To give him a sense of genesis! Eternal or ten seconds? Frivolously he fingered the silver broach pinned above her heart—a winging bird. Her glance shifted to the bird, and her lips moved in acknowledgment. He said, " *'Well, Mr.*

Flood, since you propose it, I believe I will' "—and began unbuttoning the dress.

But he didn't get far before she grabbed the hand, and his invasion proceeded as a wrestling match—at one point abetted by her gasping. "Don't unpin it! it's holding me up"—and his thanking her with a grateful grunt, as he did. He did it, albeit he needed more fingers and had to substitute his teeth.

Finally the quivering breasts stood bare, except for the lilac and purple shadows, their ocher shields, the green-gold tips. And Melanie gave way to spent weeping. He said, with abject fervor, as if it were a vindication: "I waited too long to kiss a girl once!" And her more audible tears were somehow pliantly responsive. Then he bent dramatically to bring his lips to them. But she resisted, pushing his face away before he could finish, and he blurted hoarsely between her fingers, "Seven years they hounded me!"

This shocked him: he hadn't meant to say it, didn't have it in mind. Earlier he had thought of calling them silver apples, "And pluck till time and times are done." But he lost his head. He tried to save face and regain his poise by repeating, "Ha'nted me seven years, Plump!"

Where it might have gone from there they were not then to know, however; for, at this juncture, they heard his name called out in a shrill feminine voice, close at hand. And in the next instant two dark silhouettes appeared above the glass in the door at the back of the gazebo. They came hurriedly to their feet. When Marcellus had opened up to the intruders—he did not turn on a light—Becky spoke to Melanie in a still-raised voice: "Your ride home is about to leave you!" The Vanderbilt senior, a dimly handsome youth in his self-absorbed attitude, stood beside her smiling, though not offering to speak. Marcellus pulled the plug on the heater, and shepherded them all out of the door silently.

But as they turned into the moonlight, Becky cried at them, and there still was outrage in her voice, though she tried for a tone of derision, "What were you-all *doing* out here, anyhow?" She followed with what sounded to Marcellus like the laugh of an idiot.

He muttered a gruff, "Goddamn!" but pushed them all along the path toward the Murphy camp. Becky moved on obediently, yet she leaned back at Melanie to say with oversweet solicitude, "Honey, you'd better straighten out the buttons on the front of your dress!"

Marcellus' original plans for the night struck a dyspeptic distaste in him now.

Chapter 12

AFTER HE HAD thus resurrected it ritually, the little passage in the Ransoms' back hall didn't seem to hound or to haunt Marcellus. It lost importance in the sophisticated atmosphere of Bohemia. Though he did assume that he knew about Melanie. Her emancipation. They both had backed away from their encounter overhanging the Bluff. Not that they admitted this, even to themselves—or even that there was anything to back away from. But he didn't call her for a date until the following Friday night, and then she didn't give it to him. When they ran into each other on the Bluff again, they began to get on a different footing.

To be sure, in their emancipation they must assume that they knew all they needed to know about each other. They must assume an attitude of ridicule toward their recent adolescence. Since her home had been the setting for this absurd durance, it could be spoken of only in laconic jest. Yet, in the half-dozen times he saw her out on the Bluff during the winter and spring of that year, there were confidences.

She had changed her name to Melanie when her family moved from Macon, where her father had taught mathematics at Mercer, to Dahlonega, where he became head of the department at the ag' college. It had seemed a strategic time, because she was also slimming down and seeking a new personality. Melanie was her mother's name, though her father called her mother Addie, for Addison, her surname. Her mother, as a little girl, however, had chosen Melanie for the sound of it, and that made it special. She liked Melanie. But anything would be better than her old name, Mary Ann. There was, of course, more to it than that. Her mother was blonde and long-limbed and beautiful; while she herself, she said, was the ugly duckling, superstitiously hoping she would turn into a swan. But she had remained brunette and a duck.

Marcellus had protested this, not out of mere politeness and, eventually, with vehemence. He saw finally that she really didn't think she was pretty. Obviously she suffered an inferiority complex, with her mother, he told her, adding in his half-baked assurance, maybe even a castration complex.

She agreed. Only during the previous summer had her mother become human for her—"e.g., not just the family warm morning heater"—she meant *merely* human; in fact, another woman. On second thought, perhaps, it was she who had become a woman, she said. It involved her father. Melanie had been his bright little girl always, until the last two years of high school. He had taught her Latin poetry and algebra while she was still in elementary school, and he saw to it that she won honors all along the way. And more. Once, when Melanie got a "C" on an analysis of Lady Macbeth because she had deviated from the textbook, her father wrote her English teacher a sharp note saying his daughter was being penalized for her originality. Her mother had tried to persuade him not to send the note, but he wanted to impress Melanie, he said, with the importance of original thinking. Gallatin Crosby believed that he himself suffered at the hands of the college authorities for his original work in matrix mechanics. She hadn't known she was original, Melanie said—her drawn dimple, parenthesis to a hovering smile—but he impressed her for sure: his note got the teacher down on her from there on out.

Her younger brother in grade school had been lucky enough to escape their father's attention; while she hadn't for a long time been able to do anything, anything at all, without his criticizing her. They were scarcely ever on speaking terms. He had had it in for every boy she ever dated and had eventually embarrassed her with her girl chums, too. She had accepted his breaking in on their spend-the-night parties to play his mandolin and sing to them, though she knew the girls thought it funny-strange. She had even endured his dancing with them. But finally he had patted one of her friends on the fanny. Melanie had come out of indenture on this. She called him an old goat to his face, she said. Moreover, she had gone ahead then to have a date with the football player he had forbidden her to see.

This led on in time to a deeper confidence. She had come home from Vanderbilt for the summer to find her father gone misanthrope completely. He was down on everybody, including the college and the family, and stayed by himself in his study, when he wasn't teaching a class or out hunting for gold. There had been mines in Dahlonega once. Until then it had never occurred to her that anybody could question her mother's forthrightness and loyalty and, of course, morals. But this everybody-hater had accused her—right there before Melanie—of having an affair with their own uncle, his brother. Melanie couldn't believe her ears, nor did she believe a word that he said about her mother. It was just his own filthy mind.

But what he did to her, Melanie, was even worse—out of his filthy mind. And she had never confessed this before, to anybody at all: She had a very identity-snatching experience, in the midst of her father's brainstorm. Right there in the middle of her being horrified at him, a low, contemptible, worm-turn feeling came up in *her*. She couldn't help relishing her mother's dethronement! This awful thing had not only turned her upside down, it had turned her wrong side out. She didn't know whether she despised her father or herself the more, for being his daughter. Anyhow, she had broken off relations with him for good, then.

The thing *was* Freudian, Marcellus admitted. And he did wonder if she could be a little mixed up like her father. Still, she had revolted against him. What more could she do? Her outlook about everything else was right, too. She was no peon in the groves of academe, but held conventional student standing in contempt. And she was sure hell in revolt. He didn't make up his mind exactly, but took to looking her up at her sorority house.

Before the end of her school year they knew they liked each other—solid and in depth—and found each other endlessly exciting. With him there was the usual excitement of prospect—and in her case more definitely. Yet even so, with emancipation it was a different thing, and, he was to find, she was too—her Goddamn dimple and dewy lip! But still . . .It was at the sorority house after practically everybody had left—she was manager that year and had to wait till the others had gone to close the place up. It was in the shank of the afternoon. They had been doing some rather heavy necking back in the butler's pantry and she had broken away and come into the living room. There was no one else in the house, though some of her sisters had just left. She was waiting for plumbers or electricians, and the house mother was to return.

They started all over again on a couch in the living room. Here, inadvertently, he was abetted by adequate accommodation. And, no holds barred, he was soon above her and to the point. She didn't fight back; she didn't balk, exactly. She just looked a little nonplussed, a little embarrassed, and, lowering her eyes, said, "I admit I never have—I don't quite know—a—er—" Then she looked up at him, open-eyed and at close range, and he could see, he thought, clean through her eyeballs. "Isn't there some danger?" she faltered.

He was fixed there, frozen on one ham and knee, in mingled disbelief and shock, searching her face. Could it be that David hadn't done it to her? And there was Red Lull, too. But if he knew anything about her at all, she wasn't lying. And why should she lie? he asked himself casually, he then thought. Well, hell, who could say? And what difference did it make? And he put a hand under the cheek of . . . but he knew by the stiffening in his neck it wasn't correct, wasn't sure, somehow—there, then, that way. Was he about to rush in and smash a china shop? Suddenly there was a pulse in his head and a soft swelling lift took him in the diaphragm. He backed away, saying, "Was that somebody on the walk?" and they scrambled upright and off the couch, getting themselves straight.

A glance through a front window had shown him that it was only a passerby out on the street. But he did not take hold of her again, in free love.

He followed her to the piano bench, where she had begun to pick out a tune, muttering to her by way of completing his gesture in acceptable form, " 'There's one woman he cannot rape.' " After they had embraced more casually there at the piano, he had added, "And I'll marry you without a shotgun." She had convinced him she was a virgin—little Melanie in cellophane—though he believed then it didn't matter.

Just the same, his rugged ideal of free love had been compromised for him, even if he did not formalize this in thought, and he found the pink ribbons of his imprisonment sweet. It might be said that *they* sensed it. Though perhaps she already knew it with the instinctive wisdom of her sex. Still, they wanted to make their arrangement as easygoing as possible. Indeed, they didn't define it at all, didn't even name it till the next year. She had even come back in the fall distant and wearing some klunk's diamond solitaire. Though she lied about it at first and then got rid of it. Of course, he felt himself above anything so clumsy as a ring—that was positively Victorian!

They had a devoted seminar all winter on A. E. Housman's *Last Poems,* the self-righteous apostasy of *The laws of God, the laws of man / He may keep who will and can* becoming a sort of recitative for them. And he gave himself over to the finesse of seeing how far they could go and technically maintain her virginity. She was very agreeable in this, and they went a long way. In fact, somewhere along in April they went too far or something. For whatever the technicalities may have been, she got pregnant! Well, they had meant to get married as soon as she finished school, anyhow. This, however, gave them a deadline.

More conveniently than he knew, her father had died the winter previous—had died in a mental hospital. Melanie had gone home for the funeral, leaving a note for Marcellus. But she had not allowed him to sympathize with her when she returned, and she had not spoken of her father since. Marcellus must have sensed that this unusual reticence meant something. But it had no deep significance for him then, in his obliviousness. He had never met her father, though he sometimes felt his presence with them.

Then it had been her mother who concerned them; for she was planning to come up for Melanie's graduation, and he felt that they were lucky when she got sick and couldn't get there. They were married on the next afternoon, over a downtown cigar store in the office of his favorite justice of the peace, Squire Jake Levine; Bill Trice and Bayless Lull were their witnesses. Melanie at the last minute had come up with a gold band ring that she wanted him to put on her finger. She said it had been her grandmother's and went even further back than that. He, of course, refused. Melanie was never literally consistent in such things, but he suspected her mother's hand in this. He was correct, she later admitted. But what she didn't tell him, until long afterward, was that her mother had also sent her the book with the church ceremony in it that had been used at her own wedding.

He hadn't at all been able to get away with his casual nod to Convention, however. Others more difficult barged in—thanks to Bill Trice's practical joke, or what Marcellus took for a joke. Trice had called in an account of their marrying to the opposition, the morning paper. And when Marcellus tried the next day to go on his *run* as if nothing had happened, he encountered the outpost of Society. Literally. The society editor overhauled him as he came into the city room. She was hopping mad, she said, because he had let her get *scooped*—but full of doings for them, Melanie and him. Indeed, she had been responsible for a set of flat silver from the staff—to Marcellus' chagrin. And Bunk Dooley, the assistant city editor, went to Doss, the managing editor, and arranged for him to have the week off for a honeymoon.

A honeymoon. Marcellus was furious. It was all so bourgeois! As he told Melanie, when finally he had to call her because the thing had got out of hand. When he said he couldn't afford a honeymoon, the managing editor had raised his pay—twelve dollars and a half a week. Bunk had suggested fifteen. But the twelve fifty was half as much as he was making then, and seemed munificent. Then came the fraternity circle and the camp out on Spencer's Bluff.

Melanie agreed that it was horribly bourgeois. But she didn't seem to be as hacked to pieces about it as he was. After all, she wasn't working, anyhow. And it was always fun out on the Bluff. The camp was practically luxurious and real convenient—right up to the edge of the palisade and close by the steps down to the river.

The camp was a galling mishap for him. But he didn't have money enough to get them out of town. Its three bachelor owners called it Assig—among themselves—this being a pun on the fraternity name, among other things. The thing was that he used to take his grass widow there. His brothers thought this only a good joke on him. And even Melanie, who didn't know about the widow but had heard about what they called it, thought the nickname amusing. They would rededicate the place, she said.

Rededicate? Had it been ironic? Rededicate! a gray-raftered room, a stone fireplace with antlers above it at one end and, at the other, a bas-relief brass disk pinning fraternity bunting on the wall—and them, in bathing suits, on either side of a table, standing over a picnic basket. Marcellus sensed something tainted in the distant scene now. He hadn't been allowed to forget the camp's nickname. They had, the moment before, come traipsing along the Bluff, Melanie babbling about " 'a small cabin build there, of clay and wattles,' " to find the basket just inside the screen door. Notes were pinned to its cover. One told how to open a bottle of home brew in the basket, and cautioned Melanie to look out for wasps in the girls' garden house. There was a postscript: "We policed wastebaskets, closets and cupboards, but we didn't have much time to clean up the place—sorry! Pumper."

Melanie had sniffed at this, taking fried chicken and deviled eggs out of the basket, which her sisters had fixed. She was laying things out on the table. "They didn't get around to the back room—a name painted on the wall beside the double-decker," she said. Looking up unwarily, he met her eye as she added, "Becky B."

He flushed in realization that this was the grass widow's first name with middle initial. "Becky B?" he echoed idiotically.

"Becky B," Melanie repeated. "A friend of yours?" She grinned mockingly, yet coloring a little.

To recover, he came heavily, without calculation: "Friend, hell—protection! Our security police!" He added, as an afterthought, "That second 'B' is for Backstop."

She swallowed her "oh!" to smile at his obscene joke, but the smile flickered out. After a pause, she began taking things out again, stretching across the table to reach the basket, trying to say lightly, "Do we really need anything of the sort, with me in my present *interesting condition*?"

He wondered that he and the widow had ever used the double-decker. Taking the quart bottle of home brew out of the basket carefully, feeling suddenly grim, he retorted "Don't be so fatalistic! It might turn out . . ." he started on, but with so much distaste for their surroundings and its memories (he thought then) that he faltered.

"You mean, for the better?" she took him up, and answered her own question quizzically: "For better or for worse—we married, didn't we?"

He appeared to ponder this, steadying himself against the table, trying to keep his distaste (grown acute) out of his face. Marcellus saw now that it hadn't really been the camp, but anxiety in him, an old and morbid dread coming up. Yet he managed a bland flip of the hand to say: "It's been in the papers. We'll have to pretend we did, anyhow."

They had seemed to throw it off then. "Otherwise, you'll lose your pay raise," she heckled.

He gave an exaggerated grunt. "We'd better honeymoon like hell every minute we're out here!"

"I'll race you across the river. Ten strokes, and you can't catch me." She turned to him with a pickled peach upheld. "Now—before we eat!"

Diving at her fingers, he had gobbled the peach, then whirled and run through the front door and out on the porch, yelling, "Get going!"

She followed instantly, but had managed to plump another peach into her mouth, from the sound she was making, muddled yet eloquent, to the pat of her feet on the path behind him.

Her challenge was a little reckless. The river was high and there was a current in it. It was better than two hundred yards across. And Melanie hadn't actually swum it before from bank to bank, for they had been going out in the canoe to dive from it. But she was a confident swimmer and a pretty good one. She didn't demur.

This time they went in from the foot of the steps. He allowed her a long start. Swimming along an arc, she made the mainstream on a line with the stairway. Midriver she was still ahead and about fifteen feet above him, staying with him stroke for stroke. Marcellus pulled abreast of her watchfully, keeping below. Then, thinking she would make it all right, he had turned to pull on ahead of her.

He was three-quarters of the way over before he thought to look back again. She had fallen way behind him. He slowed up. But he didn't go near her yet. She might resent it. Treading water, he moved backward to watch. And he could see then that she was drifting below him, and laboring, without making headway.

So he dived under toward her and came up alongside. He skeeted a handful of water in her direction, as if in play, then took hold of her, under the chin. Pulling with his other hand, he drew her after him. But she was swallowing the river. He slipped her into the crook of his arm, and went to work. With some digging they made it out of the current and into shallow water. It had been a pretty heavy go.

She allowed him to pull her up the strand and onto the pebble beach; then she collapsed beside him in the edge of the water. Both of them flattened out, breathing heavily. Safe harbor. They grinned at each other, then into the sun. The sky above them was high, and millions of miles blue. And they gave themselves to the endless moment, in relaxed exhaustion, her head on his shoulder, her cheek against his chest, eyes closed submissively. Her lips, a little purple, moved with a fluttery softness, as the dimple came and went. There was in her face an utter reliance upon him.

Chapter 13

OUTSIDE THIS vision bodily, bodily, Marcellus sat in the seat behind the driver on a darkened bus, shouldering swiftly over Tennessee's hills, through a rainy autumn night, headed for Georgia—just seven years (lacking six weeks) after his first return to Devil's Elbow, in search of his future. But, still viewing the inner scene, he asked himself, Wasn't there something else, too, in Melanie's eyes that day on the pebble beach on the Cumberland River? The climax to his long reverie was still vividly with him, when the lights came on and Chattanooga was called. He rubbed his eyes and stared about him in some confusion. Was it a bus he was on? And where the hell was he going? And where was Melanie? Had he been dreaming? He pressed closed eyelids with thumb and forefinger, and for a moment this did bring Melanie back: for a moment, beside him at the river's edge and her gaze on him in enigmatic inquiry, then lowered as she shrugged and said apologetically, "My extra baggage."

A dream? It had been the beginning of a nightmare!

It came about after their honeymoon (or so Melanie represented it then) that she wasn't pregnant after all. Wasn't pregnant! Evidently her household remedies, or something, proved effective, and she just lied to him about it. But he believed her—believed her then. They had come in to town from the river on Sunday, and the next day he was sent to the Cumberland Mountains on a coal-mine strike story that kept him away for a week. She *knew,* as she put it, that she was all right again by the time he got back.

She told him about it in the hallway on their flat, as he came in. And he said with feeling that was more than satiric, "I thank whatever gods may be for your—your unconquerable"—he sprung his jaw—"determination!" They kept on walking down the hall toward the living room with their arms about each other, and he said, "It doesn't take a business genius to see that we can't afford to have children."

"I didn't marry you to make you a father," she chirped, punctuating it with an embrace.

He went on, on the divan—becoming aware through her blouse of the little pink rosebuds embroidered on her brassiere—"There wasn't any shotgun behind our getting married: it's just that we want to live together and you can't do it in Nashville without a license." They looked at each other in rational agreement, and he added, "But it's got to be a limited license a long time for us!"

"I can live the rest of my life without prittle-prattle or pitter-patter, either," she had bragged, in her pink rosebuds.

He was making only thirty-seven fifty a week then, picking up ten or fifteen dollars a month more from trade magazines on the side. Even when she started teaching in the fall, it wouldn't add a whole lot. And while he had given up his efforts at poetry to try short stories with the hope that this would eventually bring in money, he would doubtless have a long apprenticeship. Such writing would always require quiet and leisure at home or somewhere—would require no children.

He had thought then that Melanie's words were probably a little boastful. When they had got in easy circumstances (had a farm or some sort of country place in which to raise children properly) they would have a few, of course, to keep Melanie from becoming a frustrated woman.

Perhaps they had been married a year before the rub and drub of it wore its way into his consciousness above the pulse of Nature—*their* consciousness, he should say. The things of the bed. Of the dark. For whatever reason he didn't have contraceptives in the drawer of his bed table, he would have to get up and go blundering to the bathroom and on through the apartment looking for them. And more often than not he didn't find any. This was bitter—actually contrary to the natural course of things. Or, if he argued it out with Melanie—as he invariably did—and she finally submitted, which she sometimes did, it was as if she were going to face a firing squad. He could recall nights when he had drunk a lot (if she took more than three drinks she got sick and upchucked) and she, sensitively sober, submitted in such fright that the thing became a sort of cold rape for him—and likely for her, too. And when he didn't go bound, she was always up and out of the bed like a whippet under the lash.

Then there were the tense days of each moon, till her relief was assured. And there was the periodic buildup, when she didn't come around—on occasion she had missed three times hard-running. He could recall such a time in the third year of their marriage, and they had been a little careless at the outset, when after the third month they'd gone to see a doctor. The relief had been well worth the money they'd put out, though God knows they were hard up. Once he had grown so cocky that they had experimented with something called rhythm—they had thought they were goners for sure that time. The thing was cumulative. They got so unnerved by the uncertainty and the household remedies that year that they went a month without intercourse.

But they had suffered more than menstrual travail—something above, something behind these things, was it not? It wasn't the game of love, to be sure. Yet its terms had suffered a subtle change. Not so much the rollaway bed, the maple-veneer chairs, and the varnished woodwork of their furnished apartment against the memory of some honey-suckle bank in the woods or hazardous divan in the dark. It wasn't their familiarity with each other, either, or their interfering with natural processes, actually. What was it?

He shook his head, peering over the driver's shoulder, along a shaft of light that revealed only clean-swept concrete coming at him. Nevertheless the spiral of experience seemed somehow to have flattened out for them.

It was that year, or the winter of the next, that he had fallen into getting drunk, not staggering but wild. It seemed to happen every time they went to a party out on the Bluff. But he sometimes got polluted at the "speak" behind the newspaper office, with the bunch. It was so much easier to talk then about what you were going to write—especially when all the return you had for your efforts was a stack of rejection slips. Anyhow, when he and Melanie would come home from a party (she had already been frightened by his driving, perhaps), with him on a tear, she would invariably be sick and sober (having already lost her lunch). She would be too sick—though mostly sick with fear. One such night—it must have been near

Christmas of that same year—she had refused him, and he had in rage quit the apartment and gone out to whore, yelling back at her, she later told him, *Double crosser* and *Vanie*. The whore was bad, sure enough, for both of them. In fact, Melanie never did get over it in a way. She either threw it up to him in bitterness when she got tight, or, whimpering, asked what it was that she lacked. And she picked at him about having called her Vanie. He never did tell her what he really had thought that afternoon at Ransoms'. When she said his face looked funny, his alibi was that he thought, until he got inside the hallway, that she was the colored girl with whom on an earlier occasion David had misbehaved, and he would suppose that he hadn't quite been able to get the sneer off his face, as he saw his mistake. Anyhow, it was just a name that got caught in his head to come out when he was blotto.

He didn't tell her what she lacked, either—except one time he did go out of control on it. But this didn't happen till after they had broken over. It was in their fifth year with intimates in the writing trade. He was an advertising copy-writer and a poet of sorts. And they were a couple in the Bluff crowd, too. And the four of them had rented a camp on the Bluff together for the summer.

But the buildup for this had been in the making over a year. As couples, they were congenial and found each other special. The Légers had lived in Paris, and had a nine-year-old daughter who stayed with his mother most of the time. The child, in a way, was the basis of the deepening intimacy between them. The Légers professed to admire the Hightowers' resourcefulness: *they* had had to get married, as she said, *shotgun*. And they had come to take a very sophisticated view of marriage.

Melanie broke over first (not counting his going to the whore), and this may have had something to do with his harsh words later.

But he viewed it with detachment at the time because Iris had just approached *him*. Couples, then, in effect, swapped about.

Iris had blonde beauty and brilliance and a hidden charm: gifted inner activity and orgasm in depth. And she was the most totally committed of any woman he had ever lain with. He got pretty infatuated with her, and thought it might build up to divorce. He did find her livelier in bed than Melanie.

Melanie had been drunk when he told her so, because she had upchucked soon afterward. He hoped that she was completely blotto. He didn't like to recall it himself. All afternoon they had been drinking home brew that had to be caught in a dishpan when you pulled the bottle cap. And they were hitting the ceiling by that time—at least he was. It was Sunday night, and the Légers had gone to his mother's to visit with their child. Some of the Bluff crowd were about the camp, however, dancing to the phonograph. Melanie had swung him out onto the porch, with intimations out of their past—the wet kiss, the tiny goose bumps on her nostrils. But he pulled back from her, his scruff rising, to say vindictively, "You started it! It's your own fault!" Then, as he turned away, "But I like it better, jellybelly!"

In time, however, he did find a flaw in his freedom, this paradise regained. There couldn't be any argument about whether contraceptives, of course. You just didn't move without condoms. And this had finally turned up the snake on the garden path. Absentminded, anyhow, he had gone out in the woods with Iris one evening, after having made too quick a change of clothes in town, only to find he'd forgotten their protection. The moment was still vivid for him. As she gathered this, she leaned at him through the dark whorl of night, eyes black and blazing. Then her slim face jerked away and, to his amazement, he felt the sting of her hand. Back and forth across his jaws, she struck him, hissing vehemently, "You trifling son of a bitch!"

That hadn't broken them up, exactly. But she set his head spinning. Actually (he would reckon) it began then to unspin—though he was too dizzy to suspect this for a while.

The slapping, he had come to see, hadn't been the only thing, however. The numb line that slipped in afterward had, perhaps, done more to disenchant him. The occasion on which they went "without." They had got tight and gone to a nightclub, where they got more so, then on to the Légers' unoccupied apartment. She said that it wouldn't make any difference because she had had a recent miscarriage. It was the next morning, she told him this, over a pick-me-up. At the moment, he felt only relieved and grateful.

But two days later he took a dumb out-of-town assignment—to cover county fairs for the whole month of August—took it with alacrity, though he might have talked the desk out of it. The crazy thing that lingered on with him was an irrational sense of her having double-crossed him.

About this time Melanie had begun heckling him. He doubtless deserved it, but he didn't appreciate it. He had by then abandoned short stories, having been able to sell but one: to a farm magazine that paid him only twenty-five dollars. He shifted his literary interest to the novel. He had now been at work on one for over a year. This labor, Melanie claimed, was comprised of his getting soused at parties and holding forth about his book to whoever would listen for as long as he could hold them. It was true that he had got but little down on paper, and that piecemeal. And he saw now that what he had got down wasn't any good. But her sharpness hadn't nurtured sympathy between them.

Moreover, there had been someone more sympathetic. Ostensibly his marriage relations with Melanie had been restored after they broke up with the Légers during the winter following their scrambled summer. He had called for a return to the ideals of their early days, and he couldn't say that Melanie didn't put her heart into the try. But they never clean got over the bruise of their first fall out of the bed. He did hold it against her, for all his saying not so. The truth was that the emotional capital of their physical love had become badly depleted.

This time he had taken on her chum who taught English at the same place where Melanie taught French and Spanish—he would have to admit, this time, without much provocation. It was partly propinquity, partly because he saw she was still a virgin long after that becomes a liability. But mixed in it was an irrational hostility to the friendship between her and Melanie, the confidential intimacy between them. A dumb thing, to be sure. He had been ashamed of it even at the time, but he didn't' seem to be able to do anything about it. It kept welling up in him, like an overloaded bile. He had told himself, however, that it was Anastasia's interest in what they—he and Anastasia—were calling *creative writing*.

Melanie's *or-else* ultimatum to him had been on his giving up the bottle and getting down to the typewriter. She was, however, already suspicious of what was going on between him and her friend.

He took her up on both points. But the Anastasia crisis had piled on top of the other one. The evening before he left, Melanie telephoned ostensibly just to chat with Anastasia at her apartment while he was there. Indeed, as it happened, while he and the girl were involved in the very act. This unnerved the chum. And he had been annoyed. He resented it—illogically, he would admit. His feeling, he could see, was a mumpish sort of thing, and there was perhaps some guilt as well as self-righteousness in it. And maybe he *was* just a trifling son of a bitch. And ought to clear out.

The bus came to a halt at an untenanted filling station, in an empty street, its lights making the outside scene pale and shadowy. They had crossed the mountains at Chattanooga before midnight, leaving the rain behind. And they had been marching through Georgia with fewer and fewer pauses for passengers, now—Marcellus consulted his wristwatch—for better than two hours. As he stepped down to the level of the driver, the rearview mirror caught his glance, and he paused impulsively to assess time's wear and tear.

Seven years! He parted his hair on the left side now, and didn't comb it so carefully. His father was supposed to have told his mother (doubtless merely to console her), when Marcellus was seven, with a brush heap on top and a bradded beezer in front, that when he got grown the hair would curl and his nose would arise. When did one get grown? But, by God, Papa was turning out to be a prophet! Of course, he'd had enough trouble to curl anybody's hair. But what had happened to his proboscis was peculiar. Maybe it was only the effect of his lantern jaw and hollow eyes. His gaze shifted. Was his glint from under the eaves hard or feverish? His belted, olive-drab velveteen suit and tan shirt were another shift. But the big change was in his cocksure stance: things didn't seem so simple now. He shrugged and moved on. No, on second thought, the complete turnabout was in his attitude: now he was eager to get back to the river country.

He found the air milder as he got down the steps. He stretched his legs for a few paces along the pavement, peering up through the velvety night at a scattering of stars; then turned back to the other passengers, lined up in three queues to drinking fountain and rest rooms. With a shrug, he wandered off down an alley toward the dark behind the building. The nightmarish thing about his bind—his bind with Melanie—was himself! He hadn't been able to control his own actions—neither with liquor nor women. It wasn't that he couldn't see trouble coming; he just couldn't run. That is, till now. He hoped the spell was broken.

He put out his fingers to the post a few inches in front of his nose, to reassure the perception of his other senses. Anastasia had spoken to him about having children, there in the bed, in the dark, night before last. It sure goosed him! A danger he hadn't foreseen. He damned sure didn't intend to jump from the frying pan into the fire. Of course, he had never had marrying her in the back of his head, anyhow.

As he looked out around his dim bulwark (he took it to be a telephone pole), the lights in the bus came on with a vivid abruptness that made his eyeballs ache. The empty red chairbacks, etched on his irises, greened out. This blindness, as suddenly, brought him into another dimension. Before him, a plump, suntanned, dark-haired little girl, in a red-dotted-Swiss dress, sat at the long table in Courtney's drugstore: the little Melanie, whom he supposedly stared through and didn't see, in that long-ago encounter. But now he did see her! Melanie and her earthquakes had been there to shatter things. And whatever the mirror may have revealed to her about their future, she had cracked the looking glass of Marcellus' boyhood, spoiling the image of his best friend. And whatever he might think of David now, it had been rankling in him, was rankling in him still.

His scene with Melanie was in their flat, where he had halted just inside the door. As he climbed back on the bus, he recovered the challenging dimness of the room. He was taking her up, he told her. . . . He meant what he said, for he was sober and had been for a month. He was headed for the little hotel in Riverton, the Ocmulgee, because he could get board there for thirty dollars a month. He had a leave of absence from the paper, and meant to chain his leg to a table and write. . . . He was on his way.

Melanie was wrapped in a Chinese red kimono and had her long dark hair in a plait down her back. The rollaway bed was already made down in their efficiency, and she leaned against the side of it to confront him. Her mouth, which did protrude slightly, was shockingly hard, he thought. "Is Anastasia coming down there?" she asked.

"That's none of your damned business!" he blurted out angrily. The "or else" of Melanie's ultimatum had remained vague, though she did imply divorce. He had not believed that either one of them wanted divorce. But he resented her threat violently. Moreover, the vindictiveness in which he concealed his sense of guilt was as touchy as a kneecap. And he was intolerant of any probing, even by himself, let alone by Melanie. He took a step toward her, folding his arms on his chest as he came. "You have said your piece, Miss!" he ground out. "You have said your piece!"—still coming, "And you can—" Yet he halted, balancing there on a toe, while they glared at each other, the moment growing long, growing tight. Then each one of them had blinked and lowered his gaze.

It seemed no more than a breath of air between them—a gasp, there, in the dim, cold, shabby, disheveled room. A defenseless thing. One more sharp word would have done it in. But something. He didn't know what. The image of a mockingbird he had inadvertently killed that afternoon, pushing along in a rented car on an emergency assignment. He had expected the bird to swoop up over the top. Instead, it had gone downward. And, after his gasp, he had heard the tiny thump against his radiator, and glimpsed the splayed wings, bearing it away upside down. Yet there had been a fraction of a second in which he might have rammed on his brakes. He went back on his heel. And, after a moment, he said, though his voice was hardly less sharp with self-righteousness: "For your information, I'm going down there to write, write! Does that get through to you? Write! There will be no liquor, no women!"

Melanie sniffed or coughed, or did both. It would be hard to say what it was, but the sound of disbelief in it could not have been plainer. And without looking at him, she rose and moved to a bureau across the room. Pausing before it, her hands on the pulls to the top drawer, she gave him her profile without her glance. "So you're running out on me!" she said bitterly. "And the apartment rent, too—I suppose? I guess you think I'll have nothing to do with my money, but pay the rent—with you off gallivanting around with—if Anastasia doesn't come down there, there's no telling who!"

He swung back to the door, under the impulse to get out and slam it behind him. He halted with his hand on the knob, and could not command the coordination to do anything. But after a moment, he chose to rattle, not to strike. "As if you cared!" he began in heavy irony. "You have your soulmate still. I know, of course, that you have never given him up. . . . I'll be out of your way now, and you won't have to pretend."

She met his gaze. After a pause, she said simply, "That isn't so." She stood still, clasping the pulls, but shaking her head in melancholy futility. "I haven't spoken to him in a year." Then she added, it seemed to him blandly: "I never was in love with him, or even thought I was in love with him. We were just playing a game!"

He barked at her, "Well, hell, it's the sort of game that gets you pregnant!" His intelligence had been insulted.

This passage between them seemed to alter Melanie's intention and her mood. She came back to the bed and, leaning against it again, meditated her fingernails with a frown, her brown face sunk in gray gloom, her lips twitching as she debated with herself. Then she looked up to say, "It didn't get me pregnant," and added with a tremble, "But I think I'm pregnant *now*. It's been almost three months. And I was sick after I got up this morning."

At this statement he jerked around from the doorknob, which he still held onto, and glared at her.

Glared at her. Glared? Was he the man who did that? And was he a man? Marcellus retreated from the headlights to glance behind him, his troubled gaze hunting along the interior of the bus above the luggage racks and returning to settle on the driver's mirror. The dark, the distant moment—though his watch disclosed that it was less than forty hours ago—began to reveal the spectrum of his white heat. His anger, his unseemly anger had risen against nausea—a frightening and, he now realized, familiar gray nausea. He drew it from the dark. He saw it now for what it was, whence it came. His disgust went back beyond Melanie. It didn't actually involve her. It went back all the way to poor Blossom Jay.

His sense of the violated taboo of a blind, spent night returned to him: he and a yellow Blossom, in a battered iron bed, on dingy sheets, in a shabby hotel room, after she had undergone the letter opener again. Earlier in the evening he had restrained himself normally. But heavy sleep, his animal gluttony, and the strange release of their being out of the world, had undone him—had undone them both. They had roused from their troubled dreams to frenzied coition—had rutted like gophers. Every night had repeated the nightmare for them—the outrageous lust, the spent remorse, the mutual repulsion. Yet even so there was more repulsive residue in his emotion. On their last day—they were then at Nora's place, after the blood poisoning had set in, as he—frightened, too—read to Blossom out of Hawthorne's *The House of the Seven Gables,* he had had to keep poulticing her swollen suppurating mound. All their past had taken on this taint. It had hung on in the dark of his mind.

And I was sick after I got up this morning.

Marcellus could finally comprehend the angry panic in which he had cried out at Melanie, "You damned well better not do that to me!"

Chapter 14

MARCELLUS BECAME the Ocmulgee hotel's star boarder in eclipse, which increased general interest in him considerably. Blind Homer had lived and begged his bread: he achieved notoriety by, in effect, blinding the public. He hadn't meant to, and in time it grew to be embarrassing. He'd been visible about the streets of Riverton the greater part of his life, and nobody had ever looked at him twice, but now he found a clutter of loiterers in the lobby and the cardroom of the old gingerbread drummers' bindle every time he appeared. Most of them, moreover, only eyed him furtively from a distance.

Martha Hazlehurst, the proprietress, was responsible for this reticence. Though her husband, Tommie, supported the family by his job as railroad telegrapher, she had to have some outlet for her diverse energies. "Running the hoh-tell" provided her challenge, and she came close to breaking even on it, too.

As star boarder, for which he paid five dollars extra a month, Marcellus had the only private bath, contrived by cutting off the end of a hall that had formerly given passage to the outside and still did, if you un-thumb-bolted the door. The bathroom had also served the room across the corridor, before the depression. But as things now stood, Martha had blocked off the whole south wing to ensure his quiet. Moreover, flanked by the shoeshine and bellboys, she stood guard over it to see that no one came near it. It wasn't so much the money, of course, as her professional pride.

She must have established a record. Marcellus had had supper with his old friends Dan and Alice Walker the day he arrived, and he only mentioned his need for seclusion. He never saw or heard from them again, except when he called them. When he tried to apologize for himself, he found they'd been warned by Martha to stay away. Nor did any other of his intimates and friends darken his door. He learned after he had been there two weeks that Adam had come by to see him and had been turned back by his adamant protectress. Marcellus probably wouldn't even have learned this if Adam hadn't had the good sense to tell her to let Marcellus know he'd been there and would be back in town on the following Saturday, if he wanted to see him.

The thing that gave bite to Marcellus' embarrassment, however, were the results of his writing efforts. The agent in New York who'd agreed to take him on, on trial, and to whom he'd sent the first draft of his novel, *World Without Words,* had been really frank, in sending it back. Marcellus had drawn on his trouble with Blossom Jay as material for his story about a teller and the girl ledger poster in a bank in a small Tennessee town. The agent said that his writing was bad enough but that he simply couldn't get by without using an abortion for the happy ending. The thing wasn't merely beyond words; it was beyond belief. Marcellus had replanned his story, kept on replanning, but he was finding it hard to make things come out any other way.

He accepted the four-blank-walls theory of working quarters for a fiction writer. And his ten-by-twelve cubicle couldn't have looked blanker, when he first sat down to his portable typewriter, under its unshaded center droplight. But a hard-bottom, leaning-backward chair and a rickety wreck of a parlor that had to be steadied by the knees proved no rocking horse to imaginative flights. And every time he did begin to lose himself and threaten to take off, he found that he was growing stiff with cold. The shotgun heater at his back had burned out, and he had to make a trip through the bathroom, out to the backyard, and cut and tote in another armful of wood. What his quarters provided for rocking—a wicker rocking chair with a limp arm and a loose joint—always let him down in a meditative climax. The lumps in his mattress were disjunctive to all thought, or even sleep, except in a state of exhaustion.

By the end of the third week, he found himself more often with his nose against the faded wallpaper, trying to figure out its illegible hieroglyphics, than at his typewriter. And the water-stain goblins on the ceiling peopled his dreams.

But these annoyances were only odd-moment, were symptomatic of his inner, his real complaint. It found imitation in his novel, to be sure. But even in this he eventually succeeded in easing his bent enough to comply with his agent's suggestions. Still, his sleep was deeply troubled.

He saw Adam on Saturday of the fourth week, and Adam's presence—his voice, his humor—helped Marcellus in a melancholy sort of way. The Hightower holding was now in the hands of a rich turpentine man, a family connection, who did more for Adam than Marcellus had ever done. He was happy for Adam. And they spoke guardedly of the time of trouble (without calling David by name) and of turkey hunting. They both knew Marcellus wouldn't find time for turkey hunting; and Marcellus was relieved, really relieved, that he didn't have transportation to get out to the scene of a past better forgotten.

But he kept waking up in the night with Blossom Jay in bed with him. A Blossom who urned out to be Melanie for a fearful moment before he identified his unoccupied pillow. There followed: *You damned well better not do that to me!* He would cringe before this memory flash and get up and go to the bathroom, telling himself (at first) that Melanie knew that he knew she was trying to get back at him—had just been putting the old ice pick in his back. Hadn't she been three months overdue twice before? She wasn't pregnant, really! When this flimsy contention wouldn't ease his mind, he tried to temporize. If it did turn out otherwise, there was Dr. Magnolia, whom their friends, the Altmans, had used. She was a graduate of a Negro medical college; and all the respectable Nashville medicos said she was the best in the business and absolutely safe; she could give a curettage, and for only fifty dollars. If worst came to worst. But none of this improved his sleep.

Marcellus had planned from the outset to spend Christmas Day with his older sister in Lancaster. By the time Christmas Eve arrived (when he would board the afternoon train) the prospect depressed him. Elinor had no reason to suspect that anything was wrong between him and Melanie, insofar as he knew. But the six weeks of silence between them was awkward to lie about, and rose in his mind, as ominous to any wavelet of hope as Gibraltar. And he lacked the heart for pretending. If his train hadn't been late, he might have backed out of the trip. But it was late; and this resulted in the southbound train getting to Riverton first to bring him needed cheer, cheer beyond all expectation: from Nashville, a postcard with the Madonna and Child on one side and on the other, in a poignantly familiar script: "No Christmas is good Christmas here. Hope your book is going well. And a merry time for all! M."

It was so late, he replied by wire (at the hazard of offending Melanie's sense of thrift, though without thought for her hazards): "Your card made my Christmas. Thanks, thanks, thanks, thanks, Gratefully, M."

At the time Marcellus took it to be a turn of fate. For he went on to Lancaster in such high spirits that he was actually able to speak of his depressing novel that he couldn't rescue; and this had provoked Elinor to say, "Why don't you try writing about the assassination of Captain McIntosh?" Her words became the hocus-pocus. Notwithstanding the fact that the assassination bore a legendary odor that had always put him off. His father, in 1889 a young lawyer for the big Yankee sawmiller employing the captain, and his mother a bride out of Charleston, had lived with the McIntoshes not long before it happened and all of the sad family lore, in high Victorian sachet, had come down to him through their mother. However, in rebuttal to his sniffing at it, Elinor had produced her mother-in-law's scrapbook of newspaper clippings on the squatter war out of which the assassination came. Marcellus saw that he had stumbled onto something quite different: he had found the dusty makings of history that wanted representation, not a threadbare parlor anecdote.

The town of Lancaster, and Coventry, the county of which it was capital, were named for those early northern promoters and had been central to their operations, about which he already knew the official story. What he was able to dig up at the courthouse the next day didn't add much. But the windfall that came to him a day later, in nearby Mackville, threw him into a fever of excitement, and in the span of seventy-two hours brought to birth a new sense of destiny. Those three days, with a few hours out for semisleep, he spent in an unused backroom of the insurance offices of a cousin, exploring the Coventry enterprise in all its litigious ramifications and bad blood, revealed in a pile of abandoned records that rose from the floor to the ceiling.

Coventry and Company, through their land titles, had laid claim to the better part of three counties, some three hundred square miles of virgin pine forests, lying between the rivers. It began to seem to Marcellus, before he got through his paper mountain, that every land lot of the way had been disputed by squatters—disputed through sabotage, guerrilla action, and assassination, as well as through the courts. Along the way his traditional "company" prejudice was overturned. Perhaps he had a natural sympathy for Georgia underdogs against rich Yankees backed by a federal court, whether they were family friends or not. But the cumulative evidence, if intricate, was convincing. By the third day he had turned squatter, found the federal court partisan, guerrilla warfare defensible. And, increasingly his conscience gnawed at him over his own family's identification in the conflict. That is, until the last afternoon, when he unsuspectingly turned over the copy of a company bill of ejection against a long list of defendants whose attorney was his father.

He had not seen his father's name on any of the corporate documents after the early days, but he assumed that he had remained a company lawyer. This bill had been filed in May of 1900, the year in which he was born and the month before it. Marcellus felt a surge of gratitude toward this dim actor on a distant scene, whose name he bore. His father was actually a stranger to him.

He dug in, to find that each side had enjoined the other against trespass, that each had accused the other of violations, and that the suit had gone on for a long time. Twenty-five of the lots of land were in Clarke County—over six thousand acres! Scanning the list of defendants, he saw that some of them must have been Hightower neighbors. Adam must have known them, known about the case.

The next morning Marcellus sat with Adam, before the hearth, in Adam's dim living quarters, reading from his notes. After a while he ceased, and lifted a questioning glance.

Adam's gaze remained on the embers for a time, the folds of his meditative face like hammered bronze. Then he raised his luminous eyes; his scraggly mustache spread and his rounding cheeks brightened into brass. "H-Hit went on a long time! I hyurd a lot of talk on it." he continued to nod as his focus returned to the fireplace. "I reckon they're all dead now."

Marcellus came up from the low rawhide chair. *But to bring them to life.* He put a hand on the high double bed beyond them, its white counterpane softly aglow, the red cross-stitching on its pillow shams spinning toward distant bull's-eyes. He had slept in this bed—he and little Walter Bruce—twenty-five years ago, the night of the big hail. Adam had rescued them from an open shed room. How vivid still! Adam kept calling the dead. Marcellus turned restlessly to a gilt-framed photographic enlargement hanging from the dingy newspaper-plastered wall. A familiar young Adam and his bride—the first. The picture was faded now, but the Adam somehow remained alive. And, in Adam, didn't his father live, too? He had told Marcellus that his father sprung him (then only nineteen years old) from the prison mines, where he'd gone under life sentence, out of a riot he didn't take part in. It had begun there.

"I told your paw, here one day: 'L-Look like everybody got something outn this lawsuit but you,' " Adam was saying. " 'And you the one done all the work.' "

Marcellus laughed and turned back to the blaze. "How was that?"

Picking up the poker, Adam met his eye. "W-Well, I don't know just how it was." He turned the backlog over. "H-Hit seem that, in during the lawsuit between them, they pretty well stole off all the timber."

Marcellus' face straightened. "You mean the squatters?"

"The company stole its share, too." Adam gathered coals about the log. "Then it would drop its case. W-Whoever might've got the timber, when a lot got cleaned off, the company would drop its claim to that lot. Most of the mens was making their claim on adverse possession; though a few had coffeepot deeds, too. But the fed'al court never did give 'em no titles. Just let 'em stay on the land. And your paw couldn't collect."

Marcellus grinned ruefully. "Are you trying to make a sucker out of him or an unwilling hero?"

Adam's acknowledgment was to center the blaze with a squirt of tobacco juice. "I said to 'im: 'Eighty-nine of 'em. L-Look like they might of chipped in and paid you sompin.' "

"He shook his head and said that under the contract they didn't have to. Then he say: 'Anyhow, I got somethin' out of it—satisfaction.'

"I said, 'That ain't going to educate that boy of your'n.' We'd talked a lot about you, in during that time: he took the case just before you come and you were done three years old then." Adam pushed back in his chair to recall mellowly: "He and your maw was awfully proud of you. You were number six, you know. Their first was a boy, but he died right off. Then there had been *four* girls."

Marcellus cleared his throat to speak, but thought better of it—one of his sisters was younger than he. He had winced, winced himself into a question mark and now he put down again in his duck-legged chair. A hell of a son he'd made. Too bad his older brother hadn't lived.

"You 'member what your paw looked like?" Adam asked, and Marcellus let out his uncertain breath, eyeing him reflectively. "Great big man. And his beard was already getting gray, then. He just pulled it slow and looked at me straight as a gun muzzle; then, like he'd done seen through me and on down the road, he say, in that quiet voice of hisn, 'You never can tell.' " Marcellus' eyes widened into a stare, and turned bloodshot.

Then he blinked and came to his feet, grinning gingerly. "Yeah, yeah!" he said, half under his breath. "Well, I'm in a rented car and I've got to be getting back."

In Atlanta, Marcellus was told at the hotel desk that Melanie was already there, waiting for him on the mezzanine. He glared at the clerk, as if he were responsible, and said in a tone of accusation, "My train was late!" But after he had filled out the registration card, he lifted his gaze to grumble, "Sorry! Just talking to myself." He didn't, however, turn around to the balcony yet to look. Here was another handicap. To add to all his other uncertainty. After four months. She wouldn't have got over his staying on after New Year's, let alone through February. Now this. He drew in his breath, straightened up, and about-faced as well as he could.

His optic nerves went into shock. Incredibly, a young woman was standing at the railing, waving to him! He couldn't seem to get his eyes into focus, but raised a hand halfway and feebly moved his fingers. Then, his eyesight clearing, he smiled and managed a smart salaam. As he was straightening up, however, his involuntary muscles took over. They sent him rapidly toward the elevator at a bucking gait.

There had been murmured, butter-mouthed word substitutes between them on the elevator, but they didn't look at each other until they were in the room, alone together. And this was less a look than an excuse for not looking: counter-facing, they batted purblind eyes brightly, broke it off, and circled.

"Well, here's your favorite son of a bitch," Marcellus intoned in a moan, coming to a stand, "late as usual."

Melanie's mouth flew open, breathing, "Oh, I'm used to it"—but with something between hiccup and a gulp, she caught it and turned it into, "You know me: always a day ahead of time."

They managed to wrinkle up their eyes at each other and let their mouths limber a little. He ducked, and shifted feet, in preface to apology. "You don't know how sharp—*dazzling,* you looked on the mezzanine!"

"On the mezzanine?" Her jerked-up black brows and too quick smile began to jell. "Maybe I'd better go back down there!"

"Oh, Goddamn, Melanie!" He yanked at his collar, heaved and rocked across the floor to the bathroom to fill a glass with water from the tap. He had really been thinking that she had on too much makeup. "Won't you have some water?" he called.

She returned, gaily singsong. "I've got a pint of red liquor in my bag!"

He shut off the tap. "Oh-ah? that's fine." He appeared in the doorway, holding up the glass. "I can't compete with that. But were you thirsty?" He saw now that her suitcase was open on the bed and she was rummaging in it. "Running on borrowed money—I haven't had a drop since I left, except Christmas Day."

He made highballs without ice; and, after they had touched glasses without words—only tight guarded smiles—each took a swig. He straddled a chair turned backward, and faced her where she sat on the edge of the bed, but before he could speak she got in, "You look positively gaunt."

He had been about to say something of the sort himself, but now it seemed dangerous. He took another swallow. "I got WWW back from my agent, for good, about a month ago. She said, 'Come with a bigger armload!' That's why I *had* to stay on." He gulped down a punctuating swig and his pace accelerated: "Ten chapters on the new one—it's probably written too fast, but I had up such a head of steam—"

She broke in, her face reflecting his excitement, "Read me some of it!"

This brought him off his chair at a jump, and he had his old gladstone half open before he could stop himself. "Nope," he said, throwing it back together. "By God, I didn't come here for this!" He wheeled about and returned to his chair. She was waving her arms futilely, in protest—a little like a dying moth, he thought. She had taken off the coat to her suit, and, exposed by a sleeveless blouse, her arms seemed pitifully thin. He scrutinized her cheeks, beneath the rouge, in some anxiety. The vague, guilty thought that she must be lying to him about her "coming around all right" shot a pain down his backbone all the way to his sphincter. "What have *you* been doing?" His tone verged on accusation.

"Oh, before I forget it!" she broke forth, coming off the bed briskly. "What time is it now? I made a seven o'clock reservation for us at a wonderful French restaurant."

He jerked backward and stared at his wristwatch blankly. Blinking, smiling dryly, he said in a noncommittal manner and a tone of uneasy admission, "It's already after six."

She now took up his question, her dark eyes suddenly blazing: "That's what I've been doing! I've been tutoring on the side. For *this*. It's my little contribution to this, this"—she smiled hard, almost covering the quiver of her uncertainty—"this little get-together. . . . I can't write novels, you know," she said, apologetic. He had come to his feet, but she waved him back to his chair. "Tell me about the land war, while I change." She gathered things from her bag. "About the squatters?"

Before he could quite resume his position astride the chair, this tocsin jerked from him, "I discovered that my father became their champion." He turned in her direction, going on with absorption, "One of the most meaningful things for me has been my reacquaintance with my father."

She paused for a moment in the bathroom doorway, a frilly pink dress on a hanger and a hairbrush in her hands. Her gaze descended, and a sullen look hovered at her brow, like a bee; then her eyes widened in a smile and their black pupils snapped as she flounced away. "Yeah. I hope you'll get reacquainted with me, too—after I get on my new dress."

Staring after the disappearing whirl of skirts, he frowned, somehow baffled by this frivolous defiance. There came over him, then, the dim sense of his being in the presence of a mystery, a hazardous mystery. What would his father have done? After it was out, the question astonished him. Two men could scarcely be more unlike, he would guess. *Done?* he suddenly asked himself, again surprised. While he was still musing, she called from the lavatory, "You were going to tell me about your reacquaintance."

He laughed. " 'Reacquaintance' is hardly the word. He was almost a total stranger to me." There were sounds of her gurgling mouthwash. A few minutes later Marcellus launched on an anecdote that, in time, made him wonder if he weren't a stranger to himself. The only conceivable reason for his telling it was that it was about the most vivid recollection he had of his father. He and his little sister, Edith, were in the family sitting-bedroom with him. There was a blazing lightwood fire on the hearth. Their father was in a rocking chair, reading the paper. Edith must have been about four: she was still wearing flannel night-drawers with feet in them. She had taken off her clothes for bed and wouldn't put on her nightclothes. Their father had admonished her twice.

Marcellus, in his own small rocker, in arc with his father, shared his disapproval of Edith's naked antics in front of the fire. "She came sashaying by, switching her little behind, and just in front of the fireplace she lost her balance and sat down in the middle of the blaze." Marcellus thrust his hand down-ward descriptively for Melanie, now dressed and standing in the doorway. He jerked it up again. "A big man never moved faster! Before I could blink my eyes, Papa had snatched her out of there. And beyond us to the bed. And was scanning her bumper, as we said then, to see if she'd been burned. And I may say, pale and dripping with cold sweat." Marcellus came up from his chair, with a gaily flung leg. "And when he found there were not fire burns, he blistered her little arse by hand!" Marcellus advanced on Melanie, chortling. He took her by the arm, and she met his gaze and joined in his charivari. As they smiled at each other, he held her out from him to exclaim, "By God, that's some pink dress!"

They found that they weren't yet late for dinner, and he poured them short drinks. Melanie took a swallow, but paused for a moment to look into her glass and turn to him. She plucked an imaginary hair from his shoulder, with a tentative yet possessive gesture. "You're nearer Daddy's size," she murmured.

They killed the whiskey before they left the room. Melanie always found a hotel room clandestine. The French restaurant was surprisingly good, though they weren't hard to please by this time.

Afterward, they went to a nightclub on the Biltmore roof. Her savings, but worth it: he'd forgotten what a dancing witch she was.

They didn't put into their hotel again until three o'clock in the morning, and then in a lordly fashion. The double bed in their room was just swaying a bit, with a muted trumpet echo along the brass tubing of the bedposts. This undoubtedly took a lot of the tongue-tiedness and tongue-untiedness out of their second wedding night—surely always more awkward than the first. But reunion, real and trackless, didn't come to them until the middle of the day. They woke to a full and abandoned relaxation, and idled in bed as if it were the first moment of creation and they had just been born into it. They got beyond the jetties of their twisted passage then, beyond all known past it seemed, and in a new spirit of recklessness allowed themselves to drift out to sea. It was a magnificent moment of imprudence.

THIRD RETURN

*

SHEILA

Chapter 15

THE TAN two-door sedan Chevrolet Marcellus was driving swayed in the sandy road beyond the gate to Adam's place. Subconsciously he increased the pressure of his foot on the gas pedal to straighten it, but his glance and thoughts were on Adam, in the seat beside him that dubious spring day. Nobody could be more contrary, when he took a notion to be. Moreover, his contrariness weighed on Marcellus heavily.

"Why'd your wife leave you?" Adam hadn't stuttered when he'd put the question. And his gaze had been direct. Marcellus had met it for a full moment, before he looked away. He had acted upon that inquiring, anxious, but observant and eventually assessing light in Adam's large, dark, liquid eyes. And he had been acted upon by it, too.

He had been sensitively self-conscious under the intelligence that appraised his lifted nose, his drawn flushed cheeks bunched at the bone, his embittered mouth, and the vindictive glare of his gaze before he lowered it. Conscious, too, of the tight crow's feet, the stringy red tendons of his straightened neck, his bloodless knuckles gripping the steering wheel with a slight tremor. But he had not answered the question.

Driving down here he had thought of his situation as a dogfall between density and disaster. Contributing to his sense of this, in the sharp April weather, were newspaper headlines of Nazi legions overrunning France and pushing British troops into the sea, against all his sympathies, prejudices, preconceptions, and beliefs. Twisted within the dogfall was the disturbing fact that he had *made* Melanie leave him. Destiny rode on a Guggenheim fellowship to keep him while he worked on another novel.

The enveloping action was to present the raftsman in the high times of Georgia's Wooden Wealth Era. Timber-running had vanished from the rivers long before. The last dribble of it had been gone for fifteen years. The only raftsmen remaining were old men, most of them with headaches, sitting in darkened rooms, having been blinded by river glare. And Adam was the key that would unlock their doors and their story to him.

For two weeks now, Adam had been riding with him over the river country to look up old raftsmen. And as they went along Marcellus undertook to refresh Adam on some of his own stories told Marcellus when he was a boy. Everything had gone amiably, or at least well enough, until the previous afternoon when Adam undertook to question him about his trouble.

Today it was Adam who wouldn't talk. A few minutes before, when Marcellus had pressed him for details on the Pete Parkerson story, Adam had become reluctant, actually evasive. He wanted Adam to tell him about those tricks at cards. Adam said he wasn't sure about those tricks at all. And if he had ever put 'em on "Mist Pete" it was reckless of him to do so, and he was sorry for it.

Marcellus found this trying. In fact, frustrating, because what he needed was details, details.

Yet his recollection of Adam's gaze somehow diminished his undertaking. Moreover, his own awareness of how he must have appeared to Adam—still appeared, clumsily approaching his fortieth birthday—made him feel more like a dogass than a dogfall.

The car swayed along the close-grown twisting trace amid the smell of bay and titi blooms for a time in silence, except for the sighing sound of the sand. Then Adam said, changing the subject, "Y-You know the S-Slitchers had a dollar bill back there at Dunk's trial they claimed was the one David loaned Grip Jackson to pay for his liquor that day at the Landing?"

Marcellus' toe let up on the gas pedal, and his head jerked about. After scrutinizing Adam's face he looked back at the road and they moved on for a moment or two before he asked, "They didn't offer it in the proof—did they?"

"That's right," Adam agreed.

Marcellus spoke without looking up, his mouth showing distaste for their subject. "I thought I didn't remember any such thing—how'd you come by that?"

"M-Mr. Slappy told me three, four years ago. You know he was pretty t-thick with the Slitchers back there."

"Hm-mm!" Marcellus sounded through his nose as he compressed his lips, adding ambiguously, "Henshaw!"

Adam was watching him out of the corner of his eye, and when he seemed about to drop it, he added, "They didn't put it on, because Grip didn't want 'em to, Henshaw said."

Marcellus grimaced at the gap in the trees approaching. "Who'd take *his* word for it?"

Adam raised his voice defensively. "He didn't have no cause to lie to me then—and he wouldn't have that much 'magination!"

"I reckon that's so."

Adam went on. "G-Grip told it first that David loaned 'im a dollar, you ricollect? And I believed it then. Hit sounded just like David's money." Marcellus frowned. Adam's stuttering was somehow grating on his nerves. He wanted to have done with the subject. He would admit, however, that Adam was probably correct. And after a moment he said to himself fiercely: David was thoughtful and generous—you can't take that away from him. The silence lengthened, and finally Adam broke it. "I believe the t-truth never has come out on Grip in that thing—not all of hit."

"Well, I reckon it never will, now." Marcellus spoke to the empty road in a tone of dismissal. He gripped the steering wheel to adjust himself in the seat, heaved a sigh, and said: "Let's get back to Pete Parkerson, Adam. *Could* he stack a deck of cards?"

Adam's tone of dismissal was quite as final as Marcellus' had been. "He never stacked none on me." The ride remained voiceless for the next mile or better as they drew into the muddy rutted swamp trail. Then, with a shrug, Adam said reminiscently, " 'Member that January day they b-brought old Buck back to the Landing? My, that was a c-cold day! You 'member that wind on the river when you and me started dragging the deep hole under the willows—sun already g-going down. Look like that wind would cut your eyeballs out."

After a pause Marcellus let his breath out into the balmy air heavily, and shivered. Indeed, he did remember. It was astonishingly vivid. That cold river sunset had drawn an iceberg down on him, an iceberg of meaningless, unanswered experience. It had both seared and frozen him. And finally soured his guts. But he had long since quit asking *Wherefore* or *Why*. It had just happened, and he had bypassed it. Perhaps he didn't even want to know, now. Shrugging, he said, "I'd just as soon not remember."

Adam went on as if he hadn't spoken. "I guess we'll never know *all* about it . . . or even all us ourselves did or didn't do." Marcellus nodded, and after a while Adam said, almost as if he were talking to himself, "There was a thing I never told anybody. It was a little thing. I forgot it at the time. But it came back to me later, and you know it didn't seem so little to me anymore. . . . About them shells David borrowed from me. It didn't take up a second hardly, when it was happening—just manners, and neither one of us paying much attention to it at the time. It was Number Six chill shot he borrowed from me."

Adam turned abruptly, lifting his head, and with a forward thrust spat tobacco juice out the car window into the swamp. After he had wiped his chin with the back of his hand, he said: "I reckon I had a dozen of 'em, chill shot. But at first he wouldn't take but two shells. You know that easy smile he had, him saying, 'I just want me a turkey—I don't want to shoot up the flock.' I urged more on him, and he shook his head. 'No, two shells'll do—I probably can't get more'n two shots in, anyhow.'

"But pushing 'em on 'im, I say, 'Hadn't you better git another turkey for your preacher'?

"And he grinned and seemed to like that. 'All right,' he say, 'for his daughter, anyhow—all right! But just gimme one more load, though.' "

Marcellus' gorge was rising, and the pit of his stomach with it—staring at him through the mind's fleeting mist was Agnes Hooker's face with callous eyes—irises showing the tarnished whites, almost the back of her eyeballs. Confusion threatened him. Swapping hands on the steering wheel with a jerk, he got a cigarette out of his shirt pocket, asking Adam for a light. Then, lifting his chin, he speeded up the car to get the ferry, to put an end to the conversation. He wondered why Adam kept on chewing the Ransom murder case over and over again. He kept on bringing it up. The other day he'd got to blaming himself for not having gone all the way to Buck's shack with David, said he should have made friends with the mammon of wickedness. And he cursed his yammering about David's body not being under the willows without his ever really trying to figure out where it was. He even damned himself for having criticized David's drinking. It was as if he, Adam, somehow felt guilty of the murder.

They came out into the clearing and saw that the ferryboat was on the far side of the river. Marcellus parked the car on the Bluff, lit another cigarette, and got out to stretch his legs. After a moment Adam followed suit, and as he drew nearby, Marcellus turned to him with a frown on his face. "When are we going to get down to talking about timber drifting? There's a lot more I want to know about Peter Parkerson." Humor and exasperation were mingled in his tone.

Adam eyed him from a distance—like a turkey gobbler in a tree. "Marcellus, you didn't come all the way down here from Tennessee for that. Not for that!" His voice lifted. "How come you had to leave up there, son?"

Marcellus flung his smoke on the ground and strode back to the car.

Adam was sure a puff adder on Parkerson. Marcellus consoled himself, however, that Adam was running down many of the other old-timers for him. From the Oconee, they drove up into the Ocmulgee country and as far down the Altamaha as the old Nightingale plantation, below the Narrows. Black and white, they talked to more than a dozen raftsmen during the last of April and the month of May. From three of them they got fragments of old rafting and river songs and chanteys.

Among the first they visited, though Marcellus felt reluctant, was Grip Jackson, just across the river from Adam. Moreover, Adam kept him more uncomfortable by bringing up the Ransom case, asking prying sorts of questions. But Grip had been one of the most colorful of the timber drifters and perhaps the most widely known of his day, and Marcellus couldn't think of leaving him out of his bone-picking. Grip's joking gab and great size went into this, for he was six foot six, a giant of a man. But it was his gift for clowning that endeared him most to rivermen. His beetling brow, Roman nose, high cheekbones, and jutting chin gave him a fierce look at the first appearance, yet a little overfierce. And he would give this away with a stagger (even when he wasn't drunk) or a hiccup, or merely by the way he smoked his corncob pipe, cocked his wool hat, or wore his denim jumper. And his name had become a byword for tall tales.

But old Grip had fallen on evil days. Now his sight came and went darkly, accompanied by splitting headaches. Moreover, he suffered rheumatism in his knees and hands. The sorriest part of his plight, however, was the strange weakening blood malady that had kept him in bed most of the time for over a year and that the doctor couldn't cure.

So it was in bed or in a big split-bottom rocker, pulled up before a fire, that they talked to Grip on their visits. On these occasions his wife, Agnes, allowed him to transgress his doctor's orders to the length of a long milk toddy—Marcellus and Adam taking their whiskey straight. While the liquor was in him, before the fire (though it might be breaking them out in a sweat), Grip would be his old self again for a little while, and tell his tales and jokes with mimicry and his provocative gutsy laugh.

There was his tale about old Cooter-Nose Dowdy who claimed to be able to tell where he was on the river, however black the night, by tasting a cupful of the water running by. And how Grip, on ahead of Cooter, shifted his watch fire to fool him, and the old fraud piled his raft up in the swamp at Devil's Elbow. Adam said his imitation brought old Cooter-Nose right into the room. There was the night when rain put out Grip's raft fire and then turned to sleet and he had had to slam away with his maul at a butting binder for four hours to keep from freezing to death.

He liked to tell about a night when the high-rolling Adair boys—one of whom was the state senator—rented a launch in Darien and filled it full of fine whiskey and hired him to pilot them up the Altamaha on a spree. They all got drunk, the younger brother passing out in the bottom of the boat. The senator got to making a stump speech, and fell overboard and Grip had to jump in after him. That left the launch plowing on up the river, in a night black as Hades, with nobody at the wheel.

Grip would groan. "And all our liquor in it!" He had never prayed before, but that night he called on the Lord in the name of every Hardshell preacher—his first wife was a Hardshell—he could remember. And he would imitate their pulpit manners. Hell, it got so serious that he told God if He'd turn the boat around he wouldn't take another drink—till after breakfast. He hadn't more than got the words out of his mouth before he could hear the launch wheeling back downstream, and here she come right between him and the senator! They latched onto either side. Adam knew to say then that he bet Grip didn't keep his promise. And Grip would wag his head and pull his handlebar moustache and shout, "Ho-no! ho-no, there! Grip might be a drunk and a fool, but he knows better'n to trifle with the Old Marster—not with Ole Man River Hisself! No siree! I kept my word." Then, sotto voce, "But I'll tell you boys, I had to start frying me some bacon and eggs before midnight."

The old galoot *was* funny, warmed your insides. He seemed convincing now when he talked about David, too—seemed to regret deeply his having got so drunk that day. And he said he hadn't testified about Dunk not being in the boat at the first trial because neither side had asked him about it. Though he had told the solicitor beforehand just what he said later on the stand. Adam took this with a grain of salt; though Marcellus wouldn't agree with Adam, he was warming up to Grip.

Moreover, they rubbed up their kinship. Grip's great-grandmother was a Hightower, and the hundred acres he still held, half in the swamp there, and the log house, were a part of her dower when she married preacher Milt Jackson. Grip laid store by his Hightower blood. And for that matter (though he didn't think so) Marcellus did, too. He took to going over the river to see Grip more and more often. Almost any evening when he was back at his base in the old winehouse he might paddle himself across and walk out to Grip's place.

Before the end of May he would have had to confess another attraction, too. Grip's wife, who was genuinely fond of him in spite of the difference in age, enjoyed sitting in on his sessions with them. She would say, in her common way, "If you boys think I'm going to embarrass you, I'll leave. But don't mind me!" She had a comic touch herself, and was still vulgarly good-looking. They'd had no children, and she had kept her figure, with the addition of a few pounds. And she still had sex appeal. She and Marcellus had rubbed up against each other in the dimness of the hallway and kitchen, and he had got a lust for her.

Throughout the whole of May it had been plain to see that Grip was growing weaker, and he complained more of the pain. In the first week of June he had a showdown with his doctor that left him in glum depression and silence. For a week he refused to see Marcellus or anybody else, and lay in his bed without uttering a word. When Marcellus got back to Adam's place from a trip up the Ocmulgee on Tuesday afternoon, however, he learned that Grip had sent for him.

Agnes told him in the hall that Grip had been out of his head, and the doctor said he didn't have many more days, but he was himself again at the moment. Marcellus found him propped up on a mound of pillows against the headboard, his face as white as the pillows except for his blue jaw and moustache. His handlebars cast shadows across his cheeks, so hollow had they grown. He didn't speak or give any sign of recognition until Marcellus stood at the bedside, leaning over him. Grip looked up at him from dark hollow eye sockets then, and all the clowning had gone out of him. He motioned Marcellus to sit down.

Agnes pushed a duck-legged chair up beside him, and Marcellus settled into it. He meant to speak lightly, something to cheer him, but the fear he had seen in Grip's eyes shook him so that he just said, "All right, Grip, I'm here."

Grip took a swallow of water from a glass his wife held to his lips, then looked up into Marcellus' face again. "My time's short, Hightower," he wheezed feebly. "I've got something to get straight before I go." Pausing, his gaze shifted past Marcellus' shoulder, and he added, "To get straight with David Ransom, before I—I—see 'im." He came back to Marcellus to say, "You're his closest friend." There was a slight movement behind him. Grip's eyes shifted and he spoke out to his wife. "No," he said, "don't leave—I want you to hear this, too."

He halted for another swallow of water, then went on with more force. "I've been mixed up in some rough things in my time. And this didn't start out that way. I don't hardly know why I lied about it now." His gaze shifted, but he didn't pause. "Partly liquor, partly something else, I'll tell about. Maybe it was murder. And maybe I'm more guilty than either one of the poor bastards who went to jail for it!" He glanced briefly at Marcellus, then away, his eyes widening in fear as he stared. "Covering it up so long, like I have! But I'm going to get it straight before I go—maybe it was murder, but nobody knew it was going to happen two seconds before it did—and I'm sure nobody could have said what he would do till after he done it. But if it's murder, the guilt lies on me."

His voice had risen in sharp self-accusation, and he slumped into silence, chin on his chest, exhausted. After a little he asked for liquor. Agnes gave him a spoonful, and he resumed. He said he had come to the landing that Saturday afternoon to find David there with Dunk and Buck as previously reported; that he had vouched for David, and Buck had got out his jug; that he, Grip, had got weaving drunk and that the whiskey in him was to some extent responsible for what he did. He said it was true that David had loaned him a dollar to pay for his drinks. But he had good reason to believe that David had made time with his girl, Agnes. He didn't like it, and as he got drunker this grudge began to work on him. First thing, just as he was getting ready to leave, he muttered to Buck that he wasn't sure of David; he had been mistaken about him.

When David undertook to help him, Grip, into the boat, he resented it, though he surely needed help. And David had knelt down in the bottom and steadied him on a forward seat, while Buck and Dunk, behind him, paddled it. They had got across and were approaching the willow piles, when David got to his feet and moved toward the bow to jump ashore with the boat chain. He, Grip, was feeling mean-drunk and huffy, and as David was stepping over the seat ahead, and off balance, Grip shook the boat.

David hit the water headfirst. A boil of freshet current took him back out, and when he came up to the surface he was athwart Fykes. He had swallowed water and was gagging, and grabbed the gunwale and tilted them pretty sharp. Buck knocked his hands off with his paddle. The next time David came up, he was behind the stern and about arm's length away. Dunk, already standing, wheeled about and let him have his heavy paddle on top of his head, and he had sunk out of sight.

All this had had a sobering effect on him, Grip—his ducking Ransom had got bad out of hand. He got hold of the pike pole in the bottom of the boat and succeeded in hooking David's clothes before the current carried him away, and finally hauled him into the boat. But he was dead.

By that time Grip was cold sober and saw that he was in the middle of a fix—though he was careful not to tell Buck and Dunk about his part in it, about his rocking the boat. It was he, Grip, who decided where David should be sunk, and he had directed the trip upriver, the weighting and sinking of the body; for which they were grateful and agreed not to involve him. He thought he had done a good job, but it's hard to trick the river! The freshet had brought the body up and lodged it on the point of Burnt Island. And then he was scareder than ever.

As he listened, Marcellus had a burning in his chest. And toward the end he felt as if his belly had caved in. When Grip paused and asked for more water, he couldn't at first get up from the low chair. But he did so in time to take the glass from Agnes' hand, and he held it to Grip's lips while he made a couple of swallows. Marcellus stood holding out the glass to see whether he would have more, but he turned aside against his pillow, murmuring, "I didn't tell your uncle John Hightower where it was till it had washed up and been there near a week. . . . I couldn't stand it any longer. And then that thousand dollars, there, in our hands! And me and John, neither one got nothing but our hat and ass!"

Staring on at Grip, Marcellus suddenly had the feeling that he was balancing on a tightwire. The glass slipped out of his hand and hit the floor. In the muddle of his trying to pick it up, he collided with Agnes, to find her broken up. "My God," she groaned, "I killed 'im, Marcellus! Letting Grip think that!"

As he stared at her, a painful gasp took him, his breathing seemed to cut off, and in the breathless quiet he heard Grip's voice again: "John split the thousand dollars with me." There followed sound that seemed a mixture of a chuckle and a rattle in his throat, and he added, "I bought timber from you with my part."

Marcellus knew vaguely that he was moving, moving away from the bed. Along with his breathing, sensibility and thought seemed suspended, too—all except the knowledge that he had to get out of the room, get out now, before he understood all of this, before he found out what it meant. He heard Agnes say, "Shorty, get the doctor!" And he nodded and kept on walking.

Marcellus walked the mile up the road to the Bede store phone at a stiff stride. He called Dr. Crabtree for Grip, and retracted his steps and still managed to keep a jump ahead of his questions. He wavered at the head of the lane to the Jackson house, but he turned in and made down it for ten paces; then, veering to his left, he was back out of it again in ten more. He halted, frowning, and shook his head, then abruptly moved off down the road for the river at a rack. He didn't slow up over the half mile of swamp to the *white* side of the Landing, and he waded into his bateau without looking to right or left, snapped up his paddle, and was halfway across before the breeze could begin to cool the sweat on his forehead or lay the fog inside. He clambered up the Bluff on the *Indian* side without locking his boat and hit the familiar old trail, holding himself back. But by the time he passed the sunken steamboat boiler he was at double time, and he cleared Adam's back gate with a cartwheel and came down the lane at a run.

Adam was seated on the step of the old winehouse, watching the sunset. Marcellus halted abruptly ten paces from him, as if seeing him for the first time. A heave took him then, and he caught his breath. Adam got up, his eyes widening and blinking, and moved out of the way—Marcellus was in motion again, up the step and into the building at a hard stride. In a moment he came back with a quart jar of corn whiskey in his hands, screwed off its top and, tilting it, took a slug.

Lowering the fruit jar, he said, "Grip is dying—if he ain't dead. The son of a bitch!" He took another short drink and held it toward Adam. "He's more guilty than anybody—than anybody, Goddamn 'im! Goddamn 'im!" Adam hadn't reached for the jar, and Marcellus brought it to his mouth again, and drank. He offered it once more, along with the top, saying, "He rocked the boat that day—it was Dunk got 'im with the boat paddle."

Now Adam took the jar and top, and, lowering them to one side, screwed the top on, saying, "He tell you this?"

"Yes," Marcellus said, his voice beginning to rise, "and, Goddamnit, it was *Grip* hid David's body—Grip told Uncle John where it was." His voice rose higher: "Hell, those sons of bitches knew it was there on the point of the island! And John split the reward with him. And me, me—a son of a bitch, too!" He began to cry. "When Carruthers, there, already damn' near broke, wanted me to claim my part of it so we could call it in and he wouldn't have to pay it—me, your finicky son of a bitch—I pretended I couldn't, because I'd already publicly said I wouldn't claim any of it. I thought I was already humiliated to death by old John taking the reward—and I let him take it all, all of it—and give half to Grip—who gave it back to me—" He sucked in his breath with a long quivering moan and began to heave. "They're on me," he said to Adam, and began vomiting.

When Marcellus had quieted, lying on his back in the yard on the gray ground that seemed to float as the dusk thickened, the cry of a whippoorwill in the swamp piercing the dark, Adam talked to him. "They say the g-good die young." He spoke from the winehouse step, leaning over his knees meditatively. "And always, us h-helps to do 'em in. Just us ordinary, selfish, 'ceitful, arrogant, heedless, sorry sons a bitches." His guttural bass gave pulse to the gloaming. "Sometimes 'e lets a good man be took out of the tangle of things. Maybe it looks like 'e cuts 'im off. But it ain't so. It ain't never blind. Hit for us. H-Hit done to show us up, to show our own meanness to us . . . and our needs." Clearing his throat, he raised his voice. "Yeah, you guilty, Marcellus . . . along with Grip. And I'm guilty too," In the swamp the whippoorwill was repeating his cry.

Marcellus shuddered and heaved a long sigh.

Chapter 16

THE GRAY EARTH, lifting out of her shadows, stirred, waking. Marcellus heard the still sleepy twittering of birds above him, felt the solid reality of the ground beneath his numbed buttocks and legs, and smelled the dawn—he had lain all night on his back in the yard! He raised up on an elbow stiffly to stare about him, reached toward a vague crumpled shadow nearby to find it a woolen shawl or blanket—Adam or some of them must have put it on him. Suddenly sleepy again, he sank back, pulling the cover over him. But he did not sleep.

Memory began to seep back into his head, images as quiet and gray as the daybreak. He saw Grip's gaunt face on the pillows, and the sequence reeled by like a sad, sickening dream. Then Adam, talking, talking in the dark—to the whippoorwill, the whippoorwill to Adam. What had it meant? The hull of it looked like last year's locust shed. But it had given him a buzz at the time. Adam's words had sounded Old Testament-like—or was it *Pilgrim's Progress?* How quaint! Marcellus writhed, turning on his side. Still, it had done something to him. It was as if he had a hard night of cholera morbus and got rid of his green plums. Yeah, a catharsis of the bowels! He felt his stiff cheeks limbering, but he fell back in a weary, easeful somnolence. Perhaps he should tell Adam about his trouble with Melanie? But where did the wrong lie? Might it not have begun here? As he lay on the ground at the beginning of day, his years with her began to take form in the depth of his being.

What was guilt? This gray dirt he was lying on had still been his when he quit it so contemptuously that January day in '26! He had imagined himself quite happy to be rid of it, to be landless, there in the new days of his adventure into Bohemia. Freedom. Down with the bourgeoisie. It had taken him a hell of a long time to find out that he was living in an idiot's utopia—or trying to—in a hooligan heaven! He hadn't realized it, even after he finally broke out of it—not for a long time. On their second honeymoon he was still flying blind with Melanie. So blind that he never suspected what had happened to him in the high moment of their imprudence. Though it wasn't what he at first feared; for Melanie later confessed to him that after he dropped off to sleep, she had gone to the bathroom. However, he now saw this, too, had a part in what did happen to him. For him, it had amounted to the conception of a new attitude, and it came to birth.

It did not stand between them until the spring of '37, more than a year later, though he had been nursing, had been gingerly dandling the idea in his mind for months. He sensed that it might appear to Melanie like a shift of ground, like an about-face even. But, hell, the depression had changed a lot of things! He had put out veiled feelers at first; then he tried insinuation through jest, but she, usually so sensitive, did not seem to get his intimations. His home-grown novel, which he had finished the previous fall, writing every morning through the spring and summer and working on the other, the morning Nashville paper, for his living—had been published in

March, and prepublication sales on it had brought him six hundred dollars. And to that had just been added two hundred more for the serialization rights. Eight hundred dollars seemed like a wad of money to him then. He had been talking all winter about owning land again, about their buying just a homesite, but out from town, with enough room for a garden and maybe chickens. He wasn't by himself in this. The depression was beginning to lift, and a lot of people came out of it talking about owning land. Though there was double-entendre in his talk.

He said he was going to open a savings account with the eight hundred dollars. It was on the morning Melanie didn't have class until ten o'clock and they were drinking a second cup of coffee in the breakfast nook of the kitchen. "Why don't we go to Paris this summer and live on the difference in the exchange?" she said.

He smiled at her like a deaf man, and went on. "I'm going to call it the farm account."

She bridled. "The farm account? What do you think you know about farming? You never plowed a furrow in your life!" He had merely smiled his complacence, and she added irritably, "What would you grow?"

This was what he'd been lying in wait for. And he tried for an innocent country grin to say, "Why, we'll raise children, honey!"

She wasn't amused. "Whose children?"

He went even more yokelish, gesturing largely with is coffee. "Oh, we'll alternate on 'em."

She said dryly, "Well, there won't be three, I can tell you—I know that joke." She put down her cup and got up. "There'll just be the one you have."

He felt so exposed, so defenseless that he forced a sickly grin to say, "I might settle for a rose garden, Mel—with sweet potatoes planted in between."

But his real discouragement had come on their wedding anniversary in June. He had remembered it with an electric blanket, bought at a sale—and on second thought not too happy an idea. He had tried lamely (at breakfast again) something about the blanket making it easier for them to go to bed and hard to get up. She'd kept on drinking her coffee in clouding silence, then lowered her cup to say, "I know, I'll swap it in for an electric fan to take to the International House with me."

This was the day before her leaving for summer school at Chicago, about which he wasn't at all happy, but he managed to work his frown around into a grunt to say, "You wouldn't wanta do that, would you, honey?"

She retorted in an ambiguous tone, "After what you've done to me!"

It came into his head, and he said without calculation, "Well, there are things I haven't done to you, Mel. A grass widow told me once that she had had her third baby before she found out her husband had been sticking pinholes in her protection!"

Her smile was quick and tight—her lips hadn't been dewy in a long time then, and were almost liver-colored—and she held him with a glittering eye, while she gave him back his own familiar words to the last intonation: " 'You damned well better not do that to me!' "

It chilled him to the marrow in his bones.

Marcellus rose from the ground in a hard shudder, shook himself, and stamped about in a circle. The echo of those words still chilled him. They had been a retribution so deeply deserved! He strode over to the pump and began to prime the plunger with water from a used coffee can. But he hadn't really understood before why their chill never left him—more, why Melanie had had to give them back to him. Water was gushing forth now, and he gazed at its revelation of truth. Actually, he had never looked at it from Melanie's viewpoint—so blinding an ego had he! He stuck a tin basin under the flow. Yet when it had filled, he did not at once use it, but turned away to face the dawn.

That night in their disheveled furnished flat, she, delaying his flight with her melancholy "But I think I'm pregnant now!" Hadn't the tremble in her voice been hope? She was trying to make a marriage out of their yoke, offering him a child. It had been his fault, not hers, that the circumstances weren't happier. He lurched forward, grasping at the empty air. A child, a child—it wasn't her fault.

He came about to the pan and began to wash his face. The incredible thing, the incredible thing about it was that she had come back to him at all. To be sure he saw now that in the beginning their inside tie, the peculiar mystique of their mutual abandon, was born in insecurity. Their insecurity, but, my God, that wouldn't take a woman back to the bed of a monster. He came up from the water sputtering, and wheeled toward the big oak tree in time to see a ghost slip behind it. He said "my God" again: Gallatin Crosby had delivered her to him. Despite his feeling of familiarity with her father, this had never occurred to him before.

During her last summer at home before he died, Marcellus had eventually learned from Melanie, her father had tried to kill her mother. Melanie, had prevented it, if barely. She had been very stupid about her father's behavior—even though she resented it. On the day before, she had chanced to uncover a big monkey wrench he had concealed under the pillow of his bed. She had thought this eccentric, but it didn't occur to her what was in his mind. Only when her mother screamed out in the dark of the night following did she grasp it, though evidently it had been very much with her. For a picture of what was happening had flashed upon her so quickly that she was in her mother's room before he could deliver a second blow. He was a slight man and, surprising him, she had been able to wrest the weapon from him.

Melanie said that, in the darkness, fortunately he had struck her mother a glancing blow that did not wound her seriously.

The county sheriff, at the say of the college, had locked her father up. Her mother hadn't opposed it, though later she got him transferred to a private sanitarium. But that morning her father had kept screaming, "Frigid bitch, she wants to kill me!" Melanie said that, the whole time, her mother had never used an unkind word in speaking of her husband. She had to admire her: she herself might feel guilty about it, but she wasn't up to her mother's forgiveness, understanding, or whatever it was. Melanie had saved her mother from her father's monkey wrench, but she hadn't been able to save herself.

He had been edging toward the trunk of the oak crab-wise, and abruptly turned to it and circled it. He did not surprise the father's ghost, if this was his intention; but beyond the tree's bare bowl, as he rounded it to the east, in the distant glow—Melanie's. It was a colorless image that communicated its intelligence quickly, unaccountably—from a day far away, indeed. There on the Cumberland's pebble beach a young bride had lifted her head from his shoulder to give him a look of inquiry that was now no longer enigmatic. "My extra baggage!" Yes, even then she was willing, was ready, and would have gone ahead at a word form him to have the baby! He stumbled over tree roots as he turned, and, teetering, tripped on the blanket that had covered him during the night. Dismally, he picked up and folded it and laid it on the water shelf. He hung up the basin, too, and raked at his hair with his fingers. The price of theories.

The dawn had dimmed, but suddenly, from the green-brown horizon, a great bulging sun popped like the pulp from a scuppernong grape. Marcellus' eyes widened under its promise and he filled his lungs with the morning air. He felt saliva flow in his mouth from hunger. The thought of breakfast gave the day new possibilities—he would take the flatness off his tongue with fried fish. He clapped on his straw hat and headed for the river, for Adam's fish basket.

Back there he didn't find the hardihood to bring up the subject of their having a child again for a year. While Melanie was at Chicago that summer he had taken his vacation and a couple of weeks' leave of absence extra and gone back to the river country to collect material for an informal history on the Altamaha for a river-book series. His job on it came out the next April. He knew that he stood to make a substantial sum of money, and he revived his talk about buying land.

He had seen in the want ads of the evening paper that the Lull place out at Spencer's Bluff was up for sale. Bohemia had long since vanished. Bob Blue had married and gone to New York; Honus Murphy's wife had divorced him and gone to Chicago. Heck Putnam had married a rich widow. And the Lulls had dissolved their brave free world in bitter acrimony. But they had had an attractive place—as he and Melanie were finally to realize so well—three acres, a little way back from the Bluff, with a brook running through it. And the main structure of their camp had been converted from a barn of pioneer days, made of hewn yellow poplar logs. He held the paper out to Melanie. "Look, they've finally cleared this out of court and're selling it. Wouldn't you like to have it? Just for old time's sake. You know it could be a bargain."

June was near, and Melanie was again getting ready to go to Chicago to work on her master's degree. Her interest was tentative, as she read the black print around his thumb. "Oh, it would be fun!" she said, pausing to add provisionally, "Wouldn't it?"

But for Marcellus, as he bored deeper into summer, digging at the prospect, dickering for the property and finally getting it—two thousand dollars down and signing notes for another two thousand—this had come to be her expressed desire.

Leaning out of the green bateau toward the feathery willow piles, he pulled at the strand of baling wire leading under the muddy surface of the Oconee and brought up a long, cylindrical wattled fish basket. He looked beyond it vaguely, and smiled. His fancy that summer had had tender stimulation. He had visited the Lull place several times. Revisited it. He now took a four-or-five pound carp and three smaller speckled cat from the fish trap, strung them on a piece of cord he had found in the bottom of the boat, and picked up his paddle. As he mounted the Bluff at the Landing, he remembered how the house sat toward the upper edge of the acreage, facing the gradual slope of a rough-grown meadow. The tree-marked brook made the far border, running into a considerable impoundment behind a rock dam at the bottom of the hill, in the corner. Gray limestone walls fenced in the plot on three sides. The burrow was the object of his romantic memories: up a way from the stream where the slope broke more abruptly at an outcropping of rock. Here it lay, concealed on three sides by buckbushes, shaded from above by the wild goose plum tree, and open only to the pool. It consisted of a shallow bed of smooth-worn limestone, on which first lichen and then bluegrass had grown—bluegrass as long and soft as a woman's hair.

On that April afternoon he and Melanie had ridden the interurban out to the Bluff ahead of the Lulls, who wouldn't get there until dark. They had roamed the woods and the meadow, in the limpid blue light, to stumble eventually upon the burrow. It was, they found, a surprising, a wonderful spot from which to watch the smooth clear water, the water of their adolescence slip over the dam. It was snug and smelled bittersweet and was cushioned like a Swinburne lyric. It was, they thought then, their find—on that afternoon of discovery—that afternoon of Melanie's expressed desire.

When she returned from Chicago late in August to learn that he had bought the old Lull camp, however, she was outraged. He was astonished at this, really, and professed to be thunderstruck; giving her back her words almost from the same spot, giving them back mildly at first. But after she got angry, he got angry, too. And they had one of the bitterest quarrels of their whole married life over it, Melanie, at the height of the thing, shrieking out incoherently, "scene of my rape, my—my miscarriage . . . plain brutality . . .trying to torture me!"

In the dim Oconee swamp, with his string of fish, Marcellus paused at a footlog to locate the slicks before stepping onto it. He reflected that that afternoon, in their burrow, it had been Melanie who wanted to go ahead. Over the dam! Of course he had made the mistake of revealing that he always carried a condom in his pocketbook—security policy. How should he know it had been there so long it had got *rotten*. He felt the buzzing in his ears even now. Still, you would hardly call it rape! Marcellus shook his head, as if he'd been hit on it. It was the first time he had heard that she had her miscarriage at the Lull's camp—Bayless had looked after her.

He mounted the log, then paused to shake his head again. He had got so mad in their argument he couldn't remember now what he'd said. But he saw that their quarrel hadn't really been about the Lull camp, though neither one of them realized it then. . . .Melanie wouldn't go out to the Bluff to look at the place even, wouldn't go near it. She had got so upset about the whole thing that she wouldn't go back to her job at the girls' academy—wouldn't stay in Nashville. She had returned to Chicago that fall to finish her work for her degree. And he had paid for it. He had been glad that he could. Her prompting, however, had been harsh. She had grown spare and gray-brown in color, for she had abandoned makeup, and she had said—a jerky undertone in her voice and her dimple now a deep furrow in her cheek—"You've never supported me a day in my life!"

Melanie had got over her rage during the fall. Before she came home for Christmas she, in her regular weekly letter, had asked his forgiveness. She had said the place did have some unpleasant associations in her mind—but a lot of pleasant ones, too. She didn't know why she felt so bitter about it then. During the holidays they had gone out there and pried about the grounds and the house and talked about renovating it. They had even had a fireside picnic there one afternoon with another couple.

But this softening, this change of attitude in Melanie didn't seem to make it any easier for him to talk to her about what was really on his mind. He was hardly a ninny with his wife, nor was he usually a stuttering man. And there were few reserves between them. Yet he couldn't work himself up to the point of speaking to her openly and matter-of-factly about them. He just couldn't propose to Melanie their trying for a child. There were too many echoes in his head. He couldn't find the right tone of voice for it. . . . He was through, however, with any more clowning on the subject.

He kept silent. He didn't say anything, but one night in January he didn't use a contraceptive, just without a word didn't. And Melanie didn't say anything, either. After this, it became their regular practice. But winter turned into spring, into summer, without the least hint of Melanie's getting pregnant. It looked to him as if privately she had decided she wasn't going to give in. Marcellus grew sullen over this intransigence, and one June night he turned the back of his hand to Melanie's approach to blurt out dourly, "You just don't intend to have any children—is that it? Vanie?"

She shuddered, and tears came into her eyes; then, lowering them, she seemed to fall into bemusement. After a while he frowned and turned away on his pillow. But she, rearing up on her hand, leaned over him and grasped his arm to say, "I haven't done anything to prevent it, Marcellus!"

The next day she went to see a doctor; then she brought word to him that they should both go. The doctor had told her that it might be her husband's fault. Both went and were pronounced sound. And that was that. Except that the doctor tried to enlarge their perspective and increase their patience (his patience at least) by telling them that many couples tried futilely for ten, even fifteen years and then succeeded in having a child.

Marcellus paused to look about him on the swamp trace, then took a leap that carried him to safety over a mudhole. With this encouragement he wouldn't guess how long they might have continued their efforts. They certainly hadn't given up at all. Indeed, what with the aid of a medical library and all of their friends' fertility recipes, it became an absorbing adventure. Though now on reflection he seemed to remember something in Melanie's subdued determination that betrayed her sense of futility—he was to know later, sense of guilt. But this, to be sure, had not stopped them—this had not made them give up. It was a uterine tumor, and the usual operation for it followed that October.

Melanie came through fine and without complications and recovered quickly. And she soon wearied of his concern for her health. Though after that they didn't seem to have much to talk about on their evenings in the house. They had moved into the old Lull camp out at the Bluff in the spring. Their remodeling of the upstairs into three bedrooms and a bath was already complete. And the extension of the shed room to include a dining room had broken down when the contractor moved to Florida and they had run low on money. Their zest had petered out then. He was preparing his application for a Guggenheim fellowship on his present venture during that gap, but that, to be sure, didn't interest her. She was back at her teaching in no time, almost. And they didn't talk to each other much. He took to canoeing alone on the river, though the wind was already sharp. He had put in some jug lines and fished 'em just for the hell of it. He really didn't know what she did with herself around the house, though she usually had papers to grade.

They tried to keep out of each other's way. But of course silence speaks louder, and maybe absence does, too. She said, after dinner in the living room one evening, "If you'd talk a little more in here, and less in bed in your sleep, I'd like it better, Shorty." He had taken his pipe out of his mouth to speak, but he merely spat in the fireplace. She went on, "And you might remember to get some liquor for the chest, if you—" She didn't finish, but after a moment broke out again.

“And it might help your insomnia to have some—if it is insomnia—I'm tire of your wandering around the house in the middle of the night!”

He had protested, then. “Look, what's the matter with you, Melanie?”

“What's the matter with me!” Her laugh went flat, then empty. “That's public knowledge. . . . But I do wish you wouldn't take it like a life sentence!”

“Life sentence?” he repeated stupidly. But he didn't know where to go from there. *His* thoughts had included something of the sort once, right after she recovered from the operation, when things had been quieting down. He had had the feeling that they had been scratched at the barrier in a race—and he'd had the impulse to say something of the sort, but he didn't. Melanie, race, yep, the human race. He got up and went on the back porch to feed the cat.

Their pent-up words had broken loose on Armistice Day, after breakfast, after he had walked out of the kitchen, where they still ate, and stood in the passage looking at the unfinished dining room. He said, turned away from her, and idly, he thought—he had no intention of making it sound portentous—“You know, I dreamed of my father last night—for the first time since I was a small boy.”

There was no sound from Melanie, but he did not sense anything ominous in her silence. He walked through the gap that was to have been the doorway, and took hold of an upright testing its stability, looking down at its moorings. “It started with the little incident I always remember about him, when I lay down on his couch with him to take a nap after lunch, and he fell asleep, and snored. As in my memory, in the dream his mouth fell open in his beard and emitted sounds like the cave of the winds.” He paused here and got no rejoinder out of Melanie, but went on without looking at her: “And I got scared, like I did really, and slipped down off the couch and ran down the back hall, through the door and out into the sunshine." There was some sort of sound from her, like a cough, though he continued, "But in my dream last night my father woke up and followed me—overtook me out in the backyard under the chinaberry trees, I thought—"

Melanie's voice broke out, unburying agony. "Don't! I can't stand it . . . again!" He gripped the upright, staring his astonishment. Glaring back at him, she burst into sudden shrillness: "All right—if you're going, go—get the hell out of here!" her face suffused to a reddish gray, and her bloodless lips rounded to sound shocking perfidy: "I might have known you would! Don't try to lay it on your father. And any of your sickly dreams—I'm sick of them!" She swallowed, gasping, emitting a whimpering undertone but to resume, "All right—yes—*you*, you ruin me—you fix it so that I can't have a child; then you want to run out on me—run off!" She swept her cup and saucer aside. "Off after some other woman!" She pushed them farther. (Marcellus was appalled: he had never seen her so in the grip of a passion before—and he felt sorry for her.) "Yes you got me pregnant, then gave your orders, and left. 'Get rid of it before I get back,' you said." He thought this unfair and swallowed, and wet his lips, but she didn't give him a chance. "And I did, and bled for seven weeks, ruined myself. And you know it. The vultures have been after me ever since. But now you'll lay it on the operation. Now you're through with me. Well, go, go get you another woman! Go!"

She was out of breath, and Marcellus finally got a chance. He jerked up his arms and thrashed down with all he had, and shouted "Jesus H. Christ!" and turned on his heel, and left.

It was dinnertime before he returned, before he stood again in the doorway, now a little rumpled and bleary-eyed, a package under his arm. He hadn't intended to go to town that morning (it was his day off), but he did and got drunk, though he was practically sober again by this hour. He had brought a couple of fifths of liquor with him to propose that they try to drink their way out of it. But Melanie had, it appeared—and miraculously to him—achieved a deep composure during the day and spoke to him quietly. She agreed to a highball, but stayed him to have her say first.

"I don't believe in divorce," she said with even weight, standing on the balls of both feet, looking at him levelly from the middle of the living room. "And I'm not going to get one. But I'm going to leave. I'm going back to Chicago and get my doctorate. Three years. I've got some money from Aunt Lizzie. And you can do what you like. I'll give you a divorce if you want it—or I'll accept any child you bring me as your own. After all, I'm more guilty than you are." She relaxed and moved toward the door to the back passage. "I just wanted to get that said at the outset. . . . I'll have a drink now."

He fumbled with his package and shuffled across the boards. She had astonished him. He never admired her more. He argued with her about her decision, argued that they go on as they were, argued half the night. She didn't budge. To be sure, it may have been that he wasn't solid all the way through in his determination to keep her there, to hold them together.

In Adam's lane, under the ripening morning sun, Marcellus opened the gate into the backyard and held up his string of fish for Adam, standing on the porch, to see. "I got a yen for some fried catfish," he called out.

Chapter 17

"HERE IT IS!" Agnes swung the dip net off the hay pileup over her head with both hands, but, overtaxed, let it down sideways, the light mesh fluttering and settling about her. "The old thing's heavier than I thought," she said, flushed from her exertion, turning toward Marcellus. She smiled with modesty. "Oh, look, it's caught on my button."

He was approaching her from the top of the ladder to the loft of the old log barn on the Jackson place. Grip was now in his grave for the third day. As pallbearer, Marcellus had helped take him there. And his excuse for being in the barn loft with his widow was to buy Grip's dip net for Adam, who once had spoken of it to him. But his thoughts were not on the net. And he judged by the prepensive poise of Agnes' movements that hers weren't either. "Wait a minute," he called to her, "let me handle that."

"It couldn't miss my top shelf," she murmured, swallowing her last word with a chuckle, as she withdrew a hand from the rim of the net to free herself.

He had come up with her now and, smiling into her still-befuddled-looking face, removed her fingers firmly from the button on her black crepe de chine blouse. “Here. Let me take you out of the net,” he said, his lips twisting in a show of detachment. He didn’t touch the mesh, but, half unbuttoning the button, paused to catch her eye as the pupil widened; finishing with the button, he drew down the blouse to uncover her breast. Naked, it trembled, grew firm, and the nipple erected under his gaze. With a calculated swoop, he bit it.

She murmured, “You son of a bitch!”

But Agnes wasn’t about to bed in the hayloft, in her best dress, she told him. She insisted on their going to the house, decently, where they could have a drink and she could cook lunch for him first. He had not seen her bed, she was at pains to say—in case he were not ghoul enough to get in a dead man’s still warm one.

She said, after they had tied the net securely on top of his car and were climbing the back steps, “It’s a funny thing how me and you are tangled up together in the web around David.” She made a weaving motion with her right hand, and shrugged. “You can hardly believe it. And our not intending him any harm. Not intending him anything—just interested in our own little selfish fish fry.” She paused on the porch at the wash shelf and dipped water from the cedar bucket into a graniteware basin. She said in another tone of voice, “Here, wouldn’t you like to wash your face and hands?” As he turned to the shelf, she resumed. “Not the same fish fries, sure. You sent him to your crosstie woods for your reasons. And I borrowed his pin for mine. . . . But, between us, we had about as much to do with putting him in the bottom of the river as anybody.”

Marcellus had been hovering above the pan, and now, precipitated by her words that struck through him like an ice pick, he plunged his face into the water with a splutter. As he turned from the shelf, she put a towel in his hands. Nodding, he dried his face to say, in an ambiguous tone, "You didn't get any of your own blood money, though."

She glanced at him curiously, her bare eyeballs and teeth glistening, before she spoke. "Oh, I don't know—I ate Grip's bread." She turned back to the bucket and drank a dipper of water before going on. "But you couldn't know the way I felt about Grip! Nor how I come to marry him." He was only a couple of years younger than her father. But Grip and her pa had drifted timber on the rivers together, and Pa had talked in the family about Grip long before she ever saw him. She grew up believing that Grip was the greatest timber runner and roisterer on the river. He was already her hero when she at the age of ten first saw him, there at their house with her father. She married him when she was still seventeen. And she had been scared he wasn't going to marry her. He wasn't the marrying kind, for he had been a widower for fifteen years. The difference in their ages hadn't been the reason why they didn't have children, though she didn't find this out till a few years ago—they didn't. Grip said he didn't know what it was till they went to the doctor. He said he got hit in the crotch by the tongue of a timber cart years before. Though she didn't know about that. He had told her then to go ahead and get her a baby by somebody else, but she knew better than to do it as long as he was alive.

In the well-scoured kitchen, one end taken by a wood range and the other by a long deal table, she brought forth a bottle of liquor from a side cupboard and, breaking the seal, set it on the table along with shot glasses and tumblers. "Will you pour the drinks while I go get off my good dress to cook you some victuals?" As he moved toward the table, she added, from the doorway, pointing, "And git that ham down hanging in the pantry, will you? Put it on the meat block!"

Marcellus gave her a dry grin, but picked up the bottle to see that it held a good Bourbon whiskey, and poured the small glasses level full, wondering with a quizzical glance down his nose how deep he was going to have to go in this. Agnes, tied to a pink calico wrapper, made biscuits by the stove. He carved slices of country ham for frying. He was aware of her dimly outlined belly and breasts, lithe in their motion at the dough tray, as he listened to her talk. "I heard you agreeing with Grip, here a while back, you coulder done with some children, too." She bore down on the elastic mixture under her knuckles, and came up with, "When Grip said no man ever admits it's his fault, you said that in your case you had a doctor's word for it that it wasn't yours." She scraped flour from her fingers. "Grip coulder said that he didn't. And maybe he was insinuating it in a joking way." She pummeled her dough. "It's never no joke to them who could and would. They got the responsibility, I figure." Her tone became speculative as she lifted her face. "And along my way it's always been the don't-haves who helped the don't-haves. Usually." She wondered, eyes back on her work but her ear shifting toward him, if he could feel the same way about it that she did? And he wondered of a feathery feeling in the top of his head whether she could be bold enough to propose marriage. He eyed with suspense the black pan of white leavened dollars, as she turned with it from her table toward the stove.

"Don't get me wrong," she halted to say. "I can stretch the 'Mrs.' I've already got to cover anything that comes in the next nine or ten months. And I got property enough to live on!"

Marcellus turned from the ham to the table to fill the shot glasses again. But she shook her head, saying she'd wait awhile. He downed his straight, and afterward felt more like listening. A son by Agnes? He said to himself, assuming the sex without thinking. Old Tom Hooker's daughter—Black Tom, common as pig tracks. Amid the expansive glow in his belly, however, Marcellus questioned this, but now was he so common? He had heard through his Uncle John and Adam that old Tom had been a henchman of his father in the dim past—a man you could depend on when you needed a man—who had the guts. Agnes had Hooker courage, too. And, as she said, the don't-haves have to turn to the don't-haves. If he was ever going to have a son?

He didn't speak, but strode to the back screen door and stood, staring out into the yard at an iron washpot overturned on the gray, sandy ground. What did he owe Melanie, anyhow? It wasn't only now, when she couldn't have a baby. Or even when they separated and she had the trouble, she said. There never was a time when she wanted children or would have had them! Was there? Didn't the double cross go all the way back? But he dismissed this with a jerk of his head and, turning to solider ground, recalled genially, Didn't she anyhow say she'd take any child he got?

"All right, now I'll have my drink," Agnes' voice sounded behind him. "With water in it. And let's go set in the parlor while the biscuits rise." After a slight pause, she added, in lower register, "And I'll play 'Yes! We Have No Bananas' on the organ for you."

There was a lengthening silence; then Marcellus turned, a tight chuckle rising in him from his navel. He fixed their drinks, then followed her through the doorway, saying, "Don't count me out too soon!"

As they walked along the dim front hall, he took her hand. She moved close in to say, in an even murmur, "It's catching for me now. That's why I'm trying to get under the cover quick."

He had an impulse to pinch her bottom with the hand she was holding, but his left arm wanted to pull away. His scruff rose and he chuckled again. Get a river-running Hooker? Well, hell, he'd know how to live in this country, this dark land! The land his father loved, his grandfather, his great-grandfather before them. The land he, Marcellus, had deserted! His father's ghost might be satisfied with Agnes' son more than another. She did not offer to sit beside him on the horsehair sofa, but took her place at the organ, and he went on with his thoughts. This way, he said to himself, this way you can sort of see what you get. And if he's fitting to be a Hightower, you can claim 'im, legitimate him.

The nasal contralto of the reed organ was too much for him, and they went back to the kitchen. None too soon at that, for by the time she'd got the ham and the eggs fried and the red gravy made, the biscuits had risen and were brown. It was a toothsome country meal, and he did his duty by it—largely in silence. Afterward she took him back to the parlor, but this time she skirted the organ and got out Grip's old box, as she called it. Strumming chords, she sang "Careless Love" for him, in about the flattest drawl in South Georgia, he thought, yet good. Then she broke off to talk about David again. He went to the kitchen and got them drinks.

She said, on the sofa behind him, looking on him but not quite seeing him: "David did try me out that night. That was while you-all were making the candy, and I took him off up in the front bedroom—you know, where the folks sat—we didn't have no parlor at our house. There was a fire in there." She took a sip of her drink, and smiled faintly. "I led 'im on, all right. And he come after me, in there by the blaze and the bed. Though he wasn't going to offer me nothing but a good time. . . . The pin come up later."

She lowered her eyes to admit: "I was already in love with Grip, as in love as I could be. . . . And he had me any time he wanted me, just about. But I couldn't git 'im to talk about marrying, though he claimed he loved me—after his fashion, he claimed it."

She looked up. "You know, David had a way with him like nobody else. I guess he saw it in my face: my holding back in spite of myself, felt the bind coming on my muscles. Anyhow, he said pretty quick, you know, in that deep-throaty nigger-fun of his, 'Who it iz, gal?' And before I could stop myself, I said, 'Grip.' He was surprised, and repeated it after me; then he laughed and said, 'Still a stout Grip, eh?' and set there close, smiling me open with those golden-harp eyes"—she wagged her head—"I would a-weakened I think then, if he'd gone at me again. Anyhow, I wanted to, but the time for it had done gone by. He said that Grip was a good fellow, a settled man. He hoped I got 'im if I wanted him. I told him he didn't know the half of it, but that Grip wasn't the marrying kind. And that wasn't all. He knew he didn't have to marry me. Then David said that any man could be had if you worked it right.

"It was while he was talking and my eye resting on that gold pin on his cream-colored silk shirt that the thought struck me. And I told him that I might work Grip into the notion, if he, David, would help me, and he said all right. But when I told him I wanted to borrow his pin, he wouldn't lend it to me. Not for a long time. I worked on him there about an hour, I reckon. I told 'im I was desperate. I would only want it for two weeks, I said. And I wouldn't let another living soul see me with it, except Grip. And I wouldn't tell him whose it was."

Marcellus came up off the sofa with a jerk and strode to the empty fireplace. His mouth was hard and his eyes incredulous when he turned around. "You claim you talked 'im out of it?" he said angrily.

Her flaring face caught him up. "You think I'd make myself his murderer if it waun't so! Just to say he didn't tail me?" Marcellus, after a moment, lowered his head. She said, "Shorty, don't be a fool!" She modulated her voice to go on: "I was upset by the killing when it happened, all right, but I didn't dream I had anything to do with it, didn't dream it! I swear before God"–her voice broke and, shaking with sobs silently, she lowered her face into her hands until she recovered enough to go on. "I never suspected it—it may have been square-headed in me, but I didn't. I didn't! And I never suspected Grip, I didn't, not until he turned loose there at the last! I believed what he said on the witness stand: he didn't tell me no different." She leaned over her thighs, shaking again, but straightened up, "Yet, yet" —her face now haggard—"that ain't quite so, Goddamnit, not quite! I'd lied to David: I did tell Grip whose pin it was; I had to! And down at the bottom all the time I'd been a little uneasy in my mind—been guilty!"

She subsided over her knees once more. While she was speaking, Marcellus' chest began to pump and he broke out in a sweat. A light blazed through his head, through Agnes, through that Hooker parlor-bedroom. It shone on a distant scene: a big boy and a little squirmy girl coming out of another bedroom into Ransoms' back hall, to clean them at last and finally of all shadow. You wart frog, he told himself, you couldn't comprehend him. He felt his knees about to give way. He moved back to the sofa and sat down beside Agnes, lifting a hand toward her shoulder, thinking how mean a thing a suspicion could be. She murmured through her fingers, "I wish to God now I'd let David have his fun that night! And—And who knows?"

He found himself with his arms about her, kissing her eyelids. Tears still coursing her cheeks, she had lifted her head in a way that seemed fine. Her talk about guilt was Gothic, but by God, where did coincidence end? Where? And every time David was dragged into the mud he came up shining like a diamond ring. Goddamnit! He felt a heave rising in his own chest, and caught his breath. She opened her eyes to him, with a lifting sweetness. He muttered, "Yes, who knows?" For blind guilt, maybe there's a blind Nature's compensation. "And what else can we do for him, anyhow?" he added.

She led the way into her bedroom and to her own pink bed. But when, naked and aroused, he moved toward her across the white sheets, at her touch he turned deathly pale with nausea and broke into a cold seat. Swaying, he shut his eyes. "Wild bees," he groaned, gone limp. Rolling off the bed, he ran out of the room.

He ran. But he reasoned that his mishap was a local thing. It wasn't until the summer of '42 that he proved it otherwise. Although he moved about the country at his writing—from San Diego to Breadloaf Mountain—he stuck close to it until he finished his novel, finished it and sent it to his publishers on the day before Pearl Harbor. In January of the next year he entered the army's volunteer enlistment officer training program, and in April came out, with some political pull, a first lieutenant—he was too old for a second lieutenancy—and was detailed to serve with the OSS, in Washington. He had his billet in Georgetown at the house of an army officer's widow, and it was by her he proved himself wrong.

It happened at the most embarrassing moment again, when she touched him. There might have been other reasons, of course, and there might have been other girls, too, but he lost his interest or his nerve. He decided he could only be sure there would be no odor with a prostitute, while he was drunk. It made him bitter, but he went slow.

Early in the spring of '43 he was made a captain, and, a little ahead of the movement of American troops to the Belfast vicinity, was sent in civilian dress to Dublin, in the new Republic of Ireland. His mission was mysterious, so mysterious, in fact, that he was never quite sure himself what he was doing there. But McAteer, head of the IRA, protested the presence of Yankee soldiers on Irish soil soon after they got there, and Marcellus' chief activity became trying to learn what he could of the sentiments of the new republican leaders toward this country and the reasons for them. But on occasion he handled certain news stories to the Dublin papers calculated to curry favor with the republicans. There was the one about generous contributions of American GI's to the "Green Cross" under the misapprehension that it was the Irish counterpart of the Red Cross, but hinting, too, that this slipup was deliberate. And others like it. He had instructions, to be sure, not to billet at the Shelbourne Hotel or to associate with English or Anglo-Irish.

He took a modest room in a small hotel called the Kevin on the opposite side of St. Stephen's Green, near a Catholic church. And finding his assignment pleasant and not very exacting, interested himself in the scene about him. Dublin rather reminded him of the deep South—Charleston or Savannah—in its leisureliness, public good manners, and shabby grandeur. He was grateful, too, that there was no war excuse here to put women into pants. The swarms of pretty, bright-skirted Irish girls on the streets, pedaling their bicycles, gave the city gaiety and an air of intrigue. He took an interest in locating the Martello tower that had figured in James Joyce's *Ulysses* and in making the public lectures at the University of Dublin and in visiting picturesque Glendaloch, once the sanctuary of the Irish saint, Kevin, for whom his hotel was named.

It was the proprietress of the hotel who told him of St. Kevin. Accompanying him in a rented car to the historic vale, she gave him graphic details of his legend. She was black Irish, a handsome young widow and a republican, and he began to take an interest in her, also.

All of it was, however, World War II for him. We were still right. But we were having to do it over again. He had been disappointed when the other fight ended for him at an aviation ground school, without his seeing action, but he was content to take part in the present one in comfort, remote from death and glory. His second-time stance comprehended more. His interest in love, as in life, took on this perspective.

He was usually the last breakfaster in the dining room (and parlor as it became between meals, for the lobby was no more than a vestibule), and the proprietress took to sitting with him for a cup of coffee. Contrary to custom she was usually in pants at this hour, having just finished her morning chores, but they looked rather like jodhpurs. She told him he was mysterious. But she was mysterious herself. She looked like horsey gentility at these times, fresh from her clerk's desk and her dust mop. Only handsomer. (It seemed odd. In the United States the claims of the shanty Irish—of every broken-nosed, square-faced, jimberjawed mick—to the blood of kings or, at the least, dukes was a standing joke. But here, every other lad you met on the street could double for William Butler Yeats, and half the girls looked like Spanish *doñas*. And their ancestry wasn't a burden here where it was hard enough to raise the price of a pint of stout. Everybody seemed to be poor; yet, however uncomfortable, they found nothing degrading about it, either.) Her blue-black hair and black-blue eyes and lower-register voice and her manner of speaking—a sort of telegraphic code, both idiomatic and poetic—made her the more mysterious—though she might be saying only that the cook mashed her finger and she had had to scramble the eggs. Indeed, in her dark poise and pensive speech, it was her unspoken depths that drew him. She brought a new dimension to his breakfast. Though of course he meant to keep his distance, she came to be as convenient and engaging a companion for his evenings, too. But he felt himself a long way from danger with Sheila Deverau at the Kevin, in Dublin—a long way from death and glory, and he liked it.

She had an educated appreciation of the drama, he found, from their trips to the Abbey Theatre. And during the summer she went with him to a series of weightily scientific lectures (though advertised as popular) by the physicist Erwin Schrödinger, at the University of Dublin. Though she did complain about them, she stuck it out. He found them tough going himself, and had to get books on genetics and the like out of the library to be able to explain them to her afterward.

He knew she liked him. As, on a Sunday drive to Cork, when it turned out a raw wet day and they found the open fire at a wayside inn welcome. She, joking and laughing about Irish girls' pursuit of husbands as they entered the empty room, had leaned down to put out her hands to the flames. And, on impulse, he cantered two fingers up her spine, on between her shoulder blades. She came up, smiling and shuddering and, leaning against him, nuzzled his jaw with her cheek. He saw she would offer no more than token resistance to his kissing her. But he didn't then. He had to be wary, wary, even if he was a long way from danger, from death and glory.

So they talked about the Mendelian law at the breakfast table. And the cells in a drosophila fly's wind. Why did the big living molecule resist the Brownian Movement? she asked him. To be sure, should he know if Schrödinger didn't? Marcellus was finding his speculations tremendously exciting. After all, what was life? Life that we were blotting out so scientifically, so partisanly. Was Schrödinger about to prove that the scientists would never know? It may be an itch, he said, but an itch about what? It may be motion, but headed where? Sheila, adding a bite of doughnut to a second cup of coffee, said through lips pursed against exposing her mouthful, " 'Slove, mr'ourse!"

That in time was what moved Marcellus, its participation mystique—moved him on the evening they went to the Green Cross benefit dance and returned about midnight to sit on Sheila's studio couch, to sit in the rhythm they felt, bodies infused. The studio couch, which the removal of the Chinese red damask cover and two gold pillows would transform into her bed, and with the letting down of a teak-like wall panel to open up her dressing table would translate sitting room to bedroom. Not that he was specifically conscious at the moment of the flimsy physical accidents or the profound spiritual substance of such a transubstantiation. He was only in rhythm with the music. Moving to her murmuring, arms about her, their hands snuggled beneath her breasts, he drew her cheek to his. After a while he lifted his face to kiss the cheek and frame it in her words: Yes, *glove mouse.* She laughed somewhere in the region of her diaphragm, and turned her lips to his.

But after a while, a while that wasn't time at all, not perspective, when the damask cover had been, not altogether removed but disarrayed and even the full creamy silk dress she wore was in disorder and her smooth narrow forehead and lowered eyelids bore a submissive wearied look against the hunger still on her mouth, she murmured as deep as ever and no louder, "Let me go, Marcellus! Let me go-o!" When he didn't, a few minutes later she raised her voice piteously to complain, "You're going to make me commit mortal sin!"

However imminent this was or wasn't, the sound of her voice, the sound of the futile anguish of her dismay affected him, brought back time, perspective. And he thought, in a delighted dismay of his own, maybe he was falling in love with her—this sudden tender transcendence of his desire! Moreover, it seemed dead certain now that he had got beyond danger, beyond the range of the "wild bees." He didn't at once relax his hold on her, but said, "It can't be a sin, Sheila—not the way I feel about you!"

Her laugh was still deep, but turned ironic. "You not the one to say—you heathen!"

"Well, suppose we got married?" he argued. Her laughter became incredulous, and he protested, "No. Sure enough. Married. I'm ready. I swear I am!" Now he did relax his hold. "Ready to settle down and raise a family. With you. Marry and have children!"

She took her hand off his knee and straightened her bodice and smoothed down her skirt. This seemed to put an entirely different face on their game on the studio couch, for she said, with a simmering gurgle that had little mirth in it, "Are you proposing bigamy, darling?"

He started blinking, then scratched his head, moving automatically into a more orderly posture himself, before exploding. "By God, you can reverse your field in a hurry!" He got to his feet. She lifted a crooked smile to him, but held to her questioning look. He said then, in a slightly hortatory manner, "I told you that it's not a marriage. She said when she left me she would give me a divorce anytime I wanted it. I just hadn't got around to doing anything about it yet." He bobbed his head a couple of times to reinforce this, and sat back down.

"Hadn't?" she said softly, reflectively, lowering her gaze to the toe of his shoe.

"No," he added. "I just didn't have anything pushing me."

"What church you married in?" she was already asking him.

"No church at all—a civil marriage. It will be easy."

"You haven't, darling, anything pushing you now," she said ambiguously.

He looked at her uncertainly for a moment, then forced a grin. "Oh, but I have, I have—pushing from within."

She clasped her hands in her lap and sat up straighter, lifting her pointed chin. "Marriage is a serious thing. It's a sacrament."

Frowning in his show of earnestness, Marcellus wagged his head. "Oh, I understand, I understand. You-all have to be married by a priest. That's all right. I'll go along on that."

She laughed in spite of herself, though it wound up flat, and she repeated, paraphrasing him, "Oh, you understand! Like a headless ha'nt, you do! What's obvious, you don't understand a thing, Marcellus."

He turned away grimacing, saying as if to himself, "I guess I got serious too soon."

Her eyes followed him, then lowered to reflect. "You haven't got serious yet. Not to yourself, serious. Why do you think you're still holding on to her—three years later—why?"

He flushed, feeling exposed, then angry. "What the hell!" he blurted, going on vehemently, "you don't understand! You don't get it at all! You don't! Sometimes it's convenient to have technical protection against another marriage. I just didn't—I—"

Her eyes, lifting to his face as he spoke, were wide and alert, yet softened in sympathy. After a pause, she said, "Darling, you're a better man than you know."

He winced and shrank as if from a blow. Her words were emasculating, and he suspected a hidden contempt. "By God, don't sneer at me. I've made you a serious offer—offered all I've got!" He came to his feet again and moved away from the couch.

She rose too, followed him solicitously, coming close. She said tenderly, "Marcellus, Marcellus. Still it's not enough." Face twisting, he turned away from her again, but she pursued him. "Look, darling, what've we got? Nothing, nothing to build on." She took hold of his shoulder to turn him.

He came around, frowning at her in open puzzlement, then shrugged. Wagging his head he said, with a try for a smile, "We've got the living molecule of love, ain't we?"

Her face dropped; he'd touched the quick. She said, "Yes, I know. Yes, I know. But it's –it's not enough, Marcellus. With us." Then she lifted her face abruptly, her eyes blazing with her intuition. "Life, yes. But it's only love when it's headed in the right direction!"

He was puzzled again, and moved as if to take her hand, but faltered, saying grimly, "Well, head us in the right direction, Sheila! I'll go—"

She broke in. "But you're not religious. And you can't be. You don't believe."

"I can be taught," he said, faltering again.

She took her head, going on. "And nothing to build on, I say—nothing to offer up. Nothing in common, like—like denial, suffering."

But she wavered, too, now that it was out, lowering her glance. He lifted his, feeling a push from the past, an unburied impulse to lead, and he took her hand, turning her arm under his and holding her fingers in his. He headed them for the door, saying, "I hear an old sea chantey." Before they reached the opening, however, he reeled and halted and loosed her, dropping the fingers. His face was twisting in nausea and fright. "Excuse me!" he said, stumbling through the doorway, hand to mouth. "It must have been the punch!"

THE WAKE

*

Adam

Chapter 18

WITHIN SIX weeks after Marcellus had faded out on Sheila—having moved out of the Kevin the next day—he got himself transferred back to the states, still mulling and "sulling" over his Irish experience. The smell of a dead man was, unhappily, still caught in his head—so what? He was, by God, going to have children anyhow! Anyhow! To be sure, Schrödinger had got life up off the ground for him, only for his Catholic girl to try to put it down in purgatory. Still, he didn't give up on Science—he was unconvinced that he couldn't find a woman as clearheaded as he was, as scientific: that is, as willing to try to rig it. Though he didn't see it in such a light then.

Sure, what the venerable physicist had presented disturbed him. He recognized that the genes in the sexual cells, uniting the begetters behind them, offered only a code copy of the new life. The life of the baby merely took off, or maybe took on form here. It was Schrödinger's demonstration of the will to live in the living cell, the capacity for self-direction that shook Marcellus. This thing statistics couldn't reach. The gratuitous seed of his loins had not merely wriggled their way out of countless forebears to take form again by sexual union, but so would give form and just form, widespread, discernible, but ever new and mysterious. Life, this first and final thing about a living man, was superphysical, supernatural—a thing religion essayed to deal with. This confused, infuriated him, and deeply unsettled him.

But he was still desperately determined to have children, to rig it. Whether the womb was a grave or a vestibule to purgatory. Children! So, in Washington where he was stationed again, he went to a psychiatrist. Here, back in '42, he had gone to see a medical man, who had told him to take a couple of aspirin, before ascending the *lit d'amour*. This had put him off the medical profession for a time.

The nutquacker (he indulged in his pun privately) proved more noncommittal, at least at first. His gold-rimmed spectacles, thinning red hair, and pale brown eyes were in harmony with the mild plumpness he presented, as he sat owlish in his swivel chair. In the early stages he let it drop that Marcellus might be psychologically impotent, to which Marcellus retorted, "How does that cover the whores when I got drunk?"

"Exception that proves the rule," he said, and then clammed up for three months just to sit there and listen to Marcellus spill his guts. He did speak of preconscious traumatic experiences, but Marcellus couldn't seem to come up with any worthy ones, even from the couch.

He had talked his way through the winter, through Washington's monolithic marble surfaces, through the doctor's tolerant auditions, the one as unproductive as the other—before he got restive enough to heckle the man. The psychiatrist gave out with thoughtful reluctance, canting his head like a rooster who has scratched up a worm for the hen: "There's a possibility of latent homosexuality here—possibly homosexual panic."

Hell, was there anything homosexual in trying to get a few children by a woman? Another woman, because the one you were married to couldn't. The only thing homosexual he had ever participated in was at the age of seven or eight, when, along with five other naked little boys, he tried pederasty. But they would sure damn quick have swapped each other for a girl, had any been available. He was disgusted. The homosexual talk made him feel that he was being had.

Something was bad wrong, all right. He was deeply crossed up inside. He was nervous and suffering from insomnia—and nightmares when he did sleep. But it was more than that. A sense of it came to him even on the sidewalks, in the diffident faces of strangers who seemed to be hiding their amusement or pity. It was as if he had been cuckolded, and everybody else knew it but him! He saw finally—saw, hanging to a strap, staring at the pale-green paisley design of the window shade on his homebound streetcar—saw that he couldn't kid himself any longer, that he couldn't longer put it off, knew he couldn't rig it. If he was going to get anywhere, get out of this maze, he had to go back to the scene of his crime, back to Oconee country, back to Devil's Elbow.

Marcellus sent Adam a wire to let him know he was coming, but got to Macon—he thumbed a ride in a military plane—rented a car and drove on down to Adam's farm before the telegram reached him. It was after five o'clock when Marcellus got to the old place, and the sun was already swinging low, already behind the scuppernong arbors, as he parked in the lane, a gold shaft breaking through here, there, and yonder. And Adam was at home, in the house. It had been four years since Marcellus had seen him. He came walking across the sandy yard at his peculiar strolling gait, apparently as straight as ever—despite his eighty-five-or-six years. He did seem a little shortened in height.

Marcellus had come inside and was pumping himself a dipper of water. After their greeting was done, they took up their familiar attitudes from old positions: Marcellus sitting on the winehouse step, and Adam squatting in the yard a few paces away. His hair was whiter, though there was still a touch of iron in it, and his scraggly moustache, grayer. But the irises of his luminous eyes had kept their rich brownness, and the liquid light of their intelligence seemed undiminished. His cheeks caved in where a tooth was missing here and there, but they were still firm, and his mouth was steady and relaxed, except when he went to speak. There was something, however. Marcellus, as he began talking, couldn't put his finger on it, yet somehow Adam seemed more remote, resigned.

Now his lips were working convulsively behind the moustache. "B-Bees?" he said.

Marcellus ducked his head, apologetic though straight-faced. "I've got so in the habit of calling it the 'wild bees' to myself, I forget—it's the smell, the smell we know like no other odor in creation that came to us that night on Burnt Island, Adam." Adam nodded, and Marcellus went on, leaning over his knees, eyeing the smooth gray ground. "It came back on me first—that is, after the beginning when it was actually there or in my early impressions—first that afternoon Grip Jackson made his deathbed confession, come on me right *here.*"

"I r-ricollect," Adam said.

"Well, it's not Grip anymore, not anymore," Marcellus said, taking Adam in briefly in the tail of his eye without shifting his gaze. "It's got mixed up, mixed up with women, somehow. Every time, unless I'm dead drunk and she's a whore, I try to lay a hand on one—"

Adam nodded, lowering his gaze, repeating as if to reassure himself, "Every time?" Then, looking back at Marcellus, he asked before Marcellus could speak, "When did it hit you the second time?"

Marcellus blinked, his eyebrows lifting, looking about him; then he began to redden from the neck. He had to drop his head to answer. "That was at Jackson's too. . . .She wanted to have a kid by me—she said. . . . It was after he died."

Adam nodded, as if he might already have known something about it, then studied the ground, marking on its hard surface with a lightwood splinter. "Your wife, she never did have a child, did she?" he said, after a time. Marcellus bridled, but Adam didn't look up. "I—I mean, in no way—dead too soon, or anything?"

Marcellus shrugged, then, collecting himself, cleared his throat. "That's right, she—we never had any." After a pause he added ironically, "We were too smart."

Adam agreed, without rising up. "Too smart—then too late when you changed your mind. Mind," he repeated, "and got too set on it—I seen that in you four years ago."

"But, Goddamnit, Adam, what's that got to do with David Ransom?" Marcellus exploded. "And this is a real smell, in my head—in my nose."

When Adam lifted his speculative gaze, when it had encountered Marcellus', his eyes began to glow with a liquid darkness that made his hair seem whiter. "You wouldn't believe it back dere when I told you, would you? Wouldn't believe it, contended hit didn't mean no more'n a sparrow in a deadfall." His jaw moved abruptly as he jerked his head about, and his mouth twisted to skeet an arc of tobacco juice at a distant doodle hole. You don't still think David died for nothing, do you, Marcellus?"

Marcellus was breathing quick, grimacing, staring like a man about to be overtaken. He swallowed hard, and his voice rose in a wavering falsetto as he spoke. "But, Goddamnit, Adam, what's that got to do with women—or having children, either?" A tic came in his left cheek, and he brusquely wiped his mouth. "And after all, Adam, God knows, we didn't mean David any harm. And it was, was almost, almost a quarter of a century ago! I scarcely remember what he looked like—I—" Marcellus broke off moodily.

"You thinks you forgit, when you just disremember!" Light shimmered in Adam's eyes; then he lifted the lightwood splinter, unlit but potent. "Hit's dere, deep. . . . Hit's dere. And hit all add up, all add together."

Marcellus jumped to his feet, scrounging his shoulders up and the back of his head down against them, stamping in protest, circling about. "But, Adam, it don't add up! This is a smell in my head! Broken off somehow—broken off—" He shrugged in frustration, still circling. "It can't be wrong for a man to want children!"

When he had subsided, had apologized for his outburst and lighted up his pipe and resumed his seat. Adam took it up again. "Marcellus, there's some hard facts in this world," he said mildly. "Some we makes it so ourselves and some we don't. But whether you responsible or whether it just come about, hit don't make no difference finally—if it's a fack and you can't change it. Some things you do you can't undo. The thing is to learn to live with 'em. Hit ain't easy, but hit's the only thing'll bring you through—hit's wise." He said then in a quick, clear monotone, "Like me being a nigger. And not only nigger, but a yellow nigger to boot—when neither side wants to trust you."

Marcellus batted his eyes. He had seldom heard Adam mention his color, and never in such bitter contempt. Adam was scratching the ground with the splinter again , and Marcellus cleared his throat to protest, but he cut him off. "You think that smell's broke off in your head—that it don't' make no sense—just aimless and got twixt you and your nature—that it can't be wrong for a cold-codded man like you to have children! . . . Anything can be wrong in this world, son—almost—can be different from what you think it is. Like that smell being in your head, you think. It ain't in your *head,* Marcellus. It ain't in your head."

Marcellus smoked silently for a time, in measured pulls at the black stem of his briar pipe. Finally he said, "All right, Adam, then I don't know, I don't know—tell me!"

Adam rose and stepped over to the pump and, dropping his tobacco cud on the ground, rinsed out his mouth. He drank a dipper of water. He turned about, speaking from where he stood. "It was hard for me to learn I was a yellow nigger. And harder still for me to stay learned about it. It put me in the penitentiary when I was a boy. And I learned some things. But it didn't all get over back there. When those white mens hired Kiger to kill me over the swamp deal and I outfoxed 'em and come out on top, I *hated* 'em, shonuff hated 'em—so I still hadn't learned. Your ma finally made me see the light. But some things, it looks like, you never get through learning, not hardly!" He moved over to let himself down on a root of the big overspreading water oak and lit his pipe. "As you know, it come up again in the killing of David Ransom, that first night we were hunting for him and I had to spend part of it in the county jail. . . . That was all right. It shook me up, but I could take it. And it come to be a high point for me afterward. For all the white people on any weight come to my aid and stuck by me. They took my word.

"But then I talked too much. I forgit again before hit was over—hit went on so long and everybody got so strained, so wore out, so baffled. When I first said hit, hit didn't seem to tax nobody. You know I said, before the second week of river dragging was out, I didn't believe we'd find 'im there where Buck and Dunk said he was. But like a numbskull I kept on saying it. Yeah, hit had done got to be a habit with me. And there in them long, cold, windy, dreary, hopeless days, hit look like I couldn't think of nothing else to say. And couldn't keep my mouth shut, neither. That river dragging went on so long and so trying that it got us all actin' curious. And it had done got to where Mr. Carruthers Ransom and Mr. Robert Bruce, both, was giving me sharp looks and short answers, before I seen what I was doing. They didn't say nothing, but they began to suspicion I knowed more about the murder than I'd told, after all."

Adam paused to shake his head, and Marcellus put in, "That's so. Carruthers spoke to me once about it."

Adam jerked up. "Did? You never told me!" He took his pipe out. "Well, anyhow, it got so plain on their faces I couldn't keep from seeing it. Then I felt like a done-bin-biggity fool! And scared, too—sho'nuff scared, because these were the men who'd always believed in me. We'd all done got so beat out and baffled over that thing it was hard to hold on to your common sense, but I knew I had to. And had to try to back off from where I'd got to, try to ease outn the close I'd done put myself into. I sweated about it. I laid awake at night. And I prayed too. I asked God to tell me what to do. And I told Him if He could see His way clear to, wouldn't He please let somebody find that body quick."

Adam tapped the fire in his pipe and dropped the ash out of the bowl. "Right about the time I was praying hardest, I dreamed one night that I found David's body. That was after they done upped the reward to a thousand dollars. When I woke up and thought about it, I broke out in a sweat, in the middle of a frosty morning. If I found his body, then nobody never would believe I wasn't in on the murder! I got scarder than ever then; I got really scared." He wagged his head. "This ain't never been told before, and you can see why. But I pretty nigh quit coming to the swamp. And I couldn't sleep at night, couldn't hardly eat my meals." Adam took out his pipe, sweeping the hand that held it toward the grapevines, glowing in the sunset. "I used to walk under them arbors before day, thinking about it and praying about it—there in the gray cold. Then one morning I dreamed again like there under the arbors. It seemed I was down on my knees, and God come up over the top of the pines, like"—his voice was suddenly labored—"like a big dim, dark man, so big he run off the picture." Adam paused. He shook his head with a flick of humor. "And hit seem like He smole a slow smile. Slow. And in the last of it a tooth showed and blinded my eyes. And I woke up with the morning sun square in my face. And I felt rested."

He was brisker when he resumed. "That day, that very afternoon—you know, after I come on back from the landing with you in the morning, a while after I'd et dinner and napped, I went out to the forks of the big road to get my mail in the box. And standing there looking up at the telephone wires that run on down the right fork toward Bright's, I began to hear 'em whine. Somehow I took it be a sign. And I just hoofed it on over there to their place, following that whine. The sun was done setting. But when I come by the front of their house, the door was open and there was Mr. Jawn, talking into the mouth of that telephone and all the Brights standing around him.

"I started to come on in the yard to ask 'em what was up, but I saw then that you waun't with 'em—I had picked up at the commissary that's where you'd gone, gone to fish shad nets. Then I walked on down to the river, to the end of the timber trace and on over to the cut. Hit's the nigh point, there across from Burnt Island. I was standing there, peering about, trying to make out something across the water, when the smell hit me. I had smelled such a smell before, and I knew what it meant. I knew before I saw anything that it was David's body, done found.

"Then's when I called out to you and you told me where the boat was chained and I paddled across. . . ." Adam knocked out his pipe and put it in his pocket. "But before I called to you, when I was standing there on the bank in the dark and that smell slipped into me like something that done happened yestidy, and it come to me what the smell was, I took my lungs full of it. I was so relieved, it was a fine smell. . . .Hit didn't bother me none over on the island, neither. Hit was a sad but saving smell to me. Has been ever since." He stood up. "Hit's not in your nose, Marcellus, nor neither in your head. Hit's in your heart!"

Marcellus had seen it coming: those last four words, had known how Adam would put it. Still, when they came they went through him like a swallow of fire just the same, and he couldn't check himself. He got out his handkerchief and wiped his eyes. He stood up, too. He stamped on the ground to wake up his right leg. He spoke in a chastened voice. "All right, Adam—I guess I had to have *you* tell me!"

Chapter 19

BACK IN WASHINGTON, he carried on as an OSS officer as usual by day, in the seedy poster-and-memorandum-plastered offices of a "temp" from World War I. But at night, after dinner, he shut his bedroom door, in a row boardinghouse—he had wanted to be alone—and lighted his pipe and eased into his rocking chair to try to figure things out. He had learned some things, though the learning came hard. He saw where he was. And he knew finally what he wanted.

Two photographs stood in front of the mirror to the golden oak bureau against the inner wall of the room, and his gaze now settled on them. He had on his recent visit dug them out of a footlocker he had left at Adam's place before the war. He'd gone into the locker, looking for a cabinet-size picture of Melanie he'd put away at the bottom of it. But he'd found too, his small portrait of David Ransom he'd thought lost. Examining now the old likeness on the narrow pasteboard, in its brown folder, he felt a new immediacy in the distant events. The photograph presented a beardless youth in olive-drab woolen uniform of World War I. It had been made while he was a freshman at college and a member of Students Army Training Corps—perhaps a year before his death. His military haircut didn't quite straighten out the wave in the thick hair on top of his head. The cheeks, the mouth, the lips were smooth and fresh and unlined, and the ears seemed to stick out a bit because of the close cropping at his temples. There was a slight manly dimple in his chin. A boy! Those dark, unsmiling, arrested eyes, however, came across the gap in time to bring Marcellus' inner situation to him with fresh poignancy and drama.

David was dead. But David lived, too—daily. It went back even beyond the uniform, the haircut—to Rawlings' pole shed. Beyond, to the fatherless beginning they faced together. It wasn't their intention, but David had laid it all on the line for him. This he had known, had proclaimed—though he'd found he didn't do it without deceit. For a time his vindictive suspicion had discredited that gaze, had—he thought—put David in the past. But David lived with him, and it was never past. What Marcellus saw now, sitting there below the blue haze of tobacco smoke, was that the eyes could ask things of him, too. He could not live at ease with himself, without David's regard—and more.

Marcellus rocked back in his chair, glimpsing Melanie's image in the larger photograph, her smile pursuing him. A sly smile? He squinted up at the ceiling, blinking at the dim, watermarked wallpaper. Crafty? Still, it bound every ounce of her, body and soul. There were no false smiles in Melanie, though all of them dissembled her meaning. Behind innocent guile! He came forward to confront her.

Staring at the chiaroscuro on the pasteboard that gave form, that was the form of giving, he felt it breathe within him, and was touched with fear. However lightly and provisionally he may have entered into it, he made a commitment to her, fifteen years ago. They made a commitment. It was hard to say how such commitments were made or what sealed them. How? Wasn't it really a part of the heedless act itself—the meaning time discovers in the thing essentially mindless, but living; because it lives? And, in right and wrong, hadn't they—to use Sheila's words—built on it? Perhaps it would be better to say that it—the commitment—had built on them.

But he had run away from their mistake only to find it was tied to his tail. He had failed Melanie. They had failed, to be sure; in the thing marriage was for—for freedom, they thought. But you don't free yourself by murder. A hard name for a wordless superstition wearing a weather-beaten derby? But it had finally to be faced. Melanie had done so already. But they had to do it together.

This made a marriage, too. Their fulfillment still lay in their marriage and through it. This was the thing. Gazing at Melanie's likeness humbly, he asked how he could reclaim their marriage. He laid his pipe on the smoking stand, and in the mirror beyond, became aware of his own image. You must move softly, he told himself, and with caution. Nobody else could tell him how to reenter his own house. He started in his seat, and his face seemed to explode. If he didn't enter discreetly, the odor might follow him in!

It had taken him until Thanksgiving Day even to get to see Melanie.

Winter rain doesn't usually set in on Saint Simons until December, but when Marcellus met Melanie's plane at the island airport that afternoon it was falling in a steady downpour, and had been all morning. The weather was raw. Because he had a storm umbrella and had parked his car beside the airfield fence, he managed to get her into the front seat without her getting wet. But the summer cottage on the beach he'd taken for the weekend was neither warm nor cheerful. He'd got there only at noontime, having been on the road since the previous morning, driving down from Washington. And he hadn't been able to do much to make the bare place comfortable. There was a wood stove in the kitchen and a fireplace in the living room, where he'd tried to build a fire out of stovewood, but the chimney wouldn't draw. The place had filled with smoke, and he had had to throw the burning sticks into the yard.

Still, he hadn't gambled on fair weather to effect their reunion. During the previous seven months, he had left as little to chance as he could, had calculated with care, employed strategy, fingered imponderables. His first letter in April opening *Darling* and ending *Devotedly,* had said only I *aint' fit for you,* but repeated it seven times, each a simile for "your son of a bitch." To make his stance clear at the outset. He figured she would take her time about answering—that is, if she wasn't getting ready to marry somebody else. So, about the middle of May, he sent number two, saying he saw she agreed with him, but did that stop all further talk between them?

As weeks slunk by, it began to look as if he weren't even a son of a bitch to her. On the morning of his forty-fifth birthday, June seventh, despite the day, he wavered, staring into his bathroom mirror at the gray hairs in the red stubble on his face. Was it more than a crapshooter's superstition for him to believe, because he couldn't get away from Melanie, that she was hooked too? What was it he was gambling on? Maybe it was his mother. He had loved, admired, and revered his mother, especially her sense of discipline. The one memento he claimed out of his family belongings was the stub of a riding whip she had worn out making a man of him. But after her death his younger sister, Edith, told him their mother confessed to her that she had always loved him the best. Melanie, too, was the sort of woman you couldn't fathom from the surface. Why hadn't she remarried? Why had she left him—turned him loose—in the first place? He suspected that whatever Melanie might say, in the last resort, she would act like Adam. Yet he wouldn't say how much longer he could have held on to this hope, if the last day of the month hadn't brought him word from her. There was only one word, and it was somewhat ambiguous, on a postal card: "No." But he was so much encouraged that he wrote at once, pointing out that they were still married, and asking whether she wanted a divorce or would consider resuming their marriage.

Then he hadn't heard from her till August, a letter written on North Carolina Women's College stationery, from Greensboro, where she was teaching at the summer school. She said that before she would try to resume their marriage she would have to know more about him, and maybe about herself, too. What he'd found out that made him write to her, he replied, was that not only was marriage supposed to bring life in but that life best rode out on it, too. This greater adventure was still open to them.

When they got to the house through the rain-beaten trees and bushes and beach and gray swirling water, the room was still smoky. And they found on shutting the door that the wind came under it, and in about the windows and even through the walls it seemed. And grains of cold wet sand, too.

Their kiss at the foot of the steps to the plane had been on the run, and perfunctory. And driving over through the rain was too saddleback for sentiment, and he had had to prepare Melanie for the house anyhow. But once inside, he defied all drawbacks—scattered chairs, bare center table, and blank walls, to hail their reunion, taking her by the forearm firmly and drawing her to him. She showed only initial reluctance, then came into his arms, murmuring something that sounded like *onyjet*. He gazed into her almost-round face, dimple gone, for the familiar assent. And was rewarded with the old look: the hinted smile behind her dark eyes and, as she lowered them, the breath of fear on her lips, then in excitement raised them to his—to give again the old belief. But her glance didn't get higher than his nose, and she said chillingly, "Oh, you haven't taken that mole off your cheek yet!"

The pumpkin was still a pumpkin, but he had a bottle of Bourbon in the kitchen and he proposed then that they start warming up from the inside. Not on your life, she said; she didn't come down here to get drunk—not yet, at any rate. Not until they'd tried to talk sensibly first. This had an ominous sound to him. So he suggested that they drive over to the house of the man who ran the rental agency to see if he couldn't do something about the chimney—at all events, the car would be comfortable. She would agree to this, she said, after she could get unpacked.

The agent's wife told them he had gone hunting, but she suggested that the fireplace might be stuffed for winter. They'd thought of this but had found nothing in it within reach. They kept on driving. There were some thirty miles of paved roads on the island, and others passable, and almost no traffic. The rain couldn't completely efface the spectacular scenery, and Marcellus' Oldsmobile was quite comfortable. He slowed down to fifteen miles an hour, and got back to the point. "So I've got a mole on my face?" he said ambiguously.

She had locked the right-hand door and sat propped against it. Leaning forward, she patted his hand on the steering wheel lightly.

"Beauty spot," she said, and, following a pause, added "after all, I'm looking for something I know, the familiar."

"You find me greatly changed?" he asked, feeling an unexpected surge of insecurity.

"Not in looks." Then, self-consciously patting her stomach, she added, "But look at me: I've got fat!" he contradicted her so stoutly that she said, "Don't take it so hard: I don't think I'm too fat." Then in the same amiable heckling tone, her eyes hiding light that glimmered through, she went on. "After all, we are strangers, almost. I don't know who you've been living with since you left me."

He frowned, "Quite alone," he said.

But she continued her chafing. "I don't know who-all you've been in love with since you left me."

He shrugged without humor. "It's as broad as it's long," he said. "And, by the way, I didn't leave you."

Oh, no, it wasn't as broad as it was long, she retorted. It was different with a woman at her age. No men had been running after her. As he had agreed, she wasn't after all, Vanie. She said this without pause, though he winced. And she hadn't time to run after them, either. She was a schoolteacher, and she had been giving it everything she had. Not without some rewards. Dubinion was only a finishing school, but she was now a full professor and head of the Department of Romance Languages. He touched his foot to the brake, bowing to her over the wheel. His congratulations were extravagant, but she wasn't taken in. "You don't believe in my work anymore than you do my love affairs!" she complained.

His tone was almost brusque. "There's just something in your nature, Melanie, makes you lie about things."

She straightened up against the door. "You haven't changed as much as I thought you had," she said.

After momentary tension they both smiled, shrugged. He said grudgingly, distantly, "It's one of the things I admire in you most, I suppose. Though it usually irritates me at the same time."

"Let's don't get irritated," she said, in a kindergarten manner.

"No," he said, "let's not. And let's talk about you and me, for a change—our love affair—that's what we came here for, isn't it?"

She sat erect, drawing up her hands and her mouth, a Japanese doll's. "What love affair? I haven't seen you in five years! You haven't wanted for women where you've been, I know."

"No, I haven't wanted for women," he said, "but that's pretty sharp irony, the way you put it. And what do you say, let's not irritate as well as not give way to irritation?" She did her kindergarten smile, nodding, and he went on: "No, I've not wanted for women, as you say. But I've tried to intimate to you in my letters about"—his voice flattened and he faltered—"about what happened to me, Melanie. And I don't find it a laughing matter, or ironic, either!"

She lifted an eyebrow soberly. "Do you mind if I find a little irony in it? that is, if I get your intimations correctly—or could believe them."

He stiffened, and they drove on in silence for a time, and there was only the pervasive roar of the sea. After a while he said, in restrained bitterness, looking dead ahead: "Maybe there is irony in it. . . . But for me, in the trap, there has been"—a shudder took him and he gripped the steering wheel, but made it—"only education."

She was moved, and put a hand on his knee. After a while she patted the kneecap, straightening up afterward. "And there seems to be something in your nature that makes you tell incredible things, too."

"But not a liar!" he said quickly.

She looked at him a long time. Her eyes darkened, her cheeks tightening and her bottom lip growing heavy. She said at last, a tremor in her voice, “No, not a liar.”

He whispered with a vehemence that almost cured it of melodrama: “I haven’t in four, almost five, years, except on desperation drunks—the prostitute I have never seen before, the bed I would not remember afterward.”

She flung up a sharpened face. “But why?” she said, in a harassed tone of voice. “Why? I didn’t stop you!”

“That’s all you know about it,” he answered with the same vehemence, and went on. “Three times at the touch, the odor came back—sickening me. It was your hand.”

She moved away from him, her eyes wide. “Not me,” she said, shaking her head tightly, “not me! It was some other woman. . . . I told you to go get you a child, go marry, if you wanted to.” She looked mystified and a little frightened. “Some other woman—it was some other woman,” she repeated. “Your old mother, Saint Lucy.” . . . After they had ridden in silence for a time in the ruck of the sea, she shook herself and tried a smile, lifting her voice to a bantering tone. “Your, your anima, Mr. Jung!”

He didn’t respond. His mouth was still hard as he turned to her. He said, in an accusatory voice, “You married me, didn’t you?”

She wriggled to resist this. Her head wobbled, but she thrust up her nose and mounted a cavalier tone. “After a fashion, married.”

“Don’t worry, we’re married!” he said menacingly. “That’s what it is—I’ve found out.” He shook his head. “I wouldn’t lie to you about it—if I could!”

She turned away, saying shakily, “Here we are!” She ran the window down on her side, and looked out “Not far from the King and Prince. I’m ready for a drink now.”

When they came out of the hotel they found that the rain had let up. They had stayed on for their Thanksgiving dinner there. Besides two drinks beforehand, they had had wines with a four-course meal, and brandy with their coffee afterward. They felt pleasantly stuffed and, as they exchanged a glance under the marquee, greatly reassured, for whatever reason. They moved to his car, but instead of opening the door, Marcellus strode on past, beyond the lights from the lobby, toward the sounding darkness that was the surf. "This is the seawall you've heard me speak of so often," he called to Melanie. She joined him, and they picked their way out onto the concrete top cautiously in the dark. The sky was still overcast, and beyond the distortion of the lights from the hotel, the moving waters were so dim as to be scarcely discernible. Off to their right a distant light buoy rose and fell, in graphic irrelevance. The breakers below their feet were uncertainly white.

They faced the sea, the sharp wind in silence for a time; then Marcellus shuddered and sighed, muttering to himself, "It's strange."

Melanie squeezed the arm she was holding on to. "What do you mean?"

He chuckled. "Oh, I don't know—it's a strange world. You can see so much farther in the dark. Or maybe it's merely that you're safer, not seeing."

"You mean safer not telling?"

"Yeah," he agreed, snorting, nodding, "especially in verse."

"Oh? Do you remember it? Say it for me. It was a moonlight night, wasn't it?"

He laughed peremptorily, "Not on your life," and hustled her back along the wall.

She resisted. "But wasn't it sort of—sacramental? Apocalyptic, for you? And maybe it still is? It shouldn't go unconfessed."

He shrugged and tried to push her along, repeating, "Not on your life."

She balked. "But what about this life together you claim you want to take up again?" She twisted her neck to get a look at him. "On Adam's advice, I gather!"

His face tightened. "He only told me why the smell of death pursued me."

Turning in his grasp, she managed to confront him. "And speaking of such: the wake you and Adam have been holding over David's murder for a quarter of a century—is that to go on?"

"A wake?" Marcellus exclaimed, his momentum arrested, going back on his heels. He lowered a blinking glance, automatically turning from her to stare off at the glimmering light buoy. The big sealed coffin where David's decomposed body rested so uneasily. He saw Adam and himself, sitting in split-bottomed chairs, one on either side of it, facing in opposite directions, each with his gaze lowered, but keeping the dully burnished box in the corner of a penitential eye. "A wake!" he repeated hoarsely, bringing himself around to look at her through the dimness in a purblind bemusement.

She did not wait for his answer. "Or is it to be supplanted by our own little wake?"

"Oh, don't Melanie!" He gripped her arm in a rigor of confusion. "My God!" he said, appalled. He pushed her along toward the car.

She apologized, as he put her in her seat, saying: "I'm sorry, Shorty. I'm sorry. But I had to bring it up." He could find no words for this, and they drove on in silence.

The rain resumed before they got back to their summer cottage, and the wind seemed to blow harder than ever. They found the floor in their windy living room wet from a leak in the ceiling. They were already chilled again, and when Marcellus offered his Bourbon this time Melanie took him up on it, and they retreated from their hurricane deck into the galley, where they managed to find good cheer. They sat on the oaken table there, under the center droplight, the bottle beside them, and swung their feet. And talked. They talked about religion. He thought it was odd that they should both have become interested in it about the same time. Yes, she agreed, though that depended on what he meant by "religion." And a coincidence that they should both have found their way to Christianity. She laughed boisterously at this, but she agreed there was an irony in their both being driven to the Church.

Here he found the table awkward, and he stood up and pulled her to her feet, the better to embrace her. She abandoned her reservations, then, saying, "All right. All right. I guess we are man and wife now till we get in the Church."

He said fervently, "If a man was ever married to a woman, God knows, I'm married to you!" And when she didn't respond, he was indiscreet enough to add, "Whether I want to be or not."

She bridled at this, trying to move out of his arms, raising her whiskey glass between them. "Well, now, do you?" she demanded.

He took the half-filled glass from her hands, swallowed it down, then rocked on his feet in make-believe drunkenness to say, "I've waited five years for this moment!"

"And all the time running as hard as you could to get away from it!" she said, laughing satirically.

But the wind blew the back door open at this point, and they decided to go to bed to keep warm. On an inspiration of the moment, Marcellus made a dash out to his car and came back with his topcoat and the rubber floor rug. This furnished the cue for Melanie to introduce her contribution to their reunion. Leading Marcellus into the bedroom where she had unpacked her things, on the white-enameled cast-iron double bed lay the old electric blanket that had been his unseasonable tenth wedding anniversary present to her. She said, "I turned it on before we left this afternoon."

The next morning the weather broke, and after breakfast the rental agent appeared, too, and took an iron lid off the top of the chimney. The scene cheered up considerably. They were sitting on the blanket in the living room, where they'd eaten breakfast, when the agent got there. And after he'd gone, Melanie got up to turn the blanket off. "I can't bring you a full moon or a spring tide," she said brightly, suppressing a little shudder, "but we did manage to keep warm under this thing, didn't we, Shorty?" He moved toward her, but she fended him off to finish. "I'm going to call it our sacramental blanket—seventh sacrament, you know—once we get under it."

He put his arms about her now, but she had changed the mood of his embrace. "At any rate our ritual will recognize what has long 'groaned for utterance,' " he said, with a smile of apology. He took a stance near the middle of the blanket, looking off through the front window at the distant beach. "Bemused by a full moon and a spring tide, at twenty and in love, and pain, I was stirred by my friend's tragedy to apotheosis. It was a poor poem, and doesn't bear repeating. Yet it did foretell something." His gaze returned to her, the crow's feet under his eyes gathering and his lips twisting in irony. "My need of apotheosis!" He met her quizzical glance for his pay line: "For the murdered hero burdens his followers with the crime—as Adam understood. It's their way to salvation."

He shook his head and moved to get off the blanket. "Your questions last night came as a shock to me. I hadn't thought of them as wakes. I can't say, of course. Perhaps both the wakes will go on.

Though maybe they are really the same wake. And we can cover it now with our sacramental blanket, and turn it into a vigil."

"A vigil?" She smiled, then almost laughed. "It can be a way to forgetting," she said.

He chuckled and picked up an end of the cover, motioning Melanie to help him fold it. "Likely David would agree that a quarter of a century is long enough to hold wake over him."

As he gave her his blanket ends, she said, "What about Adam?"

He nodded. "It can't be too long before Adam is taken to the turkey roost himself." He tossed his emptied fingers lightly. "Aren't we all on our way! And agreeably, now that we know there are no tenable Bohemias this side of it—whatever may lay beyond." He added, with a touch of tender mimicry in his voice, "The t-turkey is a wary bird." Grim vindictiveness gripped him at last: "Yet, his drowned, galling gallantries still will whirl against us!"